CAN'T FIGHT THIS FEELING

INDIGO ROYAL RESORT #1

CLAIRE HASTINGS

Can't Fight This Feeling

Indigo Royal Resort Book 1

Copyright © 2020 Claire Hastings

Cover Design by Cover Couture -www.bookcovercouture.com

Photo (c) Depositphotos/ArturVerkhovetskiy

Edited by: Happy Editing Anns

https://www.clairehastingsauthor.com/

For Drew & Denali -

For your unending, unwavering, unequivocal support in *everything*

CHAPTER ONE

THE DUDE-BRO STANDING in front of her treadmill huffed and puffed as he lifted free weights in the resort fitness suite. For the life of her, Drea Miller could not understand why people went on vacation and still got up early to work out. Why would you fly thousands of miles to paradise only to still be a slave to your alarm?

Should I ever go on an actual real vacation, you won't catch me in the gym, she thought as she continued to pound away on the moving belt, trying to keep her focus on her own breathing and heart rate rather than the borderline-disturbing noises coming from the only other person in the room. Seriously, if she could hear him over her headphones, she could only imagine what it sounded like without.

To say she'd never taken a real vacation would be a lie. Her uncles had taken her to the mainland a number of times when she was growing up; they had wanted to make sure she saw things like the Statue of Liberty, the Grand Canyon, and the Alamo. But going on a long-haul field trip with your three bachelor uncles, disguised as an adventure, wasn't exactly in the same category as the luxury all-inclusive experience that the Indigo Royal Resort was known for.

Dude-bro let out a loud grunt and dropped the weights in his hands, letting them hit the mats he was standing on just as Drea was starting to slow down to a speed-walk for her cooldown. He picked the weights up and walked them back over to the rack, looking in the mirror the whole time, and then winked at her. Well, there went her hope that he'd been eyeing himself in the mirror during the workout rather than her. She smiled back politely then quickly looked down at her phone, trying to push him out the door with her mind, hoping with all her being he wasn't going to try to engage her in conversation. After a moment of scrolling through her workout playlist she looked up, hoping he had left. Apparently, she was not going to be that lucky.

"Hey," he said, jutting his chin out with a grin, trying to be suave.

"Hi," Drea replied, not bothering to stop what she was doing, hoping he'd take a hint.

"Glad to see I'm not the only fitness enthusiast here. The last couple of mornings I was starting to think maybe I'd have the place to myself the whole time."

Drea had to stop herself from rolling her eyes at his lame attempt at a conversation starter. She had no idea how long he'd been at the resort, and didn't really care. But she couldn't exactly tell him that.

"I usually do my morning runs on the beach," she responded. "But, I've got an early excursion, so...here I am."

"Gotcha. Which one? My buddies wanna go on some boat tour thingy this morning, so we may hit that up," he said, stepping around to the side of the treadmill so that he was now immediately to her left. She could smell the booze radiating from his breath and out of his pores as he did so, making her have to stop herself from visibly cringing.

"Oh, the Turtle Cove snorkel? That one is really fun! Totally worth the extra money, since it's not technically included in the resort package."

"You've already done it? Well damn, I was gonna see if you and your girlfriends wanted to join us."

Drea stumbled over herself a little, but righted her step before he noticed. *He thinks I'm a guest! Well, shit. Ok, just let him down easy...or...*

"I could probably convince my friends to get on the boat," she smirked. "I mean, the rum punch is to die for!"

"Well then, this sounds like a party! I'll round up my dudes and we'll catch you beauties in a few!" He snapped his fingers, pointed at her with "finger guns," and winked as he walked backwards to the door leading to the lobby. Drea held up a thumbs-up as she watched him exit backwards, still looking at her.

Once the door was closed, she stopped the treadmill and just stood there, exhaling loudly, shaking her head. She should have let him down easy, should have told him the truth. But it was just too easy to play him. And maybe he and his buddies wouldn't really get on the boat. If the smell of booze emitting from him was any indication of how much they had partied the night before, it might be another three days until the rest of that group woke up.

Hopping off the treadmill, she headed for the lobby, poking her head out to make sure the coast was clear. When she was sure her new BFF wasn't hanging out, she dashed across the wide open-air space, dodging the massive round table that stood in the middle of the lobby, playing host to an exceptionally large fern as well as a number of different packets of information about the resort and the island. She had loved running circles around this table when she was little, trying to get one of her uncles to chase her. Her giggles would bounce off the walls and echo their way into the restaurant or out to the pool.

Making her way into the restaurant, she noticed there were already a few early risers already seated for breakfast. Based on the number of to-go carafes sitting on their tables, Drea guessed most had just returned from the beach, having taken advantage of the "Sip with the Sunrise" coffee service they offered their guests. It was something Drea's mom and aunt used to love to do—go sit on the beach and sip coffee while watching the sun come up. Drea loved that her uncles had taken their little indulgence and made it an everyday ritual, even if the women who inspired said ritual were no longer able to enjoy. She smiled as she took in the scene, and walked along the edge of the room toward the kitchen door in the back. She slipped into the kitchen, narrowly avoiding a server with a full tray who was headed in the opposite direction.

"Morning, baby girl!" came a shout from the other side of the kitchen.

"Morning, Uncle Miller. Wasn't expecting to see you up for breakfast this early. Didn't you do dinner last night?" Drea said, crossing over to where her favorite uncle was pulling pans of muffins out of the massive industrial oven.

Although singling him out wasn't fair, since she loved all three of the men who raised her more than anything, there was an extra special place in her heart for Uncle Miller. Maybe it was because he had been her dad's best friend, or because he was the one who had apparently been insistent that he and his brothers still be the ones to raise her, or maybe it was just his signature "magic muffins," the ones that always landed their resort on annual lists of best hotel restaurants. Uncle Vaughn, who was the general manager of the Indigo Royal, had always been the serious and strict one, pushing her to study and learn everything she could, instilling in her discipline and routine, but also always challenging her to try something new. Uncle Grayson, who she had always just called "Uncle Gray," had taken on the role of fun uncle, from the funny voices he gave to her stuffed animals when she was little to teaching her how to sail, rock climb, and any number of other outdoor activities he was in charge of as activities director for the resort.

But it had been Uncle Miller who had been the biggest influence on her growing up. He'd handled the meals, bedtimes, and all the day-to-day school and extracurricular stuff. He'd been the one nursing her back to health when she was down with the flu (although Uncle Gray wasn't ever going to let anyone forget the one time he'd been the puke receptacle when she brought home the stomach bug in the third grade). He'd been the one who very awkwardly tried to explain feminine products and "the change," as he called it, to her after an embarrassing gym class incident, before running to Vaughn's long-time girlfriend Simone and begging her to please take over before he scarred Drea for life. He'd been the one who had modeled love and loyalty and been her rock as she figured out the world. He also happened to be the most incredible chef, and made muffins that were simply to die for.

"I did. But Rafe's kiddo isn't feeling so hot so I told him to take the morning off. I remember the days of trying to wrestle a sick little one to sleep and then being up at the crack of dawn to scramble eggs," he said with a laugh. His tall frame required that he squat down all the way to pull out another pan of muffins, and Drea noticed there was a little more gray starting to appear in his dark hair. "You just come from the beach?"

"Gym actually. We're running a Turtle Cove trip this morning, so I wanted to make sure I was back and showered in plenty of time. There's a lot to do on Turtle Cove mornings and while it's not that I don't trust Dalton..." she trailed off.

"Sometimes 'living your best life' doesn't always equate with being punctual."

Drea just laughed. "That's one way of putting it. Okay, I'm off. Love you!"

"Love you too, baby girl!"

KYLE EGAN RAN through the morning checklist as he got the boats ready for the day. He didn't need to ready all three of the catamarans, but he'd had to make the quick trip to get gas for the *Runnin' Down a Dream*, so he figured he might as well gas up the *Livin' on a Prayer* and the *Don't Stop Believin'* while he was at it. He laughed to himself as he poured the gas into the fifty-two-foot day-sail catamaran; the fleet of classic rock namesakes might not match the uber posh Indigo Royal Resort on paper, but once you were on site you understood exactly why the owner-slash-operator brother trio had turned to the classic rock gods for inspiration. Everything about this high-class establishment was about enjoying the moment and living life to the fullest. One didn't get to be consistently voted one of the best resorts in the Virgin Islands by not having any fun.

Just as he was checking off the last of the items, his first mate, Dalton Sutherland, casually strolled down the pier carrying a handle of rum in each hand. Kyle looked down at his watch to see that Dalton was about fifteen minutes earlier than he had expected.

"You didn't sleep in your own bed last night, did you?" Kyle asked, grinning at Dalton.

"Now, whatever would make you say that?" Dalton drawled, his southern accent coming off strong, as he smirked in response.

"Because you're here on time. You know I think you're the best first mate I could ask for, but you only show up on time when you need to make a quick exit in the morning."

"Hey now, I resemble that comment!" Dalton said, owning up to the accusation as he handed Kyle one of the handles of rum and climbed up into the catamaran.

"You resemble what comment?" said a sweet voice that sent a flood of warmth down Kyle's whole body. He looked up to see Drea walking toward them with the stack of paperwork in hand. Her chestnut-brown corkscrew curls were still slightly wet from her morning shower and her makeup-free face radiated with an energy that was so uniquely Drea. She looked so damn cute in her running shorts and tank top, and Kyle didn't dare allow himself to linger on the thoughts of what could be if acknowledged all the things she made him feel.

"Dalton was the picture of punctuality today," Kyle said, giving Drea a 'you know what that means' look.

Drea groaned. "Ugh...please just don't let her have been one of our guests."

"Excuse you, I have standards, you know!"

"Do you, though?"

Dalton simply shrugged, not even bothering to look remotely guilty. "I didn't say they were high standards." He held out a hand and helped her step into the boat. She smiled at him and rolled her eyes playfully. "You know I would never do anything to jeopardize you, your uncles, or this establishment."

"Yes," Kyle injected. "Because that would mean he'd have to go home and get a real job."

They all erupted into laughter as Dalton tapped his nose with his index finger to indicate that Kyle was exactly right. As if taking that as his cue, Dalton headed below deck to start pulling up the life jackets and snorkel gear for the tour. Still shaking her head and laughing, Drea looked up at Kyle, the sparkle in her eyes sending a shot straight to his gut. He smiled back, secretly hoping it would keep the sparkle there just a little longer.

"Ready for another awesome day?" he asked.

"Are you kidding? You know Turtle Cove is my favorite." She flipped through the papers she was holding as she hopped down to the lower deck to the u-shaped bar where she spent most of her time while they were out with guests. "Still time for some last-minute changes, but if these numbers stick, we should only have about thirty-five on today's tour, so, perfect size for the cove."

The *Runnin' Down a Dream* had a limit of fifty-five guests, but all three members of its crew much preferred to get nowhere near that number. With that many guests, to only the three of them, it was like herding toddlers. Add in the danger of the water and of course, the rum punch, and it made for more chaos than it was worth. Well, that was until they saw the tip jar at the end of the excursion.

"Well, if that's all we have to deal with, maybe I'll tell Dalton he's stuck on deck duty and I'll hop into the water to come play," he said, giving her a little wink.

"Don't you dare tease me like that, Kyle Egan! Don't get me all excited about my favorite person coming to play in my favorite place and then back out on me." Drea pointed her finger at him accusingly and attempted to glare at him, only to have the edges of her mouth curve up slightly, giving away her amusement.

"I'm just gonna leave the whole 'playing in my favorite place' thing alone," he mused, climbing up the three little steps from the main deck into the captain's perch.

"Kyle!"

He laughed. "You said it, not me!"

Kyle settled into the seat and sighed, smiling to himself over jerking Drea's chain. He liked hearing that he was her favorite person; after all, she was without a doubt his. She'd not only been his first friend when he arrived in St. Thomas five years ago, but had been his saving grace in trying to figure out how one actually lives here full-time. She was quite possibly the best friend he'd ever had, and he couldn't imagine his life without her in it. That funny feeling niggled at his gut again as he wondered if he'd made her blush with his comment, and he had to stop himself from peeking underneath to check. He wasn't here to flirt—that was Dalton's role—he was here to do a job. Putting Drea out of his mind, and his focus back in place, he continued to prepare for the day ahead.

CHAPTER TWO

"ARE Y'ALL ready for the best day of your vacation?" Kyle yelled over the wind as they sailed out of the marina. "My name is Kyle and I'll be your captain today. The ravishing beauty up front is Dalton, my first mate, and that adorable little sprite with the effervescent giggle behind the bar is your US Coast Guard certified bartender and cruise director, Drea. She is in charge of your fun today, while Dalton and I are in charge of your safety. You have been warned!" Laughter rang out from the guests on the catamaran and Kyle could see some of the glances being thrown at both his teammates from those checking them out. "We'll be out of the marina shortly, where we shall stop to have a little chat about safety and what to expect. I promise to keep this part of the day short and sweet—just like all of Dalton's previous relationships."

"Damn right!" Dalton hollered, inciting more laughs from everyone on board, Drea included. Kyle would know that laugh anywhere, and he loved that even over the wind and the water and the voices of the guests on the boat, hers was the one he was able to hear the clearest.

Once they were clear of the marina and out in open water, he cut the engines and let them come to a slow float, bobbing up and down with the waves.

"Alrighty, if you will please turn your attention to Dalton up front, he will go over some safety basics."

Dalton launched into his well-rehearsed routine, going over the basics of the boat, and just how snorkeling worked. Kyle made his way down to the main deck, headed toward Drea when he heard her giggle in response to a deep voice.

"Convince your friends to get on the boat, huh?" the deep voice said. The voice belonged to some Jersey-shore wannabe who was leaning over the bar, looking at Drea like he'd like to eat her for lunch.

"I'm sorry," she answered. "I didn't mean to lie, but it was a little too easy. But, it got you guys up, out of bed, and on the best tour we have to offer!"

He laughed at her innocent act. "That it did, plus I get to spend time with you, and that doesn't suck." He winked.

"Sir, we need you to please pay attention to the safety demo. Coast Guard requires it, after all," Kyle said, cutting the meathead off before he could continue to crowd in on Drea. He gritted his teeth, forcing a smile so that the guest didn't see the frustration rising inside him.

"Yeah, cool," he said acknowledging Kyle. Turning back to Drea he said, "then I'll see you in a bit."

Drea looked over at Kyle with a quizzical look on her face before returning to organizing the safety waivers all the guests had turned in upon arrival at the boat.

"Friend of yours?" Kyle asked, breaking the silence.

"Not really, we met at the gym this morning."

"The gym? You hate the gym." He stood there waiting for her to continue. She made her way through the papers, filing them when finished. "He doesn't really seem your type."

"That guy? God, no. You know me better than that. But he hit on me this morning when I was on the treadmill, thinking I was a guest, and I couldn't help but mess with him. Plus, I figured if it all worked and I got him and his buddies on the boat, they'd be good for some decent tips."

"Okay, well, if he continues to bother you..."

"He wasn't bothering me. Now if you'll excuse me, I have some rum punch to mix up, to solidify those damn good tips." She stuck her tongue out at him, as she grabbed the extra-large pitcher from underneath the bar. She already had the four types of juices set out on the bar, so she started to open them one by one with the can opener, pouring in rough estimates of the "right" amount in the pitcher. When she was satisfied with the juice level, she reached for the rum, but it was just out of reach at the far corner of the bar. Drea wasn't short by any means—her curvy five-foot-six frame did place her on the taller side of average for a woman—but it didn't make reaching things down the long bar, easy, especially when she had to lean over the counter at the corner. She stood on her toes, grasping for the bottle, just grazing it with her fingertips each time.

"Wanna help?" she asked.

"You don't need my help, remember?"

"Ugh," she groaned, walking around the bar to grab the bottle. "You are such a pain."

"You love me!" he responded, making a heart with this hands. She stuck out her tongue at him again in response, and this time he returned the gesture.

DREA FINISHED POURING the rum in the pitcher just as Dalton was finishing up his well-rehearsed lesson on the finer points of snorkel gear.

"And once you have your life jacket over your head, and the waist strap around your middle, this really long fellow goes...wait for it...between your legs! Just slip it through, clip it in front here, and tighten. Gentlemen, please do not tighten this while sitting down and then go to stand up. Just trust me, it's not going to end well. Ladies, well, this is your vacation, so tighten it as much as you want!" Laughter rang out across the boat. Drea laughed too, because somehow this joke never got old, even though she'd heard Dalton say it at least once a day for the last three years.

She watched as Dalton started to hand out the life vests, making his way around the boat, flirting with each woman as he went. She didn't know how he did it, how his cheeks didn't hurt by the end of the day. He was a walking fantasy, though, to most women—tall, well-defined muscles, with dirty-blonde hair, blue eyes, and a smile that Drea was sure had turned many a world upside down. But despite the fact that he looked a lot like Scott Eastwood's twin, he never seemed to let it go to his head.

Looking to her left, she caught a glimpse of Kyle watching Dalton as well. At least she hoped he was watching Dalton, and not the gaggle of skinny little blondes that were perched up by the netting at the front of the boat, already stripped down to just their bikinis.

Their attention was fully on Dalton, but Drea was sure one smile from Kyle was all it would take and he'd have at least three of them hanging on his every word. At least, for Drea, all it took was that smile. His strong, broad-shoul-dered, six-foot frame, his square jaw and close-cropped dark hair didn't hurt either. Oh, and those deep brown eyes.

She'd loved looking at him from day one, and that feeling only magnified the closer they became while working together over the years. Her eyes followed as he started his ascent back to the captain's perch, wishing she could follow him up there.

"Now that y'all are aware of how to be safe, let's get this show on the road. Turtle Cove is about a twenty-five minute ride, so hold on to your hats, find a sunny spot, and let's roll!"

Once they got out to the cove, Drea and Dalton ushered the guests to the steps at the front of the boat where they could slowly descend into the water, or to the side, where they could jump in. Once they were all in, Drea shed her shorts and tank, righted the straps of her one-piece and grabbed her snorkel.

"Does that snorkel in your hand mean you're getting in?" dude-bro shouted at her from the water.

"Yeah, for a bit," she responded, bummed he had noticed. *Think of the tips, think of the tips.*

Knowing she couldn't keep him waiting, she put on her snorkel and hit the water. She swam past him, hoping to keep this one hundred percent professional. She was a snorkel guide and he was paying for this excursion. She saw him come up beside her and give her a thumbs-up, so she kept swimming in the direction of the biggest reef in the area, knowing that soon they could be distracted by a portion of the over five hundred different species of tropical fish, and dozen types of coral that were found in the Caribbean. This particular cove was also aptly named since they were pretty much guaranteed to see at least one sea turtle, if not three or four, hanging out around here.

After about fifteen minutes of swimming around, she felt him tap her on the shoulder trying to get her attention.

"This is pretty cool," he said, removing his mouthpiece, as they came up for air.

"Yeah," she responded, removing her snorkel from her teeth. "It's my favorite place on earth. You can't help but be happy here."

"You come here a lot?"

"Well, I mean, generally once a week for work," she laughed. "But I've been visiting this cove since I was a little girl. My uncles own the resort, so I grew up here."

"That's cool, you're a native!"

"I sure am, although—ahhh!" she shrieked, feeling arms grab her from behind. She turned around to see Kyle's great big smile and heard him chuckle through his snorkel. "Jesus, Kyle, you scared me!"

"Sorry...wait, no I'm not," he laughed. Drea rolled her eyes.

"Oh, sorry, where are my manners? Kyle, this is..." she trailed off, realizing she didn't know dude-bro's name.

"Brig," he answered, raising a hand in greeting.

"Nice to meet you, Brig. Drea, there is an older couple that is back closer to the boat. I wanna make sure they are doing okay, come with?"

"Yeah. Brig, glad you came out today. I'll see you back on the boat."

Brig gave a thumbs-up and stuck his face back in the water to go find his buddies. Drea splashed Kyle playfully before taking off toward the boat. They swam in companionable silence for a bit, circling the boat a couple of times before Drea realized there wasn't anyone over this way. *He totally made that up to make dude-bro go away*, she thought. She enjoyed being with just him, even if they were surrounded by all sorts of other people. It'd been awhile since they'd been able to go off and play like this. Their tours had been so busy and popular that guests had required their full attention for the last couple of months.

Kyle grabbed Drea's hand and pointed to a large leatherback sea turtle. As her smile widened at the sight, she noticed his did as well. She loved that smile so much—it made her feel all sorts of things. Kyle in general made her feel all sorts of things. But it didn't matter how much he made her feel, or how close they had become since he had moved to the island. Kyle was the ultimate professional; he was here focused on the job and sending money back to his mom in Florida. He also would never dream of taking up with the bosses' niece. She was just going to have to keep dreaming from afar.

Drea looked at her watch and pointed to it. "We better get back on the boat and start wrangling people in."

"I'm not sure I want to. What if I just want to stay here with you?" He pulled her close and wrapped his arms around her. Returning the gesture, she loosely wrapped her arms around his neck. She could see those deep brown eyes so clearly through his mask. She dreamed about those eyes, about getting lost in them, and seeing all the feelings she had for him returned in them. She wanted him to kiss her, to know if those lips that has just been wrapped around the snorkel were as soft as she imagined.

"And let Dalton sail the boat back?" she asked, trying to break the moment before she got too caught up in it. Kyle simply laughed in response. "Besides, it's Tuesday, so it's bonfire night."

"Fine," he relented. "Be the voice of reason."

They hopped back up onto the boat and she slipped her shorts back on, heading back to the bar to serve up rum punch. Once everyone was safely back on the boat, and they were on the way back toward the resort, she started handing out the punch. Guests were laughing and sharing some photos they got of the turtles, soaking up the last little bit of the excursion. When she got to Brig and his group, he stopped her.

"So, whatcha doing after this?" he asked her.

"Well, we have to clean up after you all and put the boat up for the night. Then it's back to the resort."

"Do you live on site?"

"I do. My uncles have this custom-made house that is basically three apartments all connected, which is where I grew up, but now I live in this little cottage across the way from them."

"So then I'll see you around? Like, tonight at the bonfire?"

"Um, maybe. I usually try to make a brief appearance."

"Good, looking forward to it."

Note to self, see if Kyle will skip the bonfire with me tonight, she thought.

CHAPTER THREE

"So, what room is he in?" Leona asked, sitting at her desk in the Housekeeping office, primed and ready to type something into the computer.

"Who?" Drea asked, looking up from the magazine she'd been flipping through, sitting on the little couch opposite the desk.

"Gym bro!" Leona answered, looking at her like it should have been obvious.

Drea just stared at her best friend in utter confusion. They had been best friends since Leona marched up to her during snack time in kindergarten and declared it so. Drea wouldn't have required much convincing, though. She was growing up on the resort that, while it wasn't explicitly stated as adults only, had no children's program and was marketed as a "grown-up playground," leaving Drea to often only have her toys and uncles for company.

"Gym bro, I like that. I'd just been calling him dude-bro," she laughed. "I have absolutely no idea what room he's in. I didn't exactly ask. Why?"

"I was gonna schedule that floor for a later servicing, so

you know, if you need to...make an exit." She made a sweeping gesture with her hand, narrowing avoiding knocking over the nameplate on the desk reading 'Leona Filipe'. "That way you could do so without Carmella or someone seeing you." Leona had worked as a housekeeper starting in high school, when her mom had gotten it in her head that she needed a job to keep her out of trouble. She'd taken over as the head of housekeeping almost eighteen months ago when the lady who had held the job since the resort opened decided to retire.

"Why would I need to 'make an exit'? What are you...Leona! Oh my God, no, just no! I'm not going back to his room. I'm not even going to entertain the idea of anything that could lead to the idea of going back to his room."

"Fine, but if you change your mind, you just let me know and I'll work some magic over here. Oh!" she exclaimed as she started typing away at the keyboard.

"Yes?" Drea asked, interest slightly piqued that her refusal to sleep with a guest sparked an idea in her best friend.

"I wonder if he's in 1227. Isobel said there are like four or five guys staying in this one room, and they have like seven jumbo boxes of condoms." Leona turned to look at her, eyes wide, an impish smile on her face. "So, they are either doing each other, or came here with plans."

Drea shook her head in exasperation, letting out a quiet laugh. "Well, that's a hell of a visual, so thanks for that. But I have zero interest in him, other than making sure he remains a satisfied guest."

"Is he hot?"

"He's not bad-looking, especially if you're really into that big muscly type. He kinda looks like he could be some evil villain's henchman, with his really dark hair and scowled facial features. But he's not..." she trailed off and looked toward the office door that was open just a crack.

"Kyle? He's just not Kyle?"

"Pretty much," she sighed. "We had an amazing day today. The group was smaller, so he left Dalton alone on the boat and came swimming with me."

"I thought you went swimming with gym bro?"

"I did, for a bit. But then Kyle came and stole me away. It would have been kinda cute and romantic if he hadn't been simply trying to protect the bosses' niece from the predatory frat boy."

"I'm sure that was not his only motivation."

"Maybe not," she shrugged, dismissing the suggestion. "But enough about him. You promised you wouldn't let me drone on about him anymore. And goodness, after he held me while we were swimming today, I could probably talk about him forever."

"He held you?" Leona asked, raising an eyebrow in suspicion.

"Right before it was time to get back in the boat. Pulled me into him and told me he didn't want to stop swimming. It was nothing. It was just that we haven't had a chance to go snorkeling, just us, in months, so it was a nice break from having to deal with guests all the time. It was a 'you're my best buddy' kind of thing, not a 'I'm secretly in love with you' kind of thing."

"Still, that's super sweet."

"It was, and it's just enough to continue to fuel my happily ever after fantasies. But, really, enough about Kyle."

"Being around him all day isn't going to help you stop thinking about it," Leona said.

"I know, but it is kinda my job."

"What about your big idea? Have you brought it up to your uncles yet?"

"Ha, ha...no," Drea answered her.

"Why not? I think it would be so awesome! A spa is exactly what we need around here!"

"I don't want to stir the pot," she said, sighing. "Everything is in the works for Uncle Gray to add in more adventure stuff and excursions, so me bringing up that I want to add on what would basically be an entire new department is not going to go over well."

"So maybe it's not a now thing," she suggested, "but a someday thing. I think you're crazy for not telling them."

"Well, maybe someday I'll bring it up, but for now, it remains a fantasy. Tucked up in there right next to Kyle," she replied. "Oh my God, I did it again. I'm talking about him. Make me stop!"

"Well, if it makes you feel better, you're not the only one with a weird guest encounter today," Leona said, thankfully changing the subject.

"Do tell."

"So, you know how your Uncle Vaughn requires me to do those random room checks, so I'm basically secret shopping my housekeepers?" Drea nodded. "So, the best way I have found to truly randomly choose which rooms I hit up is to use one of those number generator things off the internet. I put in the range and let it kick out six or so numbers and then as long as I haven't hit that room up in the last ninety days or so, I put it on the list. So on today's list pops up 1122."

"That's a fun number."

"Right? I kinda thought so too. So I'm making my rounds, checking up on things. I stopped to talk to Carmella at one point, and made my way to 1122. As is standard, I checked the indicator light above the door, and it doesn't show that the room is currently occupied. But you and I have both been around this stuff long enough to know that people don't always put their keycards into the socket like they should, especially in the daytime when they don't need the lights to turn on. So I knocked. I knocked, Drea, multiple times. Even did the stereotypical 'housekeeping!' call. Nothing, no response."

"Okay, so, I take it the room wasn't empty?"

"I walk in, pretty confident at this point that the room is vacant. I don't actually check that when I pull numbers, because technically it doesn't matter, right? So I walk in, and there, sitting on the edge of the bed, straddling the corner that faces the door, is this dude. Jacking off."

"NO!"

"Oh yes," she continued. "Just sitting there, dick in hand, like it's the most natural thing in the world. Just stroking away! And we're not talking Dalton-level looks here, where if you walked in on this there is a part of you that would be like "well, maybe I should take over!" No, we're talking old and hairy."

"How old? Like, wrinkly ballsack old?" Drea asked, a disgusted look on her face.

"Like wrinkly ballsack old. I'm pretty sure his wrinkles had wrinkles."

"What'd you do?"

"What do you mean what did I do? I sputtered out an apology and backed out of the room as quickly as I could. Then considered rinsing out my eyes with bleach."

"Oh my God, that's...that's....wow. That tops gym bro for sure!" Drea said, laughing.

"And what's worse, it was like he wasn't even fazed that I walked in. Almost like he sat in that exact spot *hoping* he would be caught. I will never be able to unsee this!"

Drea clutched her middle trying to control her laughter. Housekeeping was a beast of its own—having to maintain ridiculous standards of cleanliness and professionalism, working very hard to be damn near invisible, all while having unfettered access to strangers' personal belongings and weird little glimpses into how they lived their lives. Guests brought a wide range of items with them on vacation, and left just as wide a range of them behind when they left. There were the everyday standards of wallets, keys, phones, and laptop cords, and even your miscellaneous vibrator wasn't *that* uncommon these days.

Having been in this role for almost ten years, Leona had had some strange encounters with guests over the years, and had found some seriously strange items left behind in rooms. She kept a list posted in her office next to her desk of the top ten things she and her team had run across over the years: a prosthetic limb, an urn (complete with ashes), a bag full of sequential hundred-dollar bills totaling almost sixty thousand dollars, a journal with detailed entries of this guest's love of brussels sprouts, and a kitten (although that person had been kind enough to leave a note and an extra large tip) made appearances on the list. The number one spot had long been occupied by what the girls simply referred to as "the duck pond," referring to the time they walked into a suite to find the bathtub filled with water and seven ducklings swimming around.

Just when Drea thought she was going to be able to catch her breath, the office door flew open, causing both women to jump and burst back into giggles. Vaughn Quinlan stuck just his head into the office, looking back and forth between his niece and her best friend.

"I should tell you to stop laughing and get back to work," he said. "But I know better than to think you two would listen to me."

"Hey, Uncle Vaughn. Need one of us?" Drea asked.

"Nope, just looking for Simone. She said she wanted dinner before the bonfire, but I can't find her."

"Did you try the kitchen?" Leona asked. "I feel like every time I see her she's either in your office or there."

"That is where I am headed next, although maybe it's where I should have started. Knowing her she's probably in there harassing Miller and his staff about exactly how she wants something sautéed. Okay, back to work, you two." He winked and closed the door as he backed out.

"So, you meeting up with gym bro at the bonfire?" Leona asked, swinging her full attention back to Drea.

"Ugh, not if I can help it. If I run into him, I'll be polite and make conversation, but I'm certainly not going to seek him out."

"Maybe Kyle will come to your rescue again. Give you more fodder for those late-night fantasies of yours," Leona smirked.

"Oh, shut up. I promise you, I don't need any help in the Kyle fantasy department."

KYLE'S CELL PHONE RANG, disrupting the music playing from it while he showered. He cut the water and grabbed the towel from the rack at the far side of the tub, drying off his hand enough to reach for the phone. He answered it and put it on speaker to continue drying off.

"Hey, Mom."

"Hi, baby, how are you?" JoAnna Egan's voice called out and filled the little bathroom.

"Oh, you know, living the dream," he answered casually. He alternated between this and "just another day in paradise" every time she asked. And, really, it was true because, even on his bad days, he was still living in St. Thomas working as a charter boat captain. He worked for a family-run business instead of some big corporate monster, he was able to live in staff housing so his rent was covered, and he never had to put on a tie. Hell, most days he didn't have to put on real pants. There would be no complaints here.

"Oh, that's good. Did you have a good day? Which tour did you guys run today?"

"We went out to Turtle Cove. It was great. A little windy, but nothing that caused any major trouble. We actually had a little bit of a smaller group, too, so I got to go for a bit of a swim with Drea."

"Oh, how wonderful! I bet she loved that! How is Andrea?"

Kyle paused briefly, wrapping the towel around his waist and sitting down on the edge of the tub. "She's good. Not much has changed with her either," he answered. Talking to his mom about Drea was always a little complicated. She knew Drea was important to him, although if she had an inkling of just *how* important she never let on. He'd loved sharing stories of their adventures together over the years, and they'd had a lot. But he was still hesitant, thinking that his mom would easily be able to hear something in his voice that gave it away that Drea was more than just some girl.

"Well, please tell her I say hi. Anyway, the reason I'm calling is, I went online to pay a bill and looked at my bank statement and you made another deposit. I thought we agreed that you weren't going to do that anymore."

"No, Mom, you agreed. I did no such thing."

"Kyle—"

"Mom," he cut her off. "Does your insurance cover your anti-nausea meds? Does it cover a hundred percent of the dialysis?"

"No, but that doesn't mean—"

"But nothing, Mom. That is part of why I took this job, so that you could live stress free over your medical treatment."

He'd never forget the day he met Grayson Quinlan. Having just graduated college, he'd been working at a corporate-owned marina in Clearwater, Florida, not far from his childhood home, trying to help his mom stay afloat after being diagnosed with kidney disease his senior year. His father had died in a training exercise accident with the Coast Guard when Kyle was six, so it had just been the two of them for most of what Kyle could remember. His mom had a pretty decent job, but their health insurance only covered eighty percent of her dialysis and didn't cover the meds that helped her nausea after the treatments, since they were considered "non-critical." How not puking your guts out twice a week was "non-critical" Kyle wasn't sure, but there was no reasoning with these insurance companies.

Grayson had walked into the marina like he owned the place. Dressed in board shorts, a faded T-shirt, and a ball-cap, he didn't look like the big-deal-VIP customer Kyle had been told would be stopping by that day. Grayson had been so impressed with Kyle's knowledge of the yachts they were looking at, and the fact that he didn't kiss his ass the whole time, that when Grayson came back the next day, with his niece Drea in tow, to officially purchase one of the boats, he insisted on working with only Kyle. The sales guy hadn't been too happy about that, and let his feelings be known. While Kyle hadn't been the least bit surprised by this reaction from the sales guy, what he was surprised by was that the only offer made that afternoon was for Kyle to move down to St. Thomas and to work for him and his brothers at their luxury resort. The offer was too good to turn down, especially with that cute, curly-haired brunette urging him to accept with those sparkling brown eyes.

"I know that. But Kyle, if you're sending that much home all the time, there is no way you're saving to buy your own boat, and I know that's ultimately what you want to do," she pleaded.

"Mom, I have plenty of savings, promise. We've been over this. I can do both."

"Yes, but I got a raise at work, so I can afford this all on my own now. Think of how much faster you could be saving!"

"Or that you can now save some money, so that you could someday retire. Mom, as much fun as it is to go in these circles, I just got out of the shower and have to get dressed. It's bonfire night."

"Oh, I'm sorry, honey, you should have said something sooner! Go have fun with Andrea—we'll talk more later. I love you."

"Love you too," he said, hanging up and putting the phone down on top of the toilet bowl. He stood up and looked at the mirror across from the tub. He sighed heavily as he picked up his toothbrush and started to brush his teeth. He loved his mom and would do anything for her. After all, she'd sacrificed so much for him over the years.

It was why he couldn't do anything about the tingly feeling he got when Drea was around. It didn't matter how much he loved watching her glide effortlessly through the water when they were out swimming, or how every week at the bonfire he just wanted to hold her in his arms until they melded together from the heat of the flames. He had to stay focused on the job. He couldn't risk losing the best opportunity that had ever come his way—the one that was his ticket to someday owning his own company. Once he had enough saved to try and go out on his own, he could think about actually having a relationship. Until then, he would just have to deal with the heartache.

CHAPTER FOUR

No one remembered exactly how the weekly bonfires got started, and everyone seemed to have a slightly different version of its origins. The story always told to the guests was that it was in honor of the night Miller Quinlan and Dave Miller had met Drea's aunt and mother, who had been affectionately referred to as "the sisters" by most people since before Drea was born. After the two young men had bonded in high school when they both simultaneously responded to someone calling out "Miller!", they quickly became inseparable. So when they met sisters Marta and Sofia on a trip to Puerto Rico when they were twenty-one, the only real surprise had been that they hadn't held a joint wedding right then and there.

As legend told, the two buddies had been wandering along the beach at sunset and came upon a bunch of locals starting a bonfire, and were drawn in by the two beauties, forgoing whatever plans they had for the rest of the night and spending it right there with them. Every time Drea had asked her Uncle Miller about it, he would tell her the same thing. "I seem to remember it being more campfire than bonfire, but don't trust me—there was a lot of rum involved."

Regardless of what the genesis may have been, it was easily one of the most popular activities that the resort offered. So much so, about fifteen years ago Vaughn had invested in an area specially designed for the event, complete with an industrial fire pit built into the beach, a bar, a DJ, and a s'mores-making station. The beauty behind the bonfire was that it was truly never the same event twice. Some weeks it was low-key and subdued, others it was a raging party that went well into the wee hours of the night. This spot had seen many a vacation hookup, a couple of marriage proposals, and there was even an instance of a woman destroying her wedding photos in celebration of her divorce. Forget Vegas, what happened at the Indigo Royal stayed at the Indigo Royal.

The fire pit was located just outside the lobby, to the left of the concierge desk, just before the pool. The bar put in for the bonfire nights also served the pool during peak hours, helping offset the crowd from "Paradise City," the swim-up bar on the other side of the pool. The area flowed into the beach, which had a number of lounge chairs, umbrellas, and even a couple of cabanas permanently set up for guests to relax under. Just past the pool were the three buildings that held guest rooms. Barracuda Tower stood twelve stories high and was host to just over three hundred basic hotel rooms and suites. Just next to the tower were the Black Velvet and the Purple Rain, which housed multi-room suites only, and which Drea had always thought looked more like apartment buildings than a hotel with their open breezeways. Past the guest rooms was "The Casbah" bar, which also housed the night club that made an appearance on Friday nights. If you kept walking past the bar and down a little closer to the beach, you'd eventually find the four exclusive beachfront bungalows known as "The Villas" for those guests who wanted, and could afford, more space and privacy.

Drea hung back just outside the open-air lobby looking out at the bonfire space as some of the grounds staff finished up the last of the prep. Her Uncle Miller stood to her left, leaning against a pillar, trying to be nonchalant about spying on his team putting together the s'mores. Uncle Vaughn stood to her right, frantically typing away on his phone.

"Would you put that damn thing away, please?" Simone scolded as she walked up to the group. "You know the rules of bonfire night."

Though they weren't actually married, Simone and Vaughn had been together for twenty-one years, and Drea considered her to be her aunt, although by the time she'd had the thought to call her Aunt Simone, she was almost eleven and both she and Simone had agreed at that point it would be weird to change. The day she showed up representing the Board of Tourism, wanting to use the resort as a photo shoot location for some brochures, Vaughn had been stopped in his tracks by the tall, slender, brunette beauty. When Vaughn told his brothers later on that it was unlike anything he'd ever felt, like he was magnetically drawn to her, Miller had just laughed and responded, "Dude, you're in so much trouble. That's exactly what I felt when I first saw Marta."

"It's going away, I promise. I just have to finish...ok, done," he said, locking his phone and shoving it in his pocket.

"I don't know. Drea, what do you think, should he go lock it in his office?" Simone asked.

"Depends. Uncle Vaughn, you gonna behave?"

"I promise to be the dictionary definition of behaved, kiddo," he responded, putting his arm around Drea's shoulder, pulling her close, and kissing the top of her head.

Drea smiled up at her uncle, who released her and pulled in Simone for a long, hard kiss. They had been the only real-life example of romance in Drea's life, and she adored watching just how much they loved each other. Not only had Miller never remarried, she couldn't remember him even going on a date, ever. He still talked about her Aunt Marta like she was just the most perfect thing he'd ever seen. Listening to him talk about her, the only way you knew she was gone was that he used the past tense, and even then you'd think it'd been only a couple of years, and not twenty-five. She might not have had the most conventional upbringing, but she was surrounded by so much love she couldn't help but feel like the luckiest girl around.

"If Grayson doesn't hurry his ass up..." Miller said, pushing up from the pillar.

"I'm here, I'm here," Grayson said, jogging up to the group. "Sorry, there was a guest who wanted a private tour of the boat."

"Oh, and I'm sure you had no problem giving her the grand tour," Simone said, rolling her eyes. Grayson Quinlan was known by many for his flirting—no woman was safe from that smile of his. But for as much as people tried to create a playboy reputation around him, no one really knew much about his dating habits, including his own family.

All three of her uncles were good-looking men. Tall with dark features, all three resembled each other quite a bit in their youth, but age had helped set them each apart a bit. Vaughn had gone gray much earlier than his younger brothers and nowadays, Drea thought he resembled the guy from the Trivago commercial more than anyone. Miller's scruff had started to gray in the last couple of years, too, but since he never let it quite get to a full beard, one would have to look quite close in order to notice it. Grayson's goatee was still the same shade it had been for all of Drea's childhood, but deep down she couldn't help but wonder if that was aided by some hair dye.

"HE," Grayson emphasized the word, "was mostly interested in the engine. He was a captain in the navy like forty years ago, so he wanted to see what had changed. Sorry I'm late, doll," he finished, looking at Drea.

"I'm not a little girl anymore, you don't owe me an apology."

"You'll never *not* be our little girl!" Drea didn't have to look at all their faces to know that was true. Her uncles had changed their lives around to make sure she was taken care of growing up and that she wanted for nothing. Their little family might have looked weird from the outside, but it worked just fine for them.

"Alright, so now that we're all here, what's everyone got?" Miller asked.

"There is a group of four blondes that I call trying to entice Dalton all night. He'll flirt with all of them, but they'll all be in their own beds tonight," Drea said.

"I know the ones you're talking about, and I'll give you that, but I think this group of meatheads will try and catch some of his castoffs, so I see at least one drunken hookup between those two groups," Vaughn interjected.

"Mr. and Mrs. Prage, that really old couple from Oregon—they're gonna be the last ones standing," Miller stated.

"Oh, you think?" Simone asked. Miller nodded confidently. "Well, I'm calling an explosive fight between that weird redhead couple. With at least one chair thrown."

"Damn," Vaughn muttered under his breath.

"Uncle Gray, you wanna place your bet?" Drea asked. They had started playing this game sometime when she was in high school, once she was old enough to really understand most of what was going down. They met up before the bonfire every week to place their bets, and then had breakfast the next morning to compare notes, and see who "won." There wasn't always a clear winner and/or loser, and really the idea was to simply be the least wrong. The more specific you got, the more chance you had at losing. Winners simply got bragging rights. Whoever was deemed to have lost, though, had to wear "the shirt."

"The shirt" looked innocent enough to any bystander. It was a simple, if not fading after years of wear, heather-gray shirt that read "ask me about the bet I lost." However, when you work in the service business and interact with guests all day, you inevitably were asked, constantly, about the bet you lost. And you couldn't just answer "you didn't get blind stinking drunk and puke on yourself like I thought," now could you? So the loser was stuck making up a litany of different answers, since the rule was you couldn't say the same thing twice unless it was the truth.

"Hmmmmm," Grayson pondered. "We're gonna see a staff hookup tonight."

"With a guest, or something more incestuous?" Simone inquired.

"Nah, I'm gonna leave out specifics, but one of our staff is getting lucky tonight."

"Dude, are you asking to wear the shirt? How are we gonna know?" Vaughn scoffed.

"I'm not sure I want to," Drea inserted.

"Simone's over here calling chairs being thrown. I'm not sure I'm gonna need to go in search of a used condom."

"Ewwww, ew, ew, ew, ew ew!" Drea said, scrunching up her nose. Her uncles laughed at her reaction.

"You just keep thinking like that, baby girl," Miller commented.

"And that's why you'll always be our little girl" Grayson added.

AFTER THE FAMILY each went their separate ways—Vaughn and Simone off to secure their favorite spot on the beach, Miller to go rearrange the s'mores bar, and Grayson off to wherever it was he ventured off to during the bonfire—Drea grabbed a seat at the bar to wait for either Leona or Kyle. She looked out at the guests starting to arrive, grabbing their spots by the fire or gathering s'mores ingredients. Hoping that she blended in with the crowd, she sipped on the drink the bartender had automatically set down in front of her. Being the owners' kid had its privileges.

She watched as the group of four overly done-up, seemingly enhanced blondes from the boat arrived, umbrella drinks already in hand, clad in itty-bitty skirts (although that term was being generous) and their bikini tops. Each one seemed sexier than the last, with their long blonde hair, sparkling eyes, flat stomachs, and seriously generous busts. It was no wonder they had so much confidence, they were like walking mannequins. Just as she was about to turn away, she caught a glimpse of exactly what, or rather whom, she'd been looking for, heading right toward the hot blondes.

Drea was not the only one who had noticed him either, as the group of women turned toward Kyle and made their way in his direction. They were suddenly all smiles and giggles and hair flipping. The tallest of the four greeted him with a hug, which Kyle casually returned with only his right arm, trying to minimize full body contact. *Since when did he hug guests?* she wondered to herself. The three others followed suit and Kyle returned each hug, smiling broadly at each girl. Her stomach was tying itself in knots as she watched him stand there and chat, a new knot forming with each little giggle she heard escape from their lips. Just when she thought that maybe he might try to walk away, the music from the DJ picked up a little and "Candy," as Drea had started to refer to her in her head, the blonde who initiated the hugging, grabbed Kyle's hands and dragged him to a less-crowded area to dance.

Pulling him close and throwing her arms around his neck, "Candy" giggled as she started to move her hips in time with the music. The song the DJ was playing wasn't overly slow, but also didn't have some harsh bass beat behind it. In fact, it was the perfect mid-tempo song to simply rock back and forth to while holding another person. Drea's stomach dropped as she sat there, waiting for Kyle to pull away from the girl. She slid her eyes back to the friends left behind, who all stood there also watching the couple, whispering among themselves. She looked back over at Kyle and found him smiling. This was not his polite customer service smile, but rather his actual smile—the one that made her insides melt, the one that she had always thought was reserved just for her. He spun the girl as they continued to move to the beat and they both laughed at something she said in response to his spin. Tears started to form in the corners of her eyes and Drea thought she was going to throw up. She needed to get out of there.

She quickly slid off the barstool and turned to go. She

wasn't sure exactly where she'd go, but anywhere where she didn't have to witness her nightmare play out and feel her heart shatter would be just fine. As she turned to walk away, she smacked right into a wall. A six-foot, four-inch Dalton-shaped wall.

"Whoa there, sugar, where you off to so fast?" Dalton asked her, grabbing on to her upper arms to steady her.

She looked down quickly and shook her head, trying to rid herself of the tears that were forming. She didn't want Dalton to see her upset. She didn't want to have to explain herself. "Nowhere, just headed inside."

"How about you look at me when you say that?" She looked up at him, hoping that she could hide the fact that she was dying inside.

"Just headed inside, Dalton. Let me go, 'kay?"

"Not until you tell me what's wrong," he said. She opened her mouth to protest, but he cut her off. "And don't you dare bother telling me nothing is the matter. A) the bonfire is your most favorite thing, like ever, and you never miss it, even when you're sick. And B) I spend pretty much all day, every day with you. I know your facial expressions better than you think."

"Is that so? Then what does mine say right now?" she challenged him.

"Right now your face is telling me to go the fuck away, but your eyes are screaming heartbreak."

"Oh," Drea responded, surprised he could actually read her like that.

"And, I would bet that it has everything to do with that scene right there," he jutted his chin out, while turning her around to face the pair. "Candy" was still wrapped around Kyle, the both of them smiling like they were having the time of their lives.

"What? How...I mean...you..."

"Know? Yes, love, I know."

"But, but...HOW?!" she asked, turning back around to face him.

"Shall we return to that whole all day, every day thing? I see the way you look at him. I see how different you are with him than you are with me, or *any other* staff member here for that matter. I have known from day one that you are head over heels, ass over teakettle in love with Kyle Egan."

"Oh my God, I'm so embarrassed."

"Eh, don't be. But what I do not understand is why you don't tell him how you feel."

"Because he's not interested in me! He doesn't see me as anything other than the bosses' niece, and he would never, ever put his job at risk like that."

"How do you know he's not interested in you? Has he told you that?"

"No, but he's never acted interested in being more than my BFF either."

"Well, girl, I'm not gonna lie to you here. You give off the BFF vibe. Maybe if you wore something other than that one-piece under your tank, then he would get the idea that you're all woman and that you're interested in *all* he has to offer." Drea glared at him. "Drea, I'm serious. You're smoking hot. And you're smart, funny, and you can hang like one of us dudes, and that is super sexy. You just need to go after what you want."

"Even if I could find it in myself to do it, I'm not sure I would know where to start," she sighed.

"I'll tell you what. I'll help."

"Help? How are you gonna help?"

"I have my ways. Trust Uncle Dalton."

"I have enough uncles. Find another nickname for yourself," she smirked.

"I'll work on it. Do we have a deal?" He held out his hand.

"I don't know why I'm agreeing, but okay. I will accept your help." She slid her hand into his and they shook.

"Good deal."

"But, I still need to get out of here. I've seen enough and I just need to be alone right now."

Dalton pulled her close and gently kissed her on her forehead. "I understand. Go find Leona. Last I saw her she was prancing around the kitchen pulling out the leftover magic muffins."

Drea stepped back and started to walk back toward the hotel lobby, but stopped and turned around. "Dalton..."

"Yeah, sugar?"

"I have no idea why you're doing this, but um, thanks."

"Any time, love. Any time."

CHAPTER FIVE

KYLE WASN'T sure why he was still dancing with the tall blonde. She'd run up to him while he was on his way to meet Drea at the bar, hugging him like she'd known him her entire life. He hugged her back, mostly so she didn't break his neck from hanging off of it, but still tried to avoid any kind of body contact. As soon as he let her go, her three friends all jumped in for a hug. He thought maybe after these greetings he could make a simple escape, but the instigator inserted herself right back in his view, making it so he couldn't turn away.

"I'm Staci, with an i," she giggled, flipping her long hair over her shoulder. "I don't think we got a chance to be introduced today on the boat."

"Hi Staci, I'm Captain Kyle. Nice to officially meet you."

She giggled again, trying to make her smile even bigger. She reached out and ran her hand up and down Kyle's arm in a flirty little gesture, and he took a slight step back, trying to give himself some distance. It's not that she wasn't hot. In fact, she was the exact definition of "hot" according to most red-blooded males—tall, blonde, and blue-eyed, with long legs, a sizable rack, and an itty-bitty waist, highlighted by the strappy little heels she wore, matching her bikini top and denim skirt. But Kyle wasn't sure that, other than that sizable rack, there was much more to her. Maybe he was wrong—he shouldn't judge her based on her vacation attire.

"Look, Captain Kyle," she said, closing the couple of inches he'd put between them, giggling again. "I'm gonna be real up-front with you. You seem very sweet, and I'm sure there is someone out there who just adores you for that. But that's not gonna be me. What I want is Dalton."

Kyle barked out a laugh, not sure if it was from relief or the knowledge that he'd been right about her. He took a moment to wipe the grin off his face, looking her directly in the eye. "Um, thanks? I think there was a compliment in there. So, then, um...what exactly is it you think I'm gonna do?"

"Oh, I just hoped that if you were around, he'd be close by. Or you could lead me to him."

"Oh," Kyle said, relieved she didn't expect much more. "Well, he should be around here somewhere."

"But where somewhere?" she giggled again.

"Not quite sure, but if I see him, I'll send him your way," Kyle answered.

He went to take a step around her, finally seeing an escape from her clutches, when the music picked up tempo a bit. She grabbed his hands and pulled him over to an area where the crowd had thinned. "Let's dance! Spin me around and show me off!" she squealed.

Kyle did as he was told, lifting his right arm and spinning her as if they were ballroom dancing or something. She tripped over her own feet a bit and Kyle couldn't help but laugh. She pulled him in close so their bodies were touching and slipped her arms around his neck, swaying her hips in time with the music, forcing his body to follow along.

"You don't have to look so excited to be with me," she said, once again giggling.

Kyle wasn't sure how to respond. She was a guest, so he couldn't tell her that all he could really think about was how he hoped he didn't get VD from her. On the other hand, she was on a pretty singular track here, and only using Kyle to further her agenda, so maybe a lighter version of the truth wouldn't be such a bad thing.

"It's not you. Well, I mean, it is on some level, since you're the one kinda holding me hostage. But, it's tradition, you could say, for me to spend the bonfire with someone else."

"Let me guess, that cute little brunette from the boat? The one you hopped into the water after?"

Kyle couldn't help but smile. A real, true, genuine full smile. Staci might not be scoring off the charts on an IQ test, but she saw straight through him. He thought he'd kept all those feelings masked when they were out on the water, but maybe his actions toward the Hulk Hogan wannabe weren't as well disguised as he thought. He hadn't realized anyone even paid him and Drea that close attention, other than maybe Brig. So maybe he wasn't as stealthy as he thought. Had her uncles noticed too? There was no way. If any of them had suspected anything, they would have said something. They were all too close to not.

"I see that smile," Staci cooed. "I'm on to something, aren't I?"

"Yeah, she's um, Drea. Drea is special."

"I knew it!" she squealed again. "I just knew it! I saw the way you held her today while we were snorkeling. So, is it true love?"

Kyle laughed again, this time nervously, but never letting that smile leave his face. Did he love her? Like actual real love? There was no way—she was his best friend. So what if he wondered what was under that swimsuit and how exactly she would feel underneath him. That wasn't love, that was lust. And all that really meant was that maybe he needed to find another outlet other than his right hand. Some "inspiration" that wasn't based around Drea might not hurt the cause either.

"She's my best friend, we'll just leave it at that." As soon as he said the words, he knew that he was lying. It didn't matter though—her uncles would have his head, he'd lose his job, and he wasn't even convinced she saw him that way in return.

Staci opened her mouth to respond, but as she did, Kyle noticed movement out of the corner of his eye, over in the direction of the bar. The exact bar where he should have been standing with Drea right about now. He saw a flurry of her bright tank top as she dropped from her barstool and quickly spun around, right into Dalton. He tried to step away, but Staci grabbed hold of him again and kept them moving to the beat. He tried to focus on what was happening between Drea and Dalton—he was holding her awfully close for Kyle's taste—while not stepping on Staci's feet. Staci followed his gaze over to his friends and then turned back to him, looking concerned.

"Something wrong?"

"I'm...I'm not sure."

He stopped moving and turned fully to watch Drea and Dalton. He wasn't sure if they had seen him with Staci and he was silently praying that they'd blended in with the crowd enough. They were whispering to each other, and Drea was holding her head down like she was upset. It was a punch to Kyle's gut to see her like this and turning to Dalton of all people. Was there something going on there that he didn't know about? She couldn't be interested in him, could she? She'd never be interested in a playboy like him, at least he didn't think she would. But she never actually talked about being interested in anyone, and she did spend all day with him, just like she did Kyle, smiling and play flirting. Or Kyle assumed it was play flirting. He saw her start to walk away and pause to turn back to Dalton. She smiled as she said something to him, and he saw Dalton smile in return.

"Staci, if you'll excuse me," Kyle said, not waiting for her answer. He pried her off of him, and walked quickly toward where Drea was walking away.

"Whoa there, cowboy, where you headed off to?" Dalton asked, grabbing his arm and pulling him back from following her into the lobby.

"What's wrong with Drea? She looked upset. What happened?"

"She'll be fine, just leave her be."

"Why? What upset her? I need to go see what's wrong."

"Not sure you're the right person for the job."

"What? And you are?" Kyle snarked.

"I think there are just some things girlfriends are better for, dude," Dalton answered, looking down at him. Kyle wasn't short by any means, but at six foot four, Dalton towered over pretty much everyone. "What's up with you and Wendy Peffercorn over there?"

"Who?"

"Dude, the blonde who was just all over you? The one who looks just like the lifeguard in *The Sandlot*? Don't tell me you forgot already." They turned to look at Staci, who had made her way back to her friends and was chatting away about something. Probably about whether or not her stunt was going to work.

"Oh, her. Nothing. She's looking for you, actually."

"So why were you latched on to her?"

"For starters, she latched on to me, and she was trying to get your attention. What's going on with you and Drea?" Kyle said, turning his gaze back to his buddy.

"You think something is going on between me and Drea?"

"You know that Grayson would kick your ass, right? Not to mention what Vaughn and Miller would do."

"Dude, sometimes I just do not understand what goes through your head."

"I'm just saying, whatever you said or did to upset her—"

"Whatever *I* did to upset her?" Dalton cut him off. "Okay, dude, I'm gonna go hang with the hot blondes and I'll see you tomorrow on the boat. But take my advice, dude, just leave Drea alone tonight." He walked away, heading toward the group of women who had eagerly been awaiting his appearance all evening.

Kyle watched as the women greeted Dalton with huge smiles, giggles, and just enough body movement to make him wonder if those bikini strings would hold. He slid into the seat that Drea had been sitting in and sighed. Something had gone very wrong tonight and he had no idea what. Much less how he was going to right the ship.

CHAPTER SIX

As was fairly standard, the only one who beat Drea to family breakfast was Miller. So many years of being up for breakfast service and kiddo duty had created an internal clock that she was pretty sure he couldn't turn off even if he wanted to, and she was pretty sure there was zero desire in there. She'd gotten her love of being up early from him, she was sure of it, even if they weren't biologically related. Long gone were the days of her joining him in the kitchen to get the day going, helping make the magic muffins and set out whatever else he might need for the day. Those events were now replaced with her morning run along the beach, watching the sun come up, listening to the waves come and go. She loved having this time to herself.

Miller was settled at the family table that sat over in the back corner of the kitchen, poring over the morning paper. The "big house" where Drea had grown up, and where the brothers still lived, had a decent-sized kitchen and small living room that was the central part of the home, that all three of the separate apartments connected into. Although, other than drinks and some basic snacks, Drea had no recollection of the kitchen ever really being used. Every big family meal, and even most regular everyday meals were eaten at the table in the resort kitchen. This was the table where she had done a good portion of her homework while Miller worked, and this was the kitchen where he taught her to cook. Drea slid into a chair at the table, leaving an open spot to her right and in between her and her uncle. She reached for the carafe in the middle of the table and one of the mugs Miller had set out, pouring herself some coffee and taking a nice long sip.

"Morning, baby girl," her uncle said, looking up from his paper. "You disappeared early last night. Where'd you get off to?"

Oh shit, Drea thought. She had not been prepared to answer any questions about last night. She didn't realize anyone but Dalton and Leona knew that she had left the bonfire early and didn't return. Leona had texted her late last night to tell her that Dalton did spend a good portion of the night with "Candy" and her friends, so she knew she was in the clear on her bet. Besides, Grayson had a point—Simone called out chair throwing, so unless that went down, she was going to lose.

"I wasn't feeling good, so I just went to bed early," she said quickly. *It wasn't a complete lie.*

"Oh no, is it something you ate? Are you coming down with something?" he asked, reaching over to try and feel her forehead.

"No, it's just, I was..."

"Miller, leave the girl be!" Simone chastised, walking into the kitchen. She grabbed a mug and poured herself some coffee before sitting down to Drea's left. "She's a girl, we have girl things to deal with. Girl things we don't want to talk to our uncles about. Not to mention, she's twenty-six.

Even if she was out having hot, wild, monkey sex, she does not owe you an answer."

Miller just stared at her for a moment before saying "forgive me for being concerned," with his hands raised in surrender. He turned back to his paper, avoiding eye contact with either woman.

"She better not have been out having hot, wild, monkey sex! Someone puts his hands on her, I'll kill him," Vaughn injected, as he swept into the room.

"Uncle Vaughn, I'm—" Drea began, before being cut off by Simone.

"I repeat, she's twenty-six. She can do what she wants! Including hot, wild, monkey sex."

"Who's having hot, wild, monkey sex?" came Grayson's voice.

"Apparently Drea," answered Vaughn.

"No, I forbid it. There will be no hot, wild, monkey sex."

"OK!" Drea exclaimed. "Can we please stop saying 'hot, wild, monkey sex'? Not that I'm having any, but even if I were, not the conversation I want to have over family breakfast. Or at any point with any of you."

"So, moving on," Miller said, folding up his paper, looking exceptionally uncomfortable at all the sex talk. "Dalton held court with quite the blonde audience last night from what I saw, so, Drea is all clear."

"Mr. and Mrs. Prage were not the last ones standing, by the way," Vaughn interjected.

"Damn it," Miller cursed. He got up from the table and walked over to the oven, pulling out the French toast he'd been keeping warm in there. He brought it back over and set it on the table.

"But they were second to last, so I say we give it to you,"

he continued. Murmurs around the table agreed. "They were second to none other than that weird redhead couple. In fact, I think the Prages would have stayed longer, but they were trying to give them privacy for their argument."

"But did chairs fly?" Grayson asked. He grabbed a plate as he glared at Simone. He grabbed a few slices of the French toast and started eating.

"YES!" Simone hollered, raising her arms in victory.

"Well, slow down, babe. It depends on your definition of chair."

"Excuse you, no, it does not. Furniture flew, that is what matters!"

"What?!" Grayson said with his mouth full.

"She picked up a chaise lounge and tossed it in his direction. Since it's so much bigger than her she had some trouble getting any air." Vaughn grabbed two plates and served himself and Simone, before passing the serving utensils to Drea.

"Damn, I missed some good stuff," Drea said, plating some food. "I think a chaise lounge counts, Uncle Gray. Sorry."

"Yeah, so unless you can prove a staff hookup, you're wearing the shirt!" Simone teased, pointing her finger straight at Grayson.

"Um, hello, am I the only one who remembers that we totally skipped over Vaughn here?"

"Well, the one blonde gave up on Dalton pretty quick and headed over to the group of gym rats, so I think that one is pretty much a given," Miller stated. "Sorry man, you're wearing the shirt."

Just as Grayson was exhaling a sigh of resignation, Kyle walked into the kitchen. His head was down, like he was trying to keep a low profile, but Drea's heart skipped a beat anyway. He looked up at the table as he neared, making eye contact with her right away. Her heart started to speed up. He was wearing his usual work attire, so he at least made a stop at home, she noticed. Maybe they didn't hook up? She stopped eating and tried to catch her breath as he opened his mouth to say something.

"Sorry to interrupt family breakfast—"

He was cut off by Grayson. "Dude, you didn't happen to hook up with anyone last night, did you?"

"What? No! No, no. I slept in my own bed, promise!" Kyle said, waving his hands back and forth, looking mortified. Drea let out a sigh of relief she hoped no one heard.

"Fuck," Grayson said. "Where's Dalton, he won't let me down."

"Um, no idea."

"Sorry, son, Gray's just upset he's gonna have to wear the shirt," Miller explained. "Please, sit, have some breakfast."

"No, no, I don't want to intrude."

"You're not intruding, you're part of this family," Vaughn added. "We should really get you in on the bets."

Kyle stood there for another moment, awkwardly, not sure how to proceed. "Um, yeah, sure, sounds like fun. Anyway, I just wanted to grab Drea for a moment after you guys finish up."

"Kyle, just sit," Drea said, smiling. "If you don't eat, you know Uncle Miller will hunt you down."

"She's right, son. Sit."

He did as he was told, and took the plate that Drea made up for him. They all ate in companionable silence for awhile, and then made their way to do whatever it was that their mornings held for them.

"Got a sec?" Kyle asked as they moved their plates over to the dishwashing area.

"Sure," Drea answered. "We can go hang in Leona's office."

DREA WALKED into the housekeeping office without bothering to check to see if it was occupied. At this time of morning she knew Leona would be down in the laundry catching up with the staff down there. She collapsed down onto the couch and pulled her legs up underneath her, wishing there was some kind of throw pillow to hold close to her body as a shield. Kyle followed her in and closed the door behind himself quietly. He sat down on the other end of the couch, sitting up ramrod straight for a second, before leaning back and twisting himself so one knee rested on the couch, his body facing her and his arm draped across the back.

"Hey," he said, breaking the silence.

"Hey back."

"You okay? I didn't see you at the bonfire last night," he said, trying to leave it open for her to share what she wanted. He didn't want to come at her right away that he saw what went down with Dalton and how upset he could tell she was.

"I called it a night early. I wasn't feeling a hundred percent," she lied. He could tell it wasn't the whole truth, not only by the look in her eyes, but by the slight little shrug in her left shoulder. He'd never told her that she had the tell, but every time she wasn't being fully honest she made the slight movement.

"Something happen?" he tried to prompt her.

"Nope."

"You sure? Drea, this is me. Your favorite person. If something happened, tell me so I can fix it."

She let out a little laugh. "Kyle, there are just some things a girl needs to deal with herself. Am I making sense here?"

Kyle nodded, understanding exactly what she was trying to imply, but still knowing it wasn't the truth. His Drea had never been coy about telling him she was "hanging out with Aunt Flo," as she had so often put it. He started to do that math in his head, but stopped himself. He thought he'd gotten pretty good with her schedule, but he wasn't about to admit he tried to know her cycle so that he could be ready with a hug, or chocolate, or whatever need her PMS brought on.

"So, nothing I need to know about?" he prodded.

"Is there something *I* need to know?" she lobbed back.

"No, I just wanna make sure my best girl is okay. I missed hanging with you last night. The bonfire is kinda our thing." He reached out and took her hand from her lap. He squeezed it softly and she smiled in return.

"Well, you have nothing to worry about," she told him. There was no missing the sadness in her eyes, though. Clouds seemed to hang there, where there was normally a sparkle, one that lit up Kyle's insides. He wished he could see into that pretty little head of hers and understand exactly what was going on in there. He saw her and Dalton last night, knew that something had gone down. He couldn't understand why she wouldn't just let him in.

"Good." He squeezed her hand and let go.

"Since we have that settled," she said, pushing herself up off the couch. "I'm still sticky from my run, so I need to go home and shower and then get all the morning paperwork done before this afternoon's excursion. Shipwreck day, right?"

He nodded. "Yup, shipwreck day."

"Great, then I'll see you at the pier."

She walked out of the office without looking back, and it made Kyle feel sick to his stomach. He slouched back against the couch and sighed, not having the slightest idea what just happened, and he couldn't help but feel like the conversation he was so convinced was going to fix things had actually made them worse.

CHAPTER SEVEN

WALKING BACK TO HER COTTAGE, Drea kept replaying the conversation in her head. His best girl? Do people really say that anymore? He knew she was hurt and she knew she'd never be able to hide that part from him, but he made it pretty clear in how he approached that hurt how she ranked in his life. She wasn't worth running after in the moment—a check-in the next morning after he got laid was perfectly sufficient. Of course she wasn't totally sure that he and "Candy" had hooked up. After all, it's not like he shared any details about what he had been up to last night, but it didn't take a rocket scientist to put two and two together from watching them.

She wasn't sure if she wanted to cry or scream. Everything inside her just wanted to bust through her skin, and it was taking everything she had to not lose it. More than anything, she just wanted to feel less...stupid. Less like a stupid girl who let her feelings get in the way, like a stupid little girl who fell for someone who would never, ever return her affections. She knew she wasn't completely unfortunate looking—she got hit on. Just look at Brig yesterday morning. There had to be something about her that resonated on some level if he was willing to sign up for the excursion just because she said she might go. Sure, she had the tomboy thing going on, but her lack of makeup on a daily basis was an occupational hazard more than anything else—all that work prettying herself up would just be wasted the second the wind and the water took over.

Drea slowed down as she approached her front door, suspiciously eyeing the little brown bag oddly hanging from her doorknob. Who would have left her something? Her uncles would have just brought whatever it was to breakfast, and other than them, only the staff knew that she lived in the little cottage that had been the home of the original resort caretaker. Had Brig asked one of the staff members where she lived? Would they have told him? The cottage, as well as the "big house" next to it, was set back on the property behind some trees, down a little trail that steered you away from the main part of the resort. The only real guest spaces over this way were the Villas, but even they ended on the other side of the trees before you reached the trailhead. Unless you knew that the trail led to those houses, then you'd never think to wander there. Even though the staff knew this is where the family lived, none of them ever ventured back this way. Leona, Kyle, and Dalton had come to hang out, but the staff dorm—which was originally a short tower of guest suites that were renovated a bunch of years back to include a kitchenette along with the bed, desk, couch, and en suite bathroom—was on the other side of the trees and could be seen from the guest beach if one looked in this direction. She looked over at the "big house" and it didn't seem like her uncles or Simone had come back this way since breakfast. Cautiously taking the bag off the door handle, she saw a note poking out the top.

Drea~
Morning Sugar! Take off that one-piece and put this baby on. Today is the first day of the rest of your life...or some shit like that :) See you on the Run!

-D

Drea just shook her head as she reached into the bag and pulled out a royal-purple bikini. She shoved it back into the bag and quickly opened her door and scooted in. Once fully inside, she dumped the bag on her couch, picking up the bikini top again, turning it around in her hands. So many questions ran through her mind. Where did Dalton get it? How did he know her size? Just how exactly was she going to be able to function with only this little flimsy thing holding in her boobs?

After a quick shower, Drea towel dried her hair and went to get dressed for the day. She grabbed her usual one-piece that was hanging from the rack in the bathroom and stared at it. After a moment, she hung it back up and grabbed the bikini from the couch and shimmied into it. It took her a moment to properly adjust her breasts, but she finally got herself situated fully. Looking in the mirror, she was shocked to see just how well it fit her. The top was, thankfully, not just two small triangles like the one she wore out on her deck when she and Leona would sun themselves, but shaped more like an actual bra, complete with a little bit of underwire or something to give her at least some support while working the boat. She'd still have to be careful how she moved to not give any of the guests too much of an eyeful, but she couldn't deny that she felt good in this suit. No, scratch that—she felt sexy.

Making her way down the pier toward the *Runnin' Down A Dream*, Drea saw Kyle and Dalton standing at the front of the boat with her Uncle Gray. She hurried her steps, holding on to all the papers she had brought with her from the concierge desk, trying to not have any go flying into the water. As she approached, Dalton pulled away from the group to help her aboard.

"Morning, sugar," he greeted her, reaching out a hand. "Find what I left you?"

"Sure did," she answered as she stepped up into the boat. "And I am very confused on *many* levels. I mean, I have *a lot* of questions."

"No questions, just trust the magic!"

She eyed him skeptically as they made their way back toward Kyle and her uncle. *Just trust the magic?* She had no idea what Dalton's plan was or why she was going along with it, but since she was standing here with the swimsuit he gave her on underneath her tank and shorts, she guessed she was going along with it.

"Hey doll, how's the day lookin'?" Grayson asked as she came to stand next to him.

"Good, we're all sold out for this afternoon, so should be a busy day."

"I like the sound of that. Guess that decides if I'm tagging along." He clapped his hands together. "You set out at noon?"

"We can fit you on. If we're gonna have a full boat, having an extra set of hands wouldn't be a bad thing. Besides, when was the last time you and Drea went out?" Kyle interjected.

"Come on, Uncle Gray, it'll be fun. Kyle's right, we

haven't been out in forever. Plus, I recognize some names on today's list from yesterday's tour, some *female* names, so if nothing else, we can sit back and watch Dalton make a fool of himself with all the attention," Drea added in.

"Whatever," Dalton scoffed. "What you will witness is me at my best! My prowess knows no bounds!" He raised his hands in triumph as he backed away from the group. They all laughed as he turned stylishly and headed toward the front of the boat to check equipment.

"Well then, maybe I will." Grayson put an arm around Drea's shoulder and kissed her on the top of her head. "Let me see how the morning goes. But you're right, it'd be a good time. Until then, look after my girl here, Kyle. I'm trusting you with her life." He kissed the top of her head again and turned to disembark the boat.

"You got it, sir!" Kyle called after him, as Drea simply rolled her eyes.

"I can be trusted with my own life!" she added. Grayson simply held a thumbs-up high over his head as he headed down the pier.

"I know you can," Kyle said, turning to face her head-on. "Dalton, on the other hand..."

"Drea's life can be trusted with me. I'd never let anything happen to our princess," Dalton hollered from the front of the boat.

Drea cut her eyes to Dalton. Princess? What was he getting at? She slid her eyes to Kyle, trying to see what his reaction had been to the new nickname, but his face didn't seem to change. *Okay, then.*

The guests started to arrive a little earlier than expected, but the three of them had a routine that ensured they were ready for it. Drea only half watched as they piled on, wiping down the bar and making sure that everything was ready for once they were out on open water. She looked up as she heard some giggles that made her freeze —"Candy" and her friends were getting on the boat. Damn it, that must have been the group of female names that looked familiar. Right behind them, though, was the part of the story that she had failed to mention earlier. Brig and all his buddies were also joining them again today. She took a deep breath, watching them all settle in. One of the blondes had basically surgically attached herself to one of Brig's buddies—they must have been the pairing that Vaughn had witnessed the night before—and they settled right up at the front of the boat. The rest of the group followed, the girls smiling and winking at Kyle and Dalton as they did so.

Glancing over at the boys as they continued to help guests onto the boat, Drea couldn't help but smile to herself. The sun glistened off of Kyle's tan skin, and watching the muscles on his back move and contract as he worked caused all sorts of butterflies in her tummy. She was still so hurt by what she had witnessed last night, but thoughts of what it would be like to hold on to that back as he moved above her filled her head. Thoughts of how his tongue would feel against hers and the friction as he rubbed—

"Hi!" A high-pitched voice pulled her from her daydream. She looked over to find "Candy" standing in front of her across the bar.

"Hi," Drea answered, taken aback by the girl's sudden appearance.

"I'm Staci, with an i," she said, reaching a hand out to shake. Drea took her hand and shook back.

"Drea. Nice to see you again."

"Thanks! We just had sooooo much fun yesterday, we couldn't resist another trip!"

"Glad to hear you enjoyed it."

"So, you spend all day with these boys? You lucky girl!"

"Yeah, they're the best. I really couldn't ask for better crewmates."

"Or a better view!"

"That part isn't so bad either," Drea admitted.

"So, can you give me the inside scoop?"

Drea shook her head, startled, not sure she heard Staci correctly. "I'm sorry, the what?"

"You know, what do I need to know about him? Likes, dislikes, favorite sex position, things like that."

Drea felt like she'd been hit in the gut with a sledgehammer. This wasn't really happening, was it? This chick had not just asked her Kyle's favorite sex position. *I'm not gonna cry, I'm not gonna cry, I won't let her see me cry.* She took a deep breath, since she had to answer. Staci must have seen something in Drea's eyes that made her understand the panic Drea was suddenly feeling.

"I mean, I just figure you're the best person to know these kinds of things. We had a great time last night, and I just really want to continue to make a good impression."

"Oh, yeah, totally. Well, ummm, he's not a big fan of the rum punch," she said, trying to come up with something, pointing with her thumb at the pitcher sitting just to her left. "More of a rum and Coke guy. His favorite candy is peanut M&Ms—he won't touch the plain ones. He loves classic rock, but don't bring up Van Halen or else you'll get an earful about David Lee Roth versus Sammy Hagar that is just a never-ending cycle."

"Yeah, I don't know who that is, so I can promise not to bring that up."

"Right," Drea responded. Staci didn't know who Van Halen was? How the hell did Kyle find this girl the least bit interesting? *Because he's not interested in her mind, Drea, just those really perfect boobs.* "Well, he's a pretty typical dude, so, music, boats—always safe topics. As for the sex part, I can't really help you there."

"I probably shouldn't have asked that question. You seem like too nice of a girl to have gone down that road with him. Well, thanks for the tips!" She winked as she turned and bounced back to join her friends.

Drea just stood there, unable to move. She tried not to hyperventilate. She wanted to cry, scream, and throw up at the same time. She looked around her, looking for something, anything, to distract herself from the fact that she was pretty sure Staci had just insulted her in the sweetest way possible. She was too nice? Just what kind of raw, dirty sex did they have last night? And just why wouldn't he be interested in having it with her? Oh, that's right, she was just his best friend, not an actual girl.

"Hey, sugar," Dalton said, waving his hand in front of her face, bringing her back to the moment. "What's going on in that pretty little head of yours?"

"Nothing," she said, blinking away the sting of tears and forcing a smile.

"Those tears tell me otherwise, darlin'. But I promise you, we got this."

"I adore you, Dalton, but I think you are very, very wrong here. I can't compete with that." She pointed at Staci and her friends harshly.

"You can too, although I can't figure out why the hell you think you need to. But Drea, I told you last night, you are sexy as hell—you just need to own it. Now, we're about to get a move on, and your uncle just hopped on board, and since I'm pretty sure neither of us want to answer his questions about your tears, inhale deeply, embrace your sexy, and once we're out in open water, whip off that tank and show off those puppies, would ya?" He winked and walked away.

CHAPTER EIGHT

GRAYSON LEANED against the inside of the bar, sipping on a cup of the rum punch Drea had just finished mixing up. She was wiping down the bar again, trying to work out some nervous energy, hoping her uncle couldn't tell. The catamaran slowed down as they reached a spot out in the water to start the safety talk.

"Alright ladies and gentlemen, it's time to talk safety. I promise to keep this short and sweet, just like all my previous relationships!" Dalton said, delivering his well-rehearsed line perfectly as always. "Your safety is my number one priority, no matter the activity, so here we go! We start with a life jacket, and yes, you have to wear one. So, if you think you're gonna get out of it so the sexy little bartender back there will have to give you mouth-to-mouth, then you're gonna have to find a different excuse! Although, ladies, if you need my help getting it to fit properly, you just let me know!" He winked in the direction of the blondes.

"Does he use this spiel on every excursion?" Grayson asked Drea.

"Oh yes. He changes it up slightly from day to day, but

for the most part, I can recite it, line for line, bad jokes, winks, and all."

"He's a piece of work, that one," Grayson said, shaking his head.

"I think he's a keeper, Uncle Gray. The old ladies just *loooove* him!" Drea said, dragging out the O in love, batting her eyelashes and making googly-eyes at her uncle.

"Hey!" She turned back to the front of the bar to see Brig standing there, a flirtatious smirk on his face.

"Hi, you're back."

"We had so much fun yesterday, and I missed you at the bonfire last night. Thought this might be the only way to catch you."

Before Drea could respond, her uncle pushed up from the section of the bar he was resting against and moved up to stand right next to her. She could see a light scowl on his face and he looked Brig up and down. Grayson had to have a couple of inches on him, but wasn't near as bulky as the meathead. In a fight, however, especially if the topic of said fight was Drea, her money was solely on her uncle.

"You need to be listening to the safety talk," Grayson interjected.

"Just wanted to say hi—"

"Great. You said it, now back up front to listen."

"And what makes you think you're so special? Standing there like you own the place. Why aren't you listening to the safety talk?" Brig challenged.

"Because I do own the place. And the fucking boat you're on too. So I don't think it's uncalled for to tell you again to sit your ass down."

"Ok!" Drea interjected. "Brig, he's right, the Coast Guard requires that you listen to the safety talk, even though it's the same as yesterday. I'll make sure to come chat in a bit."

Brig nodded his head and turned to head back to the front of the boat, where all his buddies were sitting with the blondes. When she was sure he was out of earshot, she turned to her uncle and glared at him.

"Wanna explain why you just went all Uncle Vaughn on him?" Grayson just glared right back at her. "You have never, not once, gotten huffy with a guy who was interested in me, not even when I was in high school. Hell, you were the one who taught me how to sneak out so that Uncle Vaughn couldn't bitch out my dates."

"Who's the douche?"

"For one, a guest! For two, just some dude. He hit on me at the gym yesterday and then was on our excursion."

"I don't like him."

"Don't like who?" Kyle asked, coming down from his perch.

"Well, I don't particularly like him either, but whatever, he's a guest." Drea pulled her tank off, revealing her new suit. "But if you'll excuse me, I'm gonna go apologize for my asshat uncle and try and save our tip!"

———

KYLE WATCHED Drea pull off her tank top as if it were in slow motion. It wasn't a new motion, it was an act she did every day—strip down to her swimsuit to go hop in the water with the guests. But today, today was as if it was happening for the very first time. He saw her reach for the hem of the shirt and didn't think anything of it until she started to lift it higher, inch by inch, revealing her beautiful golden-brown skin instead of the lycra of her swimsuit.

When she reached the point of pulling it over her head, making her breasts shift in those small cups, he was pretty sure he'd been rendered useless. He'd seen her breasts in a bikini top before when they'd been hanging out on her porch or a couple of times when they'd taken the boat out, just them. They'd made plenty of appearances in his fantasies, and thoughts of playing with them were regularly conjured as spank bank material. But something about that shade of purple against her skin and the way they sat in that top, he could feel all the blood rushing to his groin. As she turned to go, all he could think was that he couldn't wait for her to take off the shorts too.

Stop thinking of her like that, her uncle is standing right next to you, Kyle thought, swallowing hard. If he didn't stop staring, it was going to be impossible to hide what he was feeling. Not that the sudden tenting in his board shorts was helping anything.

"This is the point where I should tell you to stop ogling my niece, dude," Grayson said, startling Kyle out of his thoughts.

"Sorry, sir, I wasn't, I mean..." he trailed off. "I'm gonna head back up and drive the boat."

Once they pulled up to the location of the shipwreck, Kyle killed the engine. He could hear Drea giggle and as he peered down he saw she was back at the bar chatting with her uncle. He hated to admit it, but he was thoroughly relieved that the giggles weren't in reaction to that meathead. It had taken every mind trick in the book—thinking about sports, picturing Margaret Thatcher on a cold day as Austin Powers would say, his parents having sex—but his boner was finally subsiding. Those giggles weren't helping, though.

He stared out over the ocean from his perch and sighed

heavily. He just needed to remind himself why he was here. He was all about the job. He was so close to being able to afford going out on his own. Once he had his own boat and was running his own charters, then maybe he could have a relationship. That was assuming Drea even wanted him. He'd seen her with Dalton last night, and then whispering again this morning. He hated the idea of them together, but if it was really what Drea wanted, he'd figure out a way to deal with it.

He closed his eyes and enjoyed the movement of the boat underneath him. It should have been more than enough to calm him down, but the last twenty-four hours had him rattled. The meathead, Staci with an i, seeing Drea run off in tears and then refuse to tell him what was wrong —it all weighed on him. How could so much change in such a small amount of time?

Kyle headed down to the main deck when he heard the guests reboarding the boat. He told himself it was because he was doing his job, that he was mingling with the guests, and not that he wanted to get a full view of Drea in that bikini. He scanned the boat to find her up front, helping someone undo their life jacket. Brig stood not far from her, obviously waiting until her attention could be back on him.

"Glaring at him won't make him go away," Dalton said, coming up behind him.

"I'm not glaring at anyone."

"Sure you're not. Just keep lying to yourself."

Kyle turned to look at Dalton next to him. He was looking at Drea with a smirk on his face Kyle couldn't quite read. "What's going on, Dalton? What am I missing?"

"If you gotta ask the question, buddy, then I don't know how to answer that."

"I know something is going on, Dalton. What happened with Drea last night?"

"You ask her?"

"She brushed me off, told me it was 'nothing,'" he answered, making air quotes with his fingers.

"Then there's your answer."

"Except I'm pretty sure you know something I don't," Kyle accused.

"Dude, I told you last night, I just don't understand what goes through your head sometimes. Take that however you want, but if she's not gonna tell you what she was upset about, it sure as hell isn't my place." He turned and walked toward an older couple who had just come up from the water, smiling flirtatiously at the woman as he offered to help her out of her life jacket.

"You didn't want to get in the water?" Grayson asked.

Kyle shifted slightly as his boss appeared to his left. "It was a full tour. Only Drea gets in on the full tour days."

"I was on the boat, you could have easily joined her. You deserve to have some fun too."

"I went yesterday. It would have been unprofessional to get in two days in a row."

"Dude," Gray sighed, shaking his head. "A little piece of advice you didn't ask for: you can't be a chickenshit your whole life. At some point, consequences be damned, you just gotta go for it."

CHAPTER NINE

THEY PULLED the boat back into the harbor and started to help all the guests disembark. The older couple that Dalton had been chatting with earlier stopped to thank him for his help and tell him about the great time they had. The wife grabbed hold of his face and kissed his cheek hard with a loud smack.

"I'll never wash this part of my face again, Margie," Dalton said, playing up his accent and winking. "George, you better get her back to your room before I try and run off with her." The couple laughed, and she swatted at Dalton as her husband grabbed her around the waist and pulled her in the direction of the resort. A few steps down the way he spun her and pulled her in for a deep kiss.

"May we be so lucky someday," Kyle remarked to Dalton, nodding his head toward the older couple, still kissing on the pier.

"Speak for yourself, dude. Well, hello..." Dalton replied, grabbing Staci's hand, helping her down. He kissed the back of her hand, and she giggled and batted her eyelashes. "I do hope to see you later this evening, Staci with an i."

"We were talking about going up to Paradise Point tonight. Have a couple of bushwackers, see what kind of trouble we can find."

"Then I guess I'll just have to find my way up to Paradise Point. And I promise, after a couple of bushwackers, we can find plenty of trouble." He waggled his eyebrows.

"I'm looking forward to it," she said low and husky, winking at Dalton. She turned to Kyle and smiled brightly. "Thanks for everything, Captain Kyle."

"See ya," he nodded. He turned to check to see if anyone was left on the boat. Much to his dismay, he saw the only guest left was Brig, standing there talking to Drea.

He climbed back onto the boat, trying to make it look like he wasn't watching them carefully. She was smiling, but only her customer service smile. Could Brig tell that it wasn't genuine? He saw Grayson come up behind Drea and say something to Brig, but couldn't quite tell what it was. Drea pushed him away, laughing, but then turned back to Brig looking a little more serious. She gave him a high five and he turned to make his exit off the boat and down the pier.

Kyle walked back to the bar where Drea was sorting through paperwork. "Hey, you."

She looked up and smiled at him. Her real smile. "Hey back."

"So, what does the rest of your week look like?" Grayson asked, coming up the stairs from the underdeck.

"Well, Dalton has tomorrow off, I think, and then spends the rest of the week over on the *Believin'* with Bobby for the booze cruises. Kyle and I have private tours every day until Sunday, when we're both off. And they are small private tours—I think our largest group is four or five guests, so that'll be really nice."

"We have a day off together?" Kyle perked up.

"Yes, just like we usually do."

"Right, it's just I've been picking up those extra tours and you've been out with Leona, so we haven't really taken advantage of those off days in awhile," he responded, stumbling over his answer. *Shit, I sound like a dumbass, and in front of the boss.*

"Dude, keys to the *Runnin'* are yours. You two wanna go out and play on Sunday, fine by me. Hell, leave Saturday night. Just as long as you're back for work on Monday," Grayson said, leaning against the bar.

Before he could answer, a symphony of trills and beeps came from their phones, which were all housed in a drawer in the bar. Drea opened the drawer, reaching for the phones and absentmindedly handing each guy their phone.

Family mtg, Big House Beach, 10 min. BE THERE. -V

"What the hell does he want now?" Grayson grumbled. "He couldn't have told us whatever this is at breakfast this morning?"

"Think he was too busy delivering the news that you had to wear the shirt. Speaking of which, don't think I'm not on to you and why you had the brilliant idea to come and join today's excursion, since it meant getting to take it off," Drea commented, looking at her uncle knowingly. "So, you better put it back on, but your secret is safe with me."

"You always were my favorite niece," he said, pushing up from the bar and kissing her forehead. He grabbed the shirt and made his way off the boat.

"Never mind I'm your only niece!" she called out. She turned to look at Kyle, smiling really big. "We should head that way. And, I'm totally down for an escape on Sunday if you are."

"Oh, absolutely," he responded without hesitation. "There is no place I would rather be than on this boat with just you." It was the truest statement he'd made all day. There was still a pit in his stomach over everything else, but things had to be turning around if she was suggesting a date. Well, not a date, but an escape as she put it, just them. He saw the light return to her for a moment and he had to stop himself before he ended up with another hard-on.

"Perfect." She grabbed her and Dalton's phones, turning to go. "Let's go, Dalton, family meeting."

"What family? I'm not family."

"You are per Vaughn's group text just now. And I'm not gonna be the one to tell the big bossman that you're opting out," Kyle responded.

"Then funny cousin Dalton at your service! So can I call him Uncle Vaughn now too?"

Drea laughed out loud at the two of them as they helped her onto the pier. Kyle didn't let go of her hand as they all headed toward the resort. She didn't pull her hand away and Kyle smiled to himself at the simple gesture. Dalton could have the harem of blondes—she was the only girl he wanted hanging off him. He wondered if this small act of bodily contact meant as much to her as it did him, if she thought about holding other parts of him in her hands, about their bodies coming together in dirtier, more intimate ways.

She hadn't put her tank back on over her bikini top when she got back on the boat after swimming with the guests. Her beautiful, perfect breasts were still on display, their slight movement as they walked holding his attention out of the corner of his eye. Gah, the things he wanted to do to her. He tried to sneak a full-on look without her noticing —he didn't want to have to lie if she asked what he was doing. *I'm thinking about how badly I want to hold those bad boys in my hands, and suck on your nipples and make you scream with desire.*

Well, so much for holding back on that hard-on.

D REA WAS SOAKING up every moment of Kyle's hand in hers on their way to Big House Beach. It'd been an emotionally exhausting day of *did they/didn't they* in her head about Kyle and Staci, keeping Brig at arm's length, and being "on" for a full boat of guests for today's outing. The quiet comfort of his hand holding hers was everything to her, and still somehow, not enough. She cherished the relationship they had built over these last five years, and if being his best friend was all she ever got, then she'd find a way to deal with that. But she wanted what she'd witnessed with Staci last night, she wanted to be able to hang on in a way that declared that they belonged to each other, she wanted to be able to dirty dance with him and kiss him. She wanted to press herself into his hard body, feel him move above her, under her, *inside* her. Board shorts only hid so much when you spent every day with a person, and he'd held her enough to know that she was not going to be disappointed with whatever she found in there. Not that she could ever be disappointed in Kyle for anything.

As they slipped through the little alley between her cottage and the big house, he squeezed her hand and smiled at her. Both houses sat right on the beach, with back porches that looked out over the crystal clear ocean water. It was just one more part of her unconventional upbringing, but she really couldn't imagine not having a beach as a back-yard. Birthdays, family bonfires, and many a lazy day had found the five of them out here, soaking up the sun or playing in the waves. She and Leona had spent "girl time" lying on the beach reading books and magazines, talking about boys, and making "plans" for the future. It'd been where she sat with Simone when she needed to talk to a grown-up that didn't have a penis and therefore understood that her teenage self wasn't "just being overdramatic."

Walking out onto the beach, they found Vaughn standing in the middle of a grouping of paper lanterns that seemed to form a heart. Leona, Grayson, and Miller were already there, so the three of them walked over to where they were standing. Drea looked around for Simone, real-izing she was the only one missing.

"What's this all about, Uncle Miller?" Drea whispered, leaning closer to him.

"No clue, baby girl, but Vaughn is most certainly up to something."

Just then, Simone came bursting through the trees, moving at a pretty impressive pace considering her four-inch heels.

"What is it? What's the emergency?" she panted. "Sorry I'm late. I hauled myself over here from the tourism office as fast as I could."

"You're not late, love," Vaughn said, stepping out of the lanterns. "Come with me." He grabbed her hands and led her to the middle of the lanterns. He turned and faced the rest of the group.

"I don't know how many of you know this, but exactly twenty-one years ago today the most stunning creature I have ever seen walked into my life, showing up completely unannounced. I was one hundred percent ready to go tell her to take a hike when Juan came into my office to tell me someone from the Board of Tourism wanted to exploit us for their advertising campaign—my words, not his. But then I walked into the lobby and saw this angel." He turned back to Simone. "I'm pretty sure you only agreed to have dinner with me to convince me to allow you to use the resort, but what I'm not sure you know is that even if you'd said no, I would have let you do the photoshoot, just so you'd have to come back."

Drea could see Simone starting to tear up as she gazed in Vaughn's eyes. She sighed, soaking in seeing her grumpy uncle being all mushy and romantic. Kyle slipped to stand behind her, wrapping his arms around her shoulders, holding her against his chest. She nestled herself in against him and rested her head back against his shoulder.

"Every time you agreed to keep seeing me seemed like a miracle. And then, somehow I convinced you to move in here with us, my weird little family. You never once balked at the idea of living in a conjoined bachelor pad slash frat house with three crazy bachelors and the little girl that we were attempting to not screw up. You've understood that the Indigo Royal is my first love and my baby all at the same time. I know you make the joke that I'm really married to the resort and that you're just the mistress, but I think maybe it's time that I make an honest woman out of you."

Simone gasped as Vaughn dropped to one knee, pulling a little velvet box out of his pocket. She raised her hands to her face and cupped them over her mouth as the tears that had simply been welling in her eyes started to stream down her cheeks. She let out a small giggle from behind her hands.

"Simone, will you marry me?"

Drea sighed and relaxed into Kyle more as she watched

Simone nod furiously and attempt to choke out an answer. Raising her hands to hold on to his arms as he squeezed her a little tighter to him, she caught herself starting to tear up.

"Yes, oh my God, yes! Yes! Yes! Yes!" Simone squeaked out, letting Vaughn take her shaking hand and slip the ring on it. She threw her arms around his neck and kissed him, hard, as he lifted her by her waist and spun her around.

"About fucking time!" Grayson shouted.

"Says the only one of us to have never actually committed to a woman," snarked Miller.

"Shut it!" Vaughn barked, putting Simone back on the ground. Still looking her in the eyes, he said, "Bet you thought I'd never ask."

"I would have been okay with you never asking. I know who your heart belongs to," she sniffed. "But I'm so fucking glad you did!"

Turning to Drea, she held up her left hand to show off the ring and let out a little squeal. Prying herself out of Kyle's arms, Drea rushed to her soon-to-be-official-aunt, and grabbed her hand to look at the ring. The stunning marquise cut was easily close to two carats and sparkled stunningly against Simone's tan skin.

"Damn, Uncle Vaughn, you went all out!"

"She deserves nothing less," he answered and he hugged his brothers and shook the hands of Kyle and Dalton.

"Now we just have to plan a wedding," Leona said, also staring down at Simone's left hand.

"Nope, already taken care of that. You've always said that if we ever did this you wanted to keep it small and simple. So, I've got it all set to be right here, on Big House Beach, a week from Saturday. All you need to do is find a dress."

"Oh my God," Simone said. "Drea, you have to be my maid of honor!"

"Really? Yes, of course!" She hugged Simone again.

"For my next surprise," Vaughn started. Everyone stopped suddenly and just stared at him. "Kidding, kidding! It's just dinner! I got Rafe to make Simone's favorite chicken. So, if you all will just give me and my beautiful fiancée a moment to ourselves, we'll meet you all at the kitchen table."

CHAPTER TEN

FAMILY DINNERS HAD NEVER REALLY BEEN quiet, low-key affairs with the Quinlans. Miller was the only one of the brothers who could be considered "quiet" or "mild-mannered," but when left with his brothers, even he was known to raise a little hell. Add in Simone, who was outgoing, bubbly, and never shied away from busting a few balls, and it was always an event. Given the excuse of a special occasion, and the addition of Leona, Kyle, and Dalton, tonight's dinner had turned into an all-out party. After four courses of Simone's favorite foods, six and a half bottles of wine, and a surprise cake that Rafe had made for the occasion, everyone was stuffed beyond compare.

When the happy, newly engaged couple excused themselves first, it was met with a litany of comments from Grayson and Dalton about how Vaughn was "so getting laid tonight." Vaughn just shook his head and escorted his bride-to-be out of the kitchen, but not without Simone turning around and remarking "you fucking know it!" in response.

Shortly after their exit, Dalton made a vague comment

about Paradise Point and swiftly exited as well. Leona simply said goodnight and left on Dalton's heels.

Kyle had always enjoyed hanging out with Drea's family and loved that they considered him part of the group. He knew it meant something that they had included him in tonight's events and it wasn't something he took lightly. But if the two men sitting at the table with him now, much less the one that just left, knew what was going through his head while holding Drea during the proposal, they would have him drawn and quartered. She was their little girl, and even though she was an adult and moved out, he knew nothing would ever change the way they looked at her and that no one would ever be good enough. Just one more reason all those fantasies about her would remain just that.

"I really never thought he would do it, much less make a production of it," Miller said, pouring more wine into his glass. He held up the bottle to see if anyone wanted the last little bit left. Kyle shook his head no—he was already feeling the effects of the other two and a half glasses he'd had and he didn't need to risk a wine hangover in the morning. Grayson held out his glass and Miller poured the tail end of the bottle into it.

"Says the man who proposed going 'So, we're getting married, right?'" Grayson shot back.

"Excuse you, that was Dave to Sofia," Miller corrected him. "Mine was something more like 'Us too?'" Everyone burst into laughter.

"She said yes to your stupid ass, so you must have done something right."

"Marta was truly something else. Your mother was wonderful too, Drea, and she loved your father like nothing else. But your Aunt Marta, she was just perfection."

Kyle looked at Drea as Miller talked about the sisters he

and his best friend had loved. He knew Drea loved hearing stories about them and her father, and that she greatly missed them, even though she'd been an infant when they died. She was smiling at her uncle—her real true smile—and her eyes were sparkling, radiating all her emotions. Kyle could look at her all day, no matter her expression, but this was one of his favorites.

"Not a day goes by I don't miss her. She and your mother, man, were they something. Someday, if I actually make it to heaven, I'm sure they will be waiting for me there to slap me silly over some of the choices I made with you, but I like to think you turned out okay."

"I think so," she beamed.

"Alright, I think I need to get you to bed before you wax poetic all night long," Grayson chimed in. "Kyle, you gonna walk Drea home?"

"Of course," Kyle answered, a little confused why she wouldn't just walk with them. But he wasn't going to argue with his boss or turn down the chance to be alone with her.

"Great, then you two can head, and I'll help Miller with cleanup."

When they were outside of the kitchen and headed back across the resort to the trail that led to her cottage, Kyle grabbed Drea's hand and pulled her to a stop.

"Did you get the feeling like we were being dismissed?"

"I think this evening was a little emotional for Uncle Miller. I mean, it's been twenty-five years since my parents and Aunt Marta passed, but there are days he still talks about her like she's only been gone a week. He still loves her so much. I mean, if he's even gone on a date since her death, I don't know about it."

"Can you imagine loving someone that much?"

"Yeah, I can," she said softly. He pulled her in close and

held her tightly against his body. She wrapped her arms around his waist in response and sighed heavily. He rested his chin on the top of her head and closed his eyes for a moment, drinking in her scent. She hadn't had time for a shower since they got back from the excursion, so she still smelled of salt water and ocean air, with the slightest hint of her citrus shampoo.

"I'm sorry you didn't get the chance to know them."

"Thanks," she said, keeping her forehead resting against his chest. He held her there for another moment before she slowly pulled away. She slipped her hand into his as they started to walk again.

His head was all over the place and solely focused on Drea all at the same time. She must not still be too upset if she's holding his hand, right? And why was she upset? What happened with Dalton? With Brig? Dalton and Staci seemed to have found each other, so maybe it was Brig after all? Had they hooked up? If they had, had it ended poorly?

He knew Drea wasn't a virgin—they had swapped virginity stories years ago hanging out on her back porch sipping rum and Coke. He had told her about how his experience had been pretty stereotypical. He had lost it the night of his senior prom to his high school girlfriend, who he already knew he was going to break up with before they left for different colleges, both of them of going through with it because they thought they were supposed to. Or maybe it had been the fear of going off to college still hanging on to their v-cards that had served as their motivation. Drea had told him not to feel too bad about a dud of a first time, since hers had been a pretty big letdown as well. She'd given in to some kid she'd been dating off and on when she was nineteen, simply because she was curious what all the fuss was about. Apparently it had been over so fast she had still been left wondering what the fuss was about, or if anything had even happened.

"Wait, so he didn't take the time to...?" he had questioned her, trailing off at the end of his question, trying not to be too crass in the moment.

Drea had just laughed. "There was zero warm-up. As soon as I said 'sure' he whipped our clothes off so fast, I barely had time to blink. Next blink he was in me, third blink he was done."

"That's...horrible," Kyle had said, holding back laughter.

"Yeah. Didn't really see him much after that. I held out hope that it would get better with the next guy, but eh. Been to a few rodeos now and I still don't quite understand all the rage."

"Wait, are you really telling me you've never had an orgasm?" he spat out, all attempt at being a gentleman gone. He couldn't believe what he was hearing.

'No, I've had one," she'd said, muffled by the fact that she was looking at her lap, not meeting his curious gaze. "They've just all been of my own making."

It had taken everything he'd had to not take her right there and rectify the situation. He couldn't believe that no one had taken the time to treat her like the queen she was. He wanted to be the one to fix that, but he didn't want to seem like he was only after one thing. Not to mention, staying employed was a priority and ravishing the bosses' niece was not a good idea.

Suddenly they were at her front door and he was brought back to the present. He was still holding her hand, still not fully sure of where they stood and how to proceed. She turned so they were face to face, standing so close they were all but touching, looking at him through her eyelashes.

"Come in?" she whispered.

"Of course," he whispered back.

———————

SHE STOOD THERE FOR A MOMENT, reminding herself to breathe. She didn't know why she was so nervous. It was Kyle, her favorite person. He had his own keycode to her house, for crying out loud. Why had she invited him in? He likely would have just followed her in anyway. But she had wanted to make sure. She wanted to know that he was there with her and not running off to join Dalton at Paradise Point.

Kyle leaned over her and punched his code into the keypad and opened the door. Reluctantly turning around, she walked into her little cottage, throwing her phone on a side table that was only a few feet from the door. She felt so awkward in her own home, not sure if she should just sit or go change or what.

"You want another drink?" she asked, walking toward the little open kitchen adjacent to the living room. Her cottage wasn't huge, just over nine hundred square feet all told, but it suited her perfectly. A bedroom big enough to fit a queen-size bed, with a step-in closet (calling it a walk-in would have been way too generous), an en suite bathroom that also opened to the kitchen, and an open concept great room that housed her little kitchen and living room. A set of French doors led to the back porch that looked out over Big House Beach.

"I don't think I could drink another drop after all that wine. Your uncles were not holding back tonight."

"It was a special night," she said, shrugging.

"It was."

"Well, we could sit—"

"Can I ask you something?" he cut her off.

"Anything. Always."

"What's going on with the Brig guy? Are you into him?"

"Brig? Oh hell, no," she answered, half laughing. She moved around the couch and plopped down on it. She pulled her legs up underneath her and grabbed a pillow to hold in her lap. "He just kept appearing. And since he's a guest I didn't want to be rude. He just wasn't picking up on any of the clues I was dropping, or at least that I thought I was dropping. This afternoon he asked if I wanted to have drinks with him and before I could let him down easy, Uncle Gray told him that if he retracted the question he wouldn't be banned from the resort," she giggled. "So, pretty sure he'll go away now."

Kyle felt relieved that the meathead had turned out to be harmless. Although that still didn't answer why she had been so upset last night. He came and sat down on the couch, turning so he was facing her, his shoulder leaning against the back of the couch. "So, what about Dalton?"

"Dalton? What about him?"

"What did he do to upset you?"

"Why on earth would you think I was upset with Dalton?"

"I saw you last night...at the bonfire. You were crying, and Dalton was holding you. I thought...I thought he did something to upset you."

"No, no, it wasn't Dalton. He was just trying to help."

"Oh."

"Yeah." She lowered her gaze to her fingers, which were picking at the seam on the pillow in her lap. "Can I ask *you* something?"

"Always. Anything. Whatever you want, sweetheart,"

he answered, reaching out to still the hand picking at the seam.

"What's the deal with Staci...'with an i'?" she said, raising her voice mockingly on the 'with an i'. "You, um, into her?"

She was still staring at the pillow. He released her hand, putting his fingers underneath her chin, raising her head so she met his gaze. He'd never, ever seen her this shy, and was having a hard time understanding it. The uneasy look in her eye told him that she was anxious, waiting to see if his answer was going to crush her.

"Not in the slightest." Her exhale was audible, and he could see her body relax as he spoke the words. "Is that why you were so upset last night?"

Drea looked away suddenly, biting her bottom lip nervously. "Um, well, it's just that, I saw you two last night, and she was hanging off you and rubbing up against you." She paused, swallowing hard. She turned back and looked at him, tears welling in her eyes.

"Oh, no, no, no," Kyle said. He reached for her and pulled her close. She curled up in his lap, wrapping her arms around his neck, burying her face in his shoulder. He raised his hand to her hair and stroked her curls slowly, trying to comfort her.

"I know it's stupid, but she was all over you and the bonfire is kinda our thing. And then today she was asking me all about what you like and your favorite sexual position. Then she told me I was too nice to get involved with you and I just wanted to die."

Favorite sexual position? Why would Staci have wanted to know...? It hit him suddenly and he burst out into a laugh. Drea looked up at him, tears still running down her face, now with anger flashing across her face. "It's not fucking funny!" She shoved his chest.

"Oh, baby, no, no. She was asking about Dalton."

"What?!"

"The reason she leeched on to me at the bonfire was because she was hoping to get Dalton's attention. What you saw was her trying to use her succubus powers to try and entrap our first mate. So today on the boat, she was asking about *his* favorite sexual position, not mine."

"I'm so embarrassed," she whispered, swiping at her tears with her fingers.

"Oh, Dre, don't be. I get it, I would have been just as upset if the roles were reversed." He held her face in his hand, wiping at her cheeks with his thumb.

She looked deeply into his eyes, hers going dark with an emotion he couldn't place. "You, you would?" she asked, breathy, pulling out of his hands and looking down.

He shifted her in his lap so that now she was full-on straddling him. She traced the outline of his pec muscles through his tee, trying to distract herself. She wanted so badly to kiss him, to grind herself against him and show him she was better than Staci. But she couldn't bring herself to look up at him. She couldn't bear to see the pity she just knew was in his eyes right now. For as much as she wanted more, she wasn't willing to risk what they did have to get it.

"Drea, look at me," he said softly. She raised her head slowly, finding his eyes. His hands found her face again, making sure she was looking at him. "Yes. You have no idea how much it killed me to watch you flirt with that meathead these last couple of days."

She let out a huge breath, relaxing her tensed muscles in the process. She leaned forward, resting her forehead against his. She was so relieved to hear that Staci meant nothing, but the part that came after that had her heart still racing. He'd gotten jealous over her talking with Brig. What exactly did that mean?

Just as she was about to pull away, he tilted his head slightly, moving his lips closer to hers. She did the same until their lips were all but touching. She could feel his breath on her lips, like it was whispering a secret to her.

"Drea..."

"Kyle..."

No sooner had she uttered his name than his lips were on hers, moving slowly, testing the waters. She slipped her arms around his neck and returned his kiss, enjoying the feel of his lips against hers. They were just as soft as she had imagined and yet somehow strong. He parted her lips with his tongue, slowly sliding it in her mouth and finding hers. He caressed her tongue softly, sweetly, like it was the only thing he had to do tonight. She let out a soft moan, urging him to continue.

His hands left her face, finding their way to her waist, toying with the hem of her tank top. She wiggled a little in his lap, deepening the kiss. He slid his hands up her sides, underneath her top, finding the bottoms of her breasts. Sliding his hands up over them, he gave a little squeeze once again, testing the waters. His thumbs found her nipples and swiftly brushed over them, which sent a lightning bolt of lust straight to her core. She whimpered, still not backing away from his mouth. She ground against his now-prominent erection, feeling it hit her clit as she did, now fully confident she would not be let down with whatever he was packing down there. Wanting to urge him on, she arched her back, pushing her chest into his hands. She could feel herself getting wetter as he continued to kiss her and play with her nipples.

As soon as he reached down into the cup of her bikini and pinched her nipple, she lost it. She pulled away from the kiss, and groaned out his name. "Kyle...shit..."

As if saying his name broke some spell, he pulled his hands out from under her shirt and shifted out from underneath her. She fell onto her side as he quickly pushed up from the couch.

"Drea, I'm sorry, I..." he stammered, covering his mouth with his hand. "I should go."

"No, Kyle. Please, please don't."

"I'm sorry, I should have, shouldn't have done that." He turned and headed toward her front door. Opening it, he paused. "I'll, um, see you tomorrow. I'm sorry." He walked out, closing the door behind him, not bothering to turn around and face her.

CHAPTER ELEVEN

SPRAWLED out on the couch in Leona's office, Drea tried to steady her breathing, her left arm flopped over her face, covering her eyes and blocking the light. She felt like shit, there was no other way to say it, and not just because of the headache she had from the almost-no sleep she got last night. After Kyle had made his lightspeed exit, she had just sat there on the couch for a few long moments, frozen in shock from what had just happened. He kissed her—kissed her good. Inside a part of her was so excited, it had been her fantasy come true. But then he ran away. Had she done something wrong? Was saying his name out loud as he played with her nipples the wrong thing to say?

She had texted Leona as soon as she was able to function, but knew it was already too late and that she was probably asleep. She'd considered calling Dalton, but what exactly was she gonna say? *Hey, your bikini got him to notice me, but how do I get him to take it off?* She couldn't do that. Not to mention, who knows what he was doing up at Paradise Point. As long as he was keeping Staci occupied, she didn't really care. She'd tossed and turned all night, replaying the whole evening in her head over and over. He had told her that he'd been jealous, right? Or had she imagined that? When her phone dinged with Leona's response at six am, she sprang to her feet and rushed off to meet her best friend, skipping her run on the beach in hopes that Leona could help her make some sense of it all.

"Here," Leona said, handing Drea a cup of coffee. "Before we get any deeper into this, this is gonna require caffeine."

"Thanks," she muttered, sitting up enough to take a sip. Leona sat at her desk, cradling her own coffee in her hand.

"So, just to recap, he walked you home, holding your hand like fucking Prince Charming, held you in his lap and told you he wanted to go all He-Man on gym bro and then he kissed you? Then he just all of a sudden up and ran away? Just like the lawyer dude in Jurassic Park who ran into the toilet."

"That's not the reference I would have come up with but, yeah, that's pretty much exactly how he ran away. Although I'm assuming he didn't get eaten by a T-Rex on his way out."

"Well, how was it?"

"Confusing. I have no idea what made him just stop all of a sudden."

"No, I mean the kiss! How was it? Everything you'd thought it'd be?"

"Lee, there aren't words," she sighed. "I have wanted to kiss him since the moment I saw him working on that yacht in Florida all those years ago. How many times have I gotten lost in thoughts of what his lips would feel like? Every time I would read one of those romance novels you give me, I would picture him doing all those dirty things to me."

"Well, that must have made for a hell of a collection in the old rub tub."

"You have no idea. But last night, with his tongue twisting with mine and his hands all over me, it was better than those books, better than anything my imagination has ever conjured up."

Just then the door to the office opened swiftly, but just far enough for Dalton to squeeze himself inside.

"Morning, sugar," he said, taking the cup of coffee out of Drea's hand and taking a sip. "Wild night?"

"Ugh!" she exclaimed, flopping back down on the couch and throwing her arm back over her eyes. "What are you even doing here?"

"Leona texted, said to get my ass over here, so I peeled myself out of bed and here I am."

"You said he knew," Leona interjected.

"He does know. Well, he knows about my feelings. The rest, well, the rest is his fault. His and Staci's." She shot back up and pointed at him. "She's not still in your bed, is she? Wait, I don't wanna know, she's a guest."

"I slept alone last night, in my own bed. I don't know what you're talking about," he smirked, taking another sip out of her mug. "So, my bikini worked, huh? Had I known that was all it would take, I would have thrown that thing at you a long time ago."

"But it didn't work!"

"Did he or did he not kiss you?"

"He did. But then he ran away! Muttering he was sorry and that he shouldn't have."

"Okay, so that's not ideal."

"Not ideal? Dalton, I texted you to help, not to provide mediocre commentary," Leona said. She shot a glare at him as if to say, *fix it now.*

"Start from the beginning, sugar. What exactly went down?" he drawled, shooting a look right back at Leona.

Drea reached over and grabbed her coffee mug back from him and took a long, slow gulp. She sighed as she started to relay the story, not sure just how much detail she should go into with Dalton. It was one thing to get graphic with Leona—they'd talked about sex since they were girls, reading romance novels and looking up things on the internet when they didn't know what something was. When she got to the part involving her boobs, she opted for a simple "felt me up," figuring Dalton had enough experience for all three of them combined and would get her meaning just fine.

"And he initiated the kiss?" Dalton asked when she was finished.

"Yes. We were both hovering right there, but the final push was him."

"And he was into it?"

"He was certainly acting like he was. He shoved his hand into my bikini top and he was sporting what seemed like a decent hard-on."

"Okay, okay," he said, waving his hands for her to stop. "I don't need details about another's dude's dick."

"But why did he run away?" Leona asked.

"I don't know." Dalton shrugged.

"You don't know?!" Leona squeaked. "You're here as the resident expert. I could have provided insight such as *I don't know*. Start proving yourself useful, or Carmella stops cleaning your bathroom."

"Carmella cleans your bathroom?" Drea asked, looking at Dalton, confused.

"What? I pay her."

"And that is technically against her employment

contract, so I can make it stop at any point," Leona said, looking smugly at Dalton.

"Look, I really don't know. I know he likes you, any idiot can see that there is something between you two, and from the sounds of it, he was enjoying himself. So my guess would be that he got up in his own head and freaked himself out."

"So, now what?" Drea asked, feeling the knots in her stomach multiply.

"Now, you leave it to me. I told you I would help and I did, and I will continue to until it's either happily ever after or you're a puddle of heartbreak and tears, in which case I'll supply the ice cream and booze to Leona over here. Can you continue to trust me, just for a little longer?"

"Is it going to involve another bikini?"

"Oh, absolutely, because that apparently worked significantly better than I thought! Just trust me, okay?"

"Okay, I think."

"I'm not so sure," Leona interjected, crossing her arms and looking skeptical.

"Well then, it's a good thing I don't require your trust, Lee, because then we'd never get anywhere. Now, shall we go get food? Because if I have to be up this early on my day off, then I deserve magic muffins that are straight out of the pan."

KYLE HAD CHECKED PRETTY MUCH ALL the places he could usually find Drea in the morning. She hadn't answered her door, she wasn't on the beach where she normally ran, and the gym was empty. That only left either Leona's office or the kitchen. *Please let her be in Leona's office, please let her be in Leona's office,* he pleaded in his head. At least in there they could be alone; Leona would excuse herself and give them the privacy they needed. In the kitchen, they'd have to deal with the staff, or worse, her family. He wasn't ready to face them, not after last night. He needed to talk to Drea first, needed to see where her head was at. He knew he was an idiot for running out the way he did, and he knew that she had to be all kinds of pissed at him. She had every right to be—it was a dick move on his part.

He just needed time to think. He certainly hadn't been thinking when he pulled her into his lap last night while they were revealing their green-eyed monsters, or when he allowed himself to lean all the way into her lips or when his hands had taken a field trip up her tank, exploring all those beautiful, soft curves she'd been unknowingly taunting him with all day. Even now, he was getting hard just reliving the memory of her slowly moving her core against him. If it had felt that good with clothes on, man, the real thing would be out of this world. But he needed her to know he wasn't just after her for sex, that it was *her* that he wanted. Her kindness, her giggles, her knowledge of sailing and the islands, her sense of adventure.

Leaving last night the way he had might have just been one of the biggest mistakes he'd ever made. He'd realized that before he was even halfway back to the staff dorms. He'd heard Grayson's advice loud and clear on that walk back. *"At some point, consequences be damned, you just gotta go for it."* This was that point. He just hoped Drea was still on the same page.

Making his way around the front desk and down the little back hallway that led to Leona's office, he was feeling pretty confident. He was just about to the office door when it flew open and Dalton walked out with his arm around Drea.

Kyle stopped dead in his tracks, his hackles coming up. What the fuck was this? He knew he screwed up in leaving last night, but had she really run to Dalton? That was low—so, so low.

"Morning, dude," Dalton said, removing his arm from Drea.

"What the fuck are you doing here? You're never up this early, much less on a day off."

"Kyle, we were just—" Drea started.

"Just what?" He crossed his arms and stared at them both.

Leona came bounding out of her office, bumping right into Drea and Dalton. "I thought we agreed on food. Why aren't you moving? Oh, hey, Kyle."

"They were just about to explain to me why they were coming out of your office all snuggled up together."

"Dude, moody much?" Dalton said.

"It's my fault. Somehow word got out about Dalton's little cleaning arrangement with Carmella and someone else asked me if they could have the same arrangement and so I had to remind Dalton it's against policy so he needs to shut his trap about it, since we don't want the uncles finding out, and I asked Drea to be here as a witness so Is are dotted and Ts are crossed, all that," she spat out.

He didn't believe her, but had to give her credit for coming up with something so quick. But the guilty looks on both Drea and Dalton's faces told him that there was way more to the story.

"Whatever," he scoffed and took off down the hall.

· · ·

KYLE BURST INTO THE KITCHEN, not bothering to care if the door slammed behind him. He wasn't entirely sure exactly why he was so mad, but seeing the two of them together had ignited something in him. She told him last night there was nothing going on...with Brig. But if there was nothing with Brig, certainly there wasn't something with Dalton. Dalton had been out with Staci. And Drea...Drea had been in his lap, kissing him back, moaning out his name. Pulling out one of the chairs from the family table, he threw himself into it and pounded his fist on the table.

"Something the matter, son?" Miller's voice came from behind him.

"No, yes. I dunno."

"Girl trouble?" Miller slid into the seat across from him, wiping his hands on his apron.

Kyle looked up at him. "No," he lied.

"We don't need to get into specifics, son, but how about we stick to the truth."

"Okay, yeah. It's about a girl."

"I'm gonna wager a guess that if it's evoking this kind of emotion, you got pretty strong feelings for her."

"I don't know what I'm feeling. I mean, I do, but, I don't know."

Miller chuckled, relaxing back into his seat, sliding down a bit. "That pretty much sums up how I felt when I met Marta. She twisted me into knots. One minute I was high as a kite, the next, I was raging because someone said 'excuse me' to her on the street."

"So what'd you do about it?"

"I told her how I felt. Told her I was crazy about her and I had no idea what I was doing, but whatever it was, I wanted her there by my side. When she told me she felt the same, well, that was easily the best damn feeling in the world," he sighed, taking a moment to relish the memory. He looked back up and straight at Kyle. "Your girl share your feelings?"

"I'm not sure. I thought so, but, now, now I'm confused."

"Well, son, you're never going to be anything but confused unless you remove your head from your ass and go talk to her. And I mean really talk with her, let her be heard. I don't mean just listening. Hear what she is telling you, with her words and her heart."

The kitchen door burst open again and Dalton plowed through, making his way over to Kyle.

"What the fuck was that, dude? Your granny panties in a wad?" he accused, stopping dead in front of Kyle.

Kyle stood up, billowing out his chest like an angry bird trying to defend its nest. "Really? You're gonna ask me what the fuck that was? I think you've got plenty of explaining to do yourself."

"Why don't you boys take this out back? I am probably not the person who you should be having this discussion in front of," Miller said, not bothering to get up from the table.

"Good call," Kyle ground out. He turned, stomping out the back door of the kitchen, with Dalton on his heels.

Once they were both outside and the door had closed, they turned to face each other, arms crossed, scowls across their faces.

"Kyle, do you really, for one fucking second, think that there was something to that back there?"

"I don't know what to think anymore."

"Well, whose fault is that?"

"Mine, damn it, I get that," Kyle shouted.

"Something you wanna share?"

Kyle turned and paced a little in the alleyway. He knew he could trust Dalton. He was his first mate and, really, his closest friend. He just wasn't so sure about saying the words out loud. But he supposed he was going to have to at some point, and better to Dalton than to any of her uncles.

"I kissed Drea last night," he answered, looking up to meet Dalton's gaze.

"Fuck yeah, dude!" Dalton held out his fist. Kyle bumped it with his. "About fucking time!"

"What's that supposed to mean?"

"Seriously? Kyle, we've been friends for three years. You think I don't see the way you look at her. Like she walks on friggin' water?"

"Oh."

"Yeah, oh. So, what's this mean?"

"How the hell am I supposed to know?"

"So, I take it you two didn't talk in the middle of all this kissing?"

"No," Kyle said, turning to pace again. "I, uh, kinda just up and left after I did it. I was on my way to find her to talk to her when I saw the two of you coming out of Leona's office and..." he trailed off.

"And lost your shit?" Dalton finished. Kyle nodded. "Well, dude, only one thing left to do now."

"Yeah?" Kyle asked. "What's that?"

"Grovel."

CHAPTER TWELVE

After a run that did nothing to help clear her head, and a shower that only left her wishing that Kyle had been in there with her, Drea made her way to the docks. On any other day she would have been thrilled that this afternoon's cruise was just an older couple who wanted to hang out on the water and relax. But knowing that she wouldn't have the buffer of guests and unsure what kind of mood Kyle was in left her feeling uneasy.

She hadn't seen either him or Dalton after they both took off. Not that she had looked very hard. Leona had pulled her back into her office to finish off their coffee, waiting to see if either one of the boys showed up. When neither of them did, they eventually made their way to the kitchen where they found Miller all by himself, other than the miscellaneous staff scurrying around him. She had to fight the urge to ask him if he'd seen the boys, and if Kyle had mentioned why he was so upset. But she knew better; just because Miller had been her go-to for many years when she needed a shoulder to cry on didn't mean he would be where Kyle turned. In fact, she would probably put money on Miller and the rest of her uncles being part of why Kyle bolted last night.

Hopping up onto the *Runnin' Down a Dream*, she pulled the little Bluetooth speaker from underneath the bar and connected her phone. While her uncles and the boys were pretty much strictly classic rock listeners, Drea's taste ventured out a little more. Not that she didn't love the epic rock ballads she'd grown up listening to, but when she was by herself her country music guilty pleasure took over. Turning to her "current favorites" playlist, she cranked the music and started on some of the cleaning they had skipped yesterday due to the family meeting. Three or four songs in she had finally found a rhythm and had started to dance around the boat as she wiped surfaces down.

As she moved, she thought about what Leona had said the other day, about her bringing up her "big idea" to her uncles. It wasn't that she didn't love working on the boats—she did. But sometimes she just wanted more. She wanted to be able to have a bigger stake in the family business and have something that was her own, like each one of her uncles did. However, she also knew, as showcased by Grayson's comments later that evening, that she was still a kid to them. The idea that she take on more responsibility was probably not something that had ever even crossed their minds. But, just as she said to Leona, maybe someday.

"You know that's not really all that long, right?" Kyle said, startling Drea out of her zone.

"What?" she asked, turning away from the bar to face him.

"Ten thousand hours—it's like, just over four hundred days or something like that. So, it's not really all that long that he's promising her."

"Well, I can't speak for Dan and Shay, but I'm pretty

sure that no one has really ever looked to the Biebs for his math skills. Kind of like how no one ever really called out those weird British guys for walking 500 miles."

"They were Scottish. And they offered to walk 500 more."

"Right, how could I forget."

She looked away from him, out over the marina, afraid to make eye contact. It was killing her to feel so awkward standing there with him. She never felt awkward with Kyle —part of the beauty of their relationship was the comfort and ease that had always been so natural. But now, she didn't know what to do. She wanted to throw her arms around him and hug him just as much as she wanted to smack him across the face and scream at him for being a jackass.

"I owe you about eighty-two different apologies right now," he started. "And I'm not entirely sure that there is anything I can do or say to make up for the way I acted last night."

"Kyle," she exhaled.

"No, sweetness, please let me finish," he said, putting his index finger up to her lips softly. "I know I acted like a dick. I know I probably made you feel so, so small and worthless and that wasn't my intent at all. And I know this is probably the worst place ever to be doing this, other than maybe the family table, but I need you to know that I would never, ever do anything to hurt you."

Drea just stood there, frozen in place. Her mind was running a million miles a minute trying to figure out exactly what he was saying. Which thing was he sorry for? Last night? This morning? Both? She opened her mouth to respond, but couldn't find words to express her wild emotions.

"I know we need to talk more, like an actual real conversation, and that we don't have time for it here and now," he added. "But before we do anything else, I need to know that you forgive me and are willing to hear me out about last night. And maybe pretend this morning didn't happen."

He cupped her face in his hands and looked directly into her eyes. She sighed, unsure if it was from relief or from just how good his hands felt on her skin. Closing her eyes, she tilted her head forward, and he did the same, until their foreheads met. They stood there like that for a long moment, just the two of them soaking in the other.

"Oops, looks like we've interrupted a moment!" they heard an older male voice say. Drea broke away from Kyle and looked over to the pier where they found Mr. and Mrs. Prage standing.

"No, no, Mr. Prage, you're not interrupting anything," she said, turning down her music, and she and Kyle headed over to help them onto the boat.

"Are you sure, dear?" Mrs. Prage asked.

"If you two need to finish making up, we can come back a little later," Mr. Prage added.

"It's not that," Kyle said.

"Don't bullshit me, boy, if you'll pardon my language," Mr. Prage said. "You don't spend fifty-seven years with a person and not know a makeup scene when it happens."

"You guys have been married for fifty-seven years?" Drea asked.

"We've been married for fifty-four, but we've been together since I was fifteen, got married shortly after my eighteenth birthday," Mrs. Prage answered proudly.

"Well, that is certainly impressive. So, where can we take you lovebirds today?" Kyle asked.

"We're just in this for a nice, calm, peaceful day out on

the water. Maybe some snorkeling, definitely some sun," Mrs. Prage answered.

"And my beautiful bride would like to watch the sunset over the water, if that's possible. If there is an extra charge for keeping you two after dark then I'll gladly pay it."

"Oh no, Mr. Prage, we will gladly take you to the perfect spot to watch the sunset. We know just the spot, don't we, Kyle?"

"We sure do."

"Please, it's Jack, and my beautiful bride is Diane."

"You're Jack and Diane?" The Prages just nodded.

"Oh, you just made his little classic-rock-loving heart very, very happy," Drea laughed.

"Well, Jack, Diane, we're gonna have a good day!" Kyle said, high-fiving them. "Let's get started!"

The Prages started to get settled in with all their stuff while Kyle and Drea went back to the bar area to do the final few things before they could set sail. When he was pretty sure the Prages weren't looking, he pulled her close again, wrapping his arms around her.

"So, are we okay? I know we need to talk, and I promise we will, but I need to know we're okay."

"Yes," she nodded. "We're okay. But I'd be lying if I didn't say that I am looking forward to what you have to say for yourself."

"Oh baby, I promise it'll be worth it." He kissed her forehead before hopping up to the captain's perch.

KYLE KEPT himself up in the captain's chair all day, fighting every urge he had to go down to Drea and scoop her up. She was wearing that purple bikini again—he was pretty sure she'd done it to punish him. Bouncing around to her music, which Diane had insisted she leave on when Drea had gone to turn it off prior to setting sail, had her shaking her hips back and forth, jiggling her breasts as she went. He had wanted to go down and dance with her while the older couple was in the water snorkeling, but felt it was probably best to give her some space while they were working.

He could hear the older couple settling in on the trampolines up front, getting ready to watch the sunset. Drea had popped open a bottle of champagne for them and Mr. Prage was wrapping his wife up in a light blanket before settling in behind her and pulling her close.

Hearing her feet on the steps up to his perch, Kyle turned to see Drea headed up to him, two cups of champagne in her hands.

"Hey," she said softly.

"Hey back," he answered.

"Figured you'd want some too."

"I do believe this is technically against policy, Miss Miller," he smirked.

"I got an in with the boss," she giggled. "But I won't tell if you won't."

He took both cups from her and put them on the little shelf next to the steering wheel, and pulled her all the way up to the top of the stairs. It took a moment of maneuvering, but he scooted all the way back in his chair and opened his legs wide to slide her in between him and the wheel, pulling her closer, his legs swinging around her legs and holding her at the knees.

"Drea," he sighed. "You know you mean the world to me, right?"

"Yeah, I get it," she said, looking down.

The devastated look on her face was like a punch to the

gut. What did she think was about to happen? He knew she was hurt and confused, and that it was all his fault, but the look on her face said more than just confusion. She was obviously a lot more upset than he realized, and he could kick himself for being the one to put that look on her face.

"Dre, just what do you think you get?" he asked, trying to not sound accusatory.

"I'm great, I'm just the coolest chick, but you didn't mean it last night, you just want to be friends, all that. I get it, it's, I—"

He cut her off, pulling her in close and kissing her. The moment his lips met hers, she let out a little whimper. He slowly moved his lips with hers, letting his tongue dip into her mouth, lightly licking the inside of her lower lip. She greeted his tongue with hers, letting them play inside her mouth for a moment, before he pulled back slightly, capturing her bottom lip with his teeth and nibbling lightly before letting go. When he finally pulled away fully, the look of sadness in her eyes was gone, this time replaced with what appeared to be a little glimmer of hope.

"Dre, if that's what you think, then no, sweetness, I don't think you do get it."

She stood there, quietly searching his eyes with hers, her fingers lightly sweeping back and forth on her bottom lip. He took in a slow, deep breath waiting for her to say something. He silently hoped that he had done the right thing, that he'd expressed to her exactly what they both had been feeling. She looked down again and then out over the ocean.

"Dre, please say something."

She slowly shifted from foot to foot as she turned her head back toward him. Just as he was letting out another long, slow breath, she forcefully grabbed his face and pushed their lips together for another kiss. She kissed him hard and fast, as if she only had so much time until they were ripped apart. He slowed down her movements with his lips, taking control and enjoying each second their lips were touching.

Ever so slowly, she stepped back again. Breathing heavy, she opened her mouth to say something, but nothing came out.

"I have wanted to do that for so long," she finally said.

"Me too, sweetness, me too," he whispered. He could feel her body relax as she leaned into him fully and rested her head on his shoulder. "And last night was anything but a mistake. The only mistake was how I handled it."

"Why did you run away?"

"Because I'm an idiot." She pulled back and looked at him. "Can we just go with 'guys are dumb'?"

"No."

"Ok, well, I tried," he shrugged. "Drea, you mean so fucking much to me and I have wanted to kiss you for what feels like forever. But I held back because I came down here for a reason, and a relationship just wasn't on the to-do list. Especially a relationship with the bosses' niece. I've had it in my head that I couldn't do both. I couldn't work and save money and be the man you needed me to be."

"So what changed?"

"Grayson called me a chickenshit."

"What?! You talked to Uncle Gray about me?"

"No, no! His advice was out of the blue, and I don't think it was really about you, but he just told me I had to stop being a chickenshit. And then I saw you with the meat-head and I wanted to deck him. Last night when you were upset about that dumb blonde, I realized that you, at least on some level, felt the same way I did. I just couldn't hold back anymore."

"So, now what?"

"You tell me, baby, you tell me. I want you. I want you so, so bad. And by that I mean you, not just your body, please know that. Although you have to stop wearing that suit into work if you think I'm going to function." She giggled, and that sound went straight to his groin, making him instantly hard. "And the giggles, we might need to cut back on those at work too." He smiled. "But seriously Dre, if you want to tell me to take a hike, I get it. You have every reason to after the way I acted last night."

"And this morning."

"I thought we agreed that never happened," he smiled guiltily.

"I agreed to no such thing. Plus, even if I did, there were witnesses."

Kyle groaned. "Touché."

"But I'm willing to let you off the hook if you continue to kiss me like you did a couple of minutes ago."

"Oh yeah?" he asked. He leaned in and gave her a quick little kiss. "I think that can be arranged."

She giggled again and reached down to grab the cups she had brought up. She handed one to Kyle. "To a new start?"

"To a new us," he corrected. "Now, let's finish watching this sunset, so that when we get back, we can steal some food from the kitchen and I can take you on a picnic on the beach. Sound good to you, sweetness?"

"Sounds perfect."

CHAPTER THIRTEEN

THE OLDER COUPLE had made for a pretty easy charter, leaving them with little to no cleanup from the day. Kyle was still buzzing from their moment up on top of the boat and watching the sunset with Drea in his arms. He enjoyed feeling her body against his, her soft curves underneath his hands, being able to kiss her neck if he desired. He really enjoyed not having to shift his hips and try to hide his blatant arousal from her. The way she snuggled into him and wiggled her hips against his made it seem like she appreciated that as well.

Once they were off the boat, they headed to the kitchen to see what they could confiscate to take with them. Kyle tried to run through schedules in his head, hoping that since he saw Miller at breakfast that he had the night off and wouldn't be in the kitchen now. He was incredibly grateful for the advice he'd been given this morning, but he didn't want to have to explain to the man that the girl in question was the niece he'd raised since she was an infant. Come time to level with her uncles, he figured it would be easy enough to convince Miller that he was good enough for

Drea. He might have been her father figure, but he was a romantic at heart and Kyle knew he wanted Drea to find what he'd had with her aunt.

Grabbing an assortment of cheese and crackers, fruit, and Drea's favorite potstickers, they headed back to Drea's. After taking a blanket from inside, they spread it out on a section of Big House Beach that extended in front of the porch on her cottage.

They enjoyed the relative quiet of the private beach as they ate, with the muted beat of the music coming from the main part of the resort blending in with the waves crashing onto the beach. Kyle kept waiting for Drea to break the silence, but she simply sat there, chowing down on the potstickers like it was her last meal. When she finally held out the plate with the last potsticker on it, motioning for him to take it, he couldn't help but let out a huge laugh.

"Oh, so now you share!"

"What? I am letting you have the last one. If I have ever done anything to let you know that you're special to me, this is it," she said, a bright smile on her face.

He leaned in and kissed her lightly, her smile never fading. "I do know how special it is that you're sharing this last potsticker with me, and I am so very honored." He took it off the plate, dipped it in the tangy brown sauce that accompanied it, and reached out toward Drea's lip, motioning for her to open her mouth. "But I also wouldn't dream of taking the last one from you."

She opened her mouth and bit down on the potsticker, slowly pulling away, leaving half of it in his hand still. She chewed methodically, as if trying to tease him. Swallowing even more slowly than she chewed, Kyle couldn't help but watch her throat, wondering if she'd always been this tempting when she ate. She leaned in for the last bite, which he gladly provided, this time her lips closing around his fingers, slowly sucking the last bit of potsticker into her mouth. He'd been sporting a semi ever since they got off the boat, but with her mouth on his fingers like that, his cock instantly grew harder than he thought possible.

"You're killing me," he said, through slightly gritted teeth, not wanting to let his lust take over. This night was about the two of them being together, figuring out what the new them looked like. As much as he wanted to take her right here, he didn't want her to feel that he was only in this for the sex.

"What? Did I do something wrong? If you wanted the last one you should have said something, or just eaten it!" she exclaimed, looking horrified.

"Oh sweetness, what am I going to do with you?"

"Kiss me more?" She leaned in toward him, and he gladly obeyed.

"If I didn't know better, I'd start to wonder if you weren't just after my body," Kyle joked.

"Well, I, um," she muttered, her cheeks starting to blush.

"Hey, no secrets. We've never held back before, now would be a pretty bad time to start."

"I was just going to comment that I may have spent a fair amount of time wondering what exactly you were packing in those board shorts of yours."

He reached over, grabbing her arm, and pulled her into his lap, sending the last of the crackers flying all over the blanket. He situated her so her legs were wrapped around his waist, his arms circling her, his hands coming to rest on her lower back. He ground up into her core so she could feel exactly what he was packing, and just how much she had its attention. She reached up and looped her arms around his neck, clasping them so she could hold on. Leaning in for a couple of chaste kisses, he pulled back again and gazed into her eyes.

"Confession, I have spent a fair amount of time thinking about what was under your swimsuit too."

"Really?"

"Really. Another confession: I should probably be ashamed to admit this, but I have spent plenty of nights jerking off to thoughts of you."

"Confession," she whispered, looking away from him. "That makes two of us."

"Slow your roll there, sweetness. Are you telling me that cute, sweet, angelic Drea not only has a need for a spank bank, but that I'm in it? Well damn," he exhaled. Just when he thought it was not possible for his cock to be any harder, she said things like that.

"Leona refers to it as the "rub tub," but yeah..." she trailed off. "Sorry if that's an overshare."

"Not at all. I could go on for days about all the things I have dreamed of doing to you." He pulled her in for a kiss, taking a moment for deepening it, sweeping her tongue with his. She whimpered, pushing her core against his erection. Her hands moved to his hair as they continued to kiss, slowly moving across his scalp in rhythm with his lips.

He moved his hands around to her sides, grabbing the hem of her shirt and lifting it, inch by inch, until it required they break away from each other to pull it over her head. She looked down at her swimsuit, biting her bottom lip. Kyle released her shirt, throwing it off to the side somewhere, then returned his hands to her breasts.

"These babies, oh man. The endless hours I have thought about them."

"What about them?" she asked shyly. He wasn't sure

where this side of Drea had come from, but he knew one thing, he needed to make it go away. He wanted his fun, confident Drea back.

"What haven't I thought about? I've thought about touching them, squeezing them," he answered, running his hands over them lightly. He ran his hands back down them, cupping a boob in each hand, giving them a firm but gentle squeeze. He reached around and unclipped the back of her bikini top, slipping it from her arms. His gaze fell to the two stunning orbs before him, sending his pulse into rapid-fire with excitement.

"These might be the most beautiful tits I have ever seen," he muttered. "So much better than I imagined. Oh, have I ever imagined taking these nipples between my fingers, stroking them, loving them, tweaking them." His actions followed his words, as he slowly ran his fingers over her pert nipples, letting them pebble under his touch. Taking each between his forefinger and thumb he pinched each one. Drea felt a bolt of lust shoot through her, and she moaned as he continued.

"More than anything, though," he said, lowering his head, "I've pictured myself burying my face in them. Getting lost in your cleavage, sucking on each nipple until you cried out my name and begged for my cock." Just as he finished his words, he drew in her left nipple, sucking hard. She gasped in pleasure, rocking her hips as he continued to suck, never letting up on playing with her right one either.

"Kyle," she groaned.

"Yes, sweetness?" he said, from around her nipple.

"Don't stop, don't ever stop."

"Never, baby." He briefly unlatched himself, but only long enough to switch sides, taking up his oral assault on her right side now. This was better than any of the one-handed sessions that he'd had through the years. Actually holding her, feeling her heat against his cock as he worshipped her glorious breasts was like nothing else. He could stay like this all night long.

She was rocking against him at a pretty good pace now, and he wasn't sure if he should reach down in between them and help push her over the edge. He wondered just how wet she was. If he reached into her bikini bottoms would he find that she was ready and wanting? He had to know.

He removed his hand from her left breast, and slowly traced his way down her body toward her pussy. She slowed her hips as he neared her suit line, waiting for him to breach the line. Slipping his hand down into her suit, his hand was quickly met with his answer. Her pussy was warm and slippery with her desire. His middle finger easily found her clit, ever so slightly sweeping across it, causing her to cry out.

"Kyle!" she breathed out heavily. "Take me inside. Please."

DREA WASN'T ENTIRELY sure what fantasy planet she was on at the moment, but she was sure that she didn't want to ever return from it. The feel of Kyle's lips against hers, and all those things he was doing with his hands—she read about things like this in books, but she had been so sure that people didn't really experience these kinds of feelings.

Kyle pulled his mouth away from her nipple, returning his mouth to hers. He kissed her slowly, brushing his finger across her wet center again, resulting in her gasping into his kiss. Freeing his hand from her shorts, he shifted so that both his hands were under her butt, supporting her as he stood up. Wrapping her legs around his torso, she kissed him harder, pulling him close so her bare breasts brushed up against his shirt. Turning toward her cottage porch, he started to make his way to the gate.

"Wait," she said, pulling away quickly. "The blanket!"

"I'll come back for it later."

"But what if my uncles see it? I don't want to have to explain why my bikini top is just hanging out by itself."

Kyle wanted to argue, but she made a good point. He didn't want to give anyone any reason to come near the cottage right now. "It'll require putting you down."

She grumbled in response, but unhooked her legs and slid down his body. Running over to the blanket, her beautiful breasts jiggling as she moved, she folded up the blanket, not bothering to clear the food and plates off of it. Kyle took it from her, leaning down and kissing her.

"I enjoyed watching you do that way too much," he said, a sly smile on his face. "Seriously Dre, your tits are a dream."

She blushed, biting the corner of her bottom lip. She loved hearing him say that; it excited a part of her deep inside, a part of her that she really, really wanted to act on. Grabbing his hand, she turned and opened the gate to step up onto the porch. Another few steps and they were entering her living room via the French doors. Kyle dropped the blanket, dishes and all, as soon as they were inside and the door was closed. He picked Drea back up again and immediately returned to assaulting her nipples with his mouth.

Each swipe of his tongue sent a bolt of lust down her body, straight to her center. Her nipples were so sensitive and he seemed to know exactly what to do to them. She could feel her heartbeat thrum through her entire body and her sex pulsed with every beat. Arching her back, forcing her breasts closer to his mouth, she wiggled her hips against his, trying to find the friction she needed. Kyle laughed lightly as she did so, thrusting slightly into her gyration, teasing her.

"Trying to tell me something, sweetness?" he asked, his eyes dark with need.

"Bedroom," she growled.

"As you wish." He kissed her, lightly at first, then harder as he started to make his way to the bedroom. He covered the small cottage in just a few steps, kissing his way down her neck and across her clavicle. Thankful the door was already open, he stepped inside and closed the door with his foot. When he reached the bed, he laid her down slowly, leaning over her.

"Lights?" he asked.

"I don't know. What do you want?"

"This is about you, sweetness. I'll do whatever you want."

"How about the little lamp on the nightstand? So it's not too bright, but I can still see you."

He reached over and turned the switch on the lamp. A low, soft light illuminated their faces but not much else. He nudged her over making room for him to join her on the bed.

"You are so beautiful," he said.

"You're not so bad yourself," she answered, smiling. Reaching back out for him, pulling him back in for a kiss, she let her hands wander up his shirt, feeling all his hard muscles underneath. "This needs to come off."

Without any hesitation he sat up enough to pull off his shirt and rolled over and rested on his hands so he hovered over her. She reached up, gliding her hands across his pecs and down his abs. She reached for the hem of his board shorts, pulling at the drawstring.

"Ladies first," he said, sitting back on his haunches, pulling off her bikini bottoms, revealing her smooth, completely bare mound. "Oh, fuck," he exhaled.

"What?"

"You're bare."

"I wear a swimsuit all day, waxing is just easiest."

"I don't care about the reason," he answered, still staring at her sex. "But it's a fucking dream come true."

He ran his hand up the inside of her right thigh, before running it back down her left. She shivered at his touch, waiting for him to move closer to where she wanted him. He cupped her center and ran his palm down it, coating his whole hand with her wetness. She groaned as he made contact, shifting herself trying to find his hand again. She felt as if she would explode if he didn't touch her soon. Spreading his fingers, he rubbed up and down her folds, creating a V around her clit. When he finally made the contact she needed, she whimpered every time he hit the sensitive little nub, fueling him on.

When she felt him slide two fingers inside her, she bucked her hips. He leaned over her and started sucking on her nipples again, heightening everything she felt tenfold. She could feel the start of an orgasm forming in her belly and she couldn't believe that it was really happening. Was she really going to come at the hands of someone other than herself? Continuing to stroke her inside and out, Kyle's thumb found her clit again and that was all Drea needed to be pushed over the edge.

She cried out, louder than she intended. But she didn't care who could hear her as the most intense orgasm she'd ever had rolled through her entire body. She could feel it from the top of her head all the way down to the tip of her curled-up toes. It was all she could do to continue to breathe through this all-consuming feeling.

When she finally came back to earth, she opened her eyes to find Kyle gazing at her with a sly, but proud smile on his face. She sat up and found his lips, kissing him as hard as she could. She was still so turned on from what he had just done to her, she needed to feel him, now.

Fumbling with the waist of his shorts again, not wanting to break the kiss, Drea finally got the drawstring loose. Kyle stood up, quickly dropping his shorts, his hard dick now on full display. Drea's eyes widened as she took in the impressive shaft in front of her. She had figured out that he had to be well-endowed based on what she had felt through his suit, but nothing could have prepared her for the beast she was staring at now. Reaching out for it as he stepped closer, she gently wrapped her hand around it, impressed to find that her fingertips barely touched. Slowly stroking up and down, she was mesmerized; none of the other guys she'd been with had anything near this impressive below the belt. Just how he was going to feel inside her was all she could think about.

"Oh shit," she muttered, looking up at him. "I don't have condoms."

Kyle smirked at her and picked up his shorts from the floor, reaching into the pocket, pulling out two little foil packets.

She quirked her brow at him. "Just walking around with those in your pocket there, cowboy?"

He climbed back on her bed and pulled her close, kissing her softly. "I 'borrowed' them from Dalton's stash on the boat. I wasn't expecting anything, but didn't want to be caught empty-handed either. I figured I could put them back if they had gone unused."

She laughed, grabbing one of the packets from his hands. "Can I put it on you? I've never put one on before."

"Be my guest, beautiful."

She took his cock in hand again, softly stroking up and down a few times before trying to rip open the condom wrapper. Kyle pulled it from her hand and ripped it open with his teeth, handing her the open wrapper. Slowly rolling it down his cock only excited her more, and she could feel herself getting wetter as she went. Once it was finally on, she looked back up at him. His gaze was glued to her hand on his length, his breathing heavy with desire.

She scooted back on the bed, allowing him to climb back on, positioning his body between her legs, his hard cock pressing against her opening. He placed a hand on either side of her upper body and leaned down into her, giving her a kiss before pressing his forehead to hers.

"Hey," he whispered.

"Hey back," she whispered in response. She looked deep into his eyes, which were dark with emotion and lust. She hoped hers radiated the same back to him, as her heart nearly beat out of her chest. She shifted below him, trying to angle herself so his dick would break the barrier at which it hovered.

"Dre..."

"Yes, please," she exhaled, answering the unspoken question.

Without another word, he slowly pushed inside her. It had been so long and he was so big that for a moment she felt like she might be ripped in two as her insides adjusted to him, gripping his erection as he moved. She groaned loudly, throwing her head back in both pleasure and pain.

When he was fully inside he paused for a moment, kissing along her jawline and down her exposed neck, giving her a moment to adjust to him. Just when she thought she couldn't take the wait any longer, he slowly withdrew from her, making her feel every last inch of him again.

"You are so, fucking, tight," he said through gritted teeth. "Your pussy feels so good." He thrust inside her again, this time a little faster, then withdrew almost right away.

"Just don't stop," she managed to breathe out. He grinned at her wickedly and picked up his pace.

He found his rhythm quickly, a mixture of hard and fast thrusts with a few long, slow strokes mixed in. He was hitting her in all the right spots, spots she didn't even realize that she had inside her, making her whine and whimper with need. Trying to match him thrust for thrust along the way, she could feel the stirring of another orgasm building inside her.

"Kyle, Kyle," she cried. "I think I might..." she trailed off, unable to finish her sentence from the glorious feel of his cock inside her.

"Oh baby, yes you will!" he growled. He reached down between them and quickly found her clit with his thumb, applying just the right amount of pressure, swirling it around with the pad of his finger.

That was enough to send her flying, and she screamed out a sound she had never heard before, something so incomprehensible she wasn't really sure it was a word. She wasn't sure if her eyes were open or closed as all the colors around her swirled into a bright light. *This must be what it means to see stars*, she thought.

Her orgasm seemed to be all the inspiration Kyle needed to pick up the pace yet again and drive into her even harder. A few more pumps and he groaned as he hit his own release, collapsing on top of her.

They both lay there for a moment, breathing heavy, letting their bodies return to their normal state. Drea's thoughts raced, thinking about a thousand and one things all at once. *Holy shit, that was amazing. I hope he doesn't regret it. Should I be the one to break the silence?*

"I can hear your brain racing, sweetness," Kyle finally said, pushing himself up, rolling off of her, and standing up next to the bed. He rolled off the condom, tied it up and walked to the bathroom to dispose of it. As he walked back into the room, she noticed he had a washcloth with him.

"What's that for?" she asked, feeling a little self-conscious.

"For you," he said, climbing back on the bed. "Unless you don't want me to clean you up?"

"No, I um, just wasn't expecting it." He reached between her legs again, this time with the warm cloth in his hand, and gently wiped her down.

"Well, isn't that what all those men do in your books?" he grinned at her.

"My books? How would you know what they do in books?"

"I might have opened one once when I was waiting for you or something," he said sheepishly. "I opened it up randomly and happened to land on a good part."

Drea shook her head, laughing loudly. When he finished cleaning her, he threw the washcloth on the floor, and pulled back the covers on her bed, wrapping them around the both of them. He reached over her to turn off the table lamp and then pulled her in close to him so they were spooning. Feeling secure in his arms, his heat warm against her back, her eyes started to feel heavy. She snuggled against him, wanting to give in to the sleep she felt approaching.

"This is going to come off sounding cheesy and I might lose my man card, but I need you to know that what we just did—it means something to me, Drea. It means a lot." He swallowed hard. "You mean a lot, and this wasn't just about getting us off."

"You mean a lot to me, too, Kyle," she murmured sleepily. "But I enjoyed the getting off part too."

He laughed softly, stroking her hair, lulling her to sleep. "I'm glad, sweetness. Because there is more where that came from. Promise."

CHAPTER FOURTEEN

Drea rolled over in bed, finding herself alone. A momentary wave of panic passed through her until her hand glided over the currently unoccupied pillow and found a piece of paper.

Morning Sweetness - I didn't run away, but I did sneak out a little early to avoid some prying eyes and dodge some questions we might not want to answer just yet. I'll see you in the kitchen for breakfast. -K
PS: last night was amazing ;)

She sighed, reading the note all the way through a couple of times before finally placing it in the nightstand drawer. She was so relieved to find it wasn't a dream, and that last night did happen. Grabbing her phone, which had somehow made its way to the charging cord on the nightstand, she turned it on, hoping she didn't miss anything major. Other than a text from Simone about settling on a dress, an unexplained winky face from Dalton, and a "so, what happened?" followed by a few "???" from Leona, it seemed to have been a pretty uneventful evening. Well, for everyone else at least.

Sitting up, she realized she was a little sore from last night's activities. She pressed her palms lightly against her chest, her sensitive nipples still hard from Kyle's relentless attention. An energy flowed through her like she couldn't ever recall feeling. She knew she should get up and go run, but the slight, although wonderful, ache in her core was enough to dissuade her. She scrolled to Leona's texts and responded.

Drea: Morning
Leona: oh, look who's alive!
Drea: Very ;)
Leona: What's that supposed to mean? DID SOMETHING HAPPEN?
Drea: You in your office?
Leona: OMG, something did!
No, I'm down in laundry, India called out.
Drea: Be there in 10

STROLLING down the hall toward the laundry room, Drea tried to hide the ridiculous smile she knew was on her face. It had taken her a couple of steps to tone down the extra little pep she felt on the way over here. She didn't want anyone to look at her and think that something was up. But she couldn't help the giddiness she felt. Turning into the laundry room, she saw Leona changing out a load of towels.

"Welcome to the Indigo Royal Fluff and Fold!" Leona sang as she looked up to see Drea walking in.

"Morning."

"Don't you look like the cat that ate the canary!"

"Do I? I was trying to hide it."

"And what exactly is there to hide?"

"Well, Kyle and I talked last night," she said coyly.

"Girl, based on that dopey look on your face, you did a lot more than talk," she said, glaring knowingly at her best friend.

"Yeah..."

"Yeah?"

Drea nodded. She wanted to just word vomit the whole story out, but she didn't dare just start unloading. Not without knowing who might be listening.

"Girl, spill, now!!!" Leona hissed, grabbing a basket of freshly dried towels and dumping it on the folding table.

"Are we alone?"

"Of course we're alone, we're in the laundry! Now stop stalling!"

Drea picked up a towel and started to fold, taking in a deep breath. "Where do you want me to start?"

"Well, I can assume he apologized."

"Yes, he did. And the Prages picked that moment to get on the boat and disrupt the moment. But that actually was kinda cute, because Mr. Prage totally called us out on it!" She giggled thinking about the look on the older gentleman's face when he looked at her and Kyle yesterday afternoon. "But then later, while they were watching the sunset, he kissed me."

"Just kissed you?"

"Well, we were on the boat, working, with guests present," she pointed out. Never mind that Drea was pretty sure had they looked at those guests she would have found them making out too.

Leona just looked at her, waiting for her to continue. She pushed a stack of folded towels down the long table and grabbed another bunch to continue the fold process.

"So then when we got back, we grabbed some food from the kitchen and took it for a picnic out behind the cottage. We ate and talked and then one thing led to another..."

"OH MY GOD!" Leona whisper shouted. "You did not have sex on Big House Beach!"

"No, we made it to the bed."

"Wait, hold on. You slept with him? Like actual sex, not just heavy petting until you both were happy puppies?"

"Yup. We kinda skipped straight to the good stuff."

Leona let out a little shriek and scurried around the table. She grabbed Drea in a big hug, jumping up and down.

"Holy shit, Drea! How was it? Did it live up to your fantasies? Did you come? What does all this mean...are you together?"

"It was...I don't even know how to describe it, Lee," she said, stopping midfold. "Amazing doesn't begin to cover it. It was like, a Lauren Layne book come to life. We were like, actually in sync with each other and on the same page."

"So, did you come?"

"Twice. Turns out Kyle is really good with his hands." She blushed at her last comment, hoping it wasn't too much of an overshare.

"Damn girl, I'm borderline jealous. Of the multiple orgasms, not the Kyle part."

Drea laughed. "Thanks."

"You feeling okay about all of this? That was zero to sixty in like, no time flat," she commented, turning serious.

"I am actually. And that's not just the post-orgasm high speaking. Speaking of which, I had no idea that they were a whole hell of a lot better when not self-induced."

"Oh yes," Leona responded, waggling her eyebrows up and down. "You might want to take out your own trash though, so no one else sees what's in there. Not that I think Margarita or whoever takes care of your cottage this week would say anything, but around here, with your uncles, you probably don't want to take the risk."

"I didn't even think of that."

"Speaking of your uncles, you plan on telling them?"

"We haven't talked about that yet. Truth be told, we haven't even really discussed if we're together."

"Might want to figure that one out." She motioned for the towel Drea had stopped folding. She handed it over and leaned against the table behind her.

"Yeah."

"But I'm so happy for you, Drea. I know this is what you've wanted for a long time."

"It is," she said, looking at her watch. "Speaking of uncles and Kyle, I gotta go meet them all in the kitchen for breakfast."

"Kyle and your uncles together for a meal, the morning after he fucked you senseless? Oh, this I can't miss."

THE TWO WOMEN walked into the kitchen, still giggling about something. Kyle looked up from the coffee carafe he was filling when he heard Drea's giggle. The sound was music to his ears and sent a tingle down his spine.

Climbing out of bed while it was still dark this morning to creep back to his room was possibly one of the hardest things he'd ever done. Watching her fall asleep in his arms and feeling her lying there, snuggled up against him as they slept last night, had been absolute heaven. Everything about her had been perfection, from her tan skin, to her reaction to his touch, to the way that beautiful bare pussy gripped his cock while he was inside her.

He had to fight the urge to walk over to her, wrap his arms around her, and pull her in for a kiss. It seemed so natural to have this desire, but he was fully aware, out of the corner of his eye, of Miller standing at the oven. There was a part of him that thought about walking over to Miller and saying, "You know that girl we talked about yesterday? It's Drea, and she's perfect and I want nothing more than to sweep her off her feet," but he knew there was no way it would end the way he wanted it to while he was still an employee of the Indigo Royal Resort.

"Morning, girls!" Miller called out, not turning around from where he was working.

"Morning, Uncle Miller," Leona called out. "Kyle." She smirked in his direction, giving him an I-know-your-secret smile. He shook his head—of course she knew.

"Leona," Kyle responded, handing her a knowing smile right back. He carried the carafe over to the family table and picked up a mug, pouring coffee into it. He handed the mug to Drea, who took it, her smile lighting up her whole face. "Morning, Drea. Sleep well?"

"I did. Yourself?"

"Like never before."

He pulled out a chair from the table and motioned for her to sit. She slid into the seat, trying to hide her emotions from taking over her face as she did. Trying not to look obvious, he did the same for Leona, pulling out the chair to Drea's left and then sitting in the one to her right. Reaching over to her underneath the table, he gripped her thigh just above her knee and gave it a little squeeze. He could see the little shudder her body gave as he made contact, and he hoped it was because she was reliving last night in her head.

Vaughn, Simone, and Grayson all paraded in together and sat in various spots around the table. Vaughn was on his phone typing furiously while Grayson flipped through a stack of papers, furrowing his brow trying to make sense of something.

"Did you see my text about the dress?" Simone asked Drea as she poured herself some coffee.

"Yes! You decided just to wear that champagne one you have?"

"I did. It's my favorite and what better day to wear your favorite dress than on your wedding day, right?"

"Perfect. So, what do you want me in?"

"I'm thinking black if that works for you. I figured you could pull that off," she laughed.

"Absolutely!"

"Hey, would you two mind running a booze cruise today?" Grayson chimed in. "It'd be a small one."

"Sure," Kyle shrugged. "Something happen with Bobby or Kenny?"

"No, but somehow paperwork got screwed up, and I can't figure out how, but basically, we have three scheduled for today. Good news is, if you're willing to do this, I can make it so you have nothing tomorrow and Sunday, so you can take the *Runnin'* as early as you want tomorrow."

"That's fine," Drea answered, looking at Kyle. He smiled back at her, thrilled at the idea that they could have two whole days away, just the two of them. He just hated hiding said excitement in the moment.

"Where are you two going?" Vaughn asked skeptically, looking up to eye Drea and Kyle.

"I don't know, we haven't figured that out yet. But we

have Sunday off so we thought it might be fun to go sailing, and Uncle Gray said we could borrow the *Runnin'*."

"I was thinking maybe we'd head over to San Juan and hit up that empanada stand. We could bring you some back if you want," Kyle injected, hoping the mention of Simone's favorite street food would be a good distraction.

"I don't know how I feel about the two of you being gone for an entire weekend," Vaughn said.

"Why, you need her for something?" Miller asked, leaning over him to place pans of eggs and breakfast meats in the middle of the table.

"No. But just the two of them?"

"We're right here, Uncle Vaughn," Drea said.

"Oh no. Our twenty-six-year-old niece is going away for the weekend with her twenty-seven-year-old best friend!" Grayson snarked sarcastically.

"Well, when you put it that way."

"She's an adult, Vaughn. As much as it kills me, you know, having raised her and all, as your lovely bride-to-be pointed out the other day, she owes us no explanations," Miller stated, finally sitting down at the table.

Kyle could feel the heat of embarrassment rising up his neck. He wanted to chime in, but he didn't want to intrude on a family discussion. He knew that Vaughn had always been the serious one in the family, the worrier, and that his overprotectiveness of Drea stemmed from his own methodical way of handling life. He also knew it wasn't personal, that he'd be just as concerned if it were Leona and Drea going away for the weekend. Although if he knew all the things Kyle had imagined doing to his sweet little niece on that boat, he might never let him near her again.

"Can everyone stop talking about us like we're not here?" Drea exclaimed. Leona looked down, stifling a giggle.

"Look, if it's that big of a deal, we won't go. But we both haven't had many days off lately, so when Uncle Gray floated the idea of a weekend away, it sounded nice. But not if it's going to be a great debate at breakfast!"

Kyle inhaled slowly, and reached over to squeeze Drea's hand lightly, in what he hoped looked like a best friend move and not something more. He wanted to lean over and kiss her temple to help calm her, but instead just kept holding her hand.

"Vaughn, Miller, Grayson, I promise to not let anything happen to your baby girl," he said calmly. "Or the boat."

Everyone at the table laughed, even Vaughn.

"So, back to the real problem at hand," Grayson said sternly, glaring at his brother. "Booze cruise today? It's those blondes and their meathead counterparts."

"Ugh, no," Drea grumbled. "Give us someone else. Make Dalton take them."

"Dalton was specially requested by some very hot-to-trot old ladies," Dalton said, referring to himself in the third person as he walked into the kitchen. He grabbed a mug from the rack and poured himself a cup of coffee from the pot.

"Well done, dude," Kyle replied, holding out his fist for Dalton to bump. He saw Drea roll her eyes out of the corner of his and he laughed.

"Why, thank you! But that does mean you all get to spend the day with Staci with an i."

"Is she gonna be less hot-to-trot today?" Drea asked.

"Maybe," Dalton replied, making a clicking noise and winking.

"I take it back, Uncle Gray. I'll work the next six weekends, no days off, if it means I don't have to get on a boat with her for the third time this week," Drea said, pleading with her uncle.

"She's not that bad," Dalton shrugged.

"Based on your reaction she must not have been that good, either," Leona snarked under her breath.

Dalton just shrugged in response, refusing to confirm or deny Leona's assessment. Leona simply shook her head—Kyle just wasn't sure if it was in amazement or disbelief.

"It'll be fine," Kyle said, putting his arm around her, trying to make it look casual. "We got this, you and me versus the airheads and the meatheads."

"My money's on you kids," Miller interjected.

"Oh, are we taking bets, because I'm totally in if we are," Leona piped up.

"We only bet on Tuesdays," Vaughn said sternly.

"Spoilsport," Simone said, taking another swig of coffee as she stood up. "But I'm late, so I will see you all tonight for Friday night dinner."

"We're having your favorite roast beef tonight, Kyle, so why don't you join us?" Miller said.

Kyle looked at Drea, unsure of how to answer. Friday night dinner was a big deal with the Quinlans. While most of the other family meals were a come-and-go deal and really open to anyone who happened to be hanging around at the time, Friday night dinner was by invite only.

"He's making your favorite, you can't say no," she said, looking Kyle in the eye, a little twinkle in them saying more than she could out loud.

"Say no more! It's a date."

CHAPTER FIFTEEN

Drea stood behind the bar singing out loud to her playlist, mixing up the rum punch, and debating whether or not she should make it strong enough to drown a rhino. She poured in a good portion of the handle of rum before stopping herself; she didn't want to have to deal with a man overboard situation.

She didn't particularly like booze cruises. Even with the smaller crowd she always felt overwhelmingly outnumbered. There was rarely any activity other than hanging out on the boat and drinking, so she was generally locked behind the bar furiously mixing up some kind of drink, which at least gave her a barrier from hands that she was sure would have liked to wander if given the chance.

The type of guests who usually signed up for them tended to be demanding and snobbish when sober, often turning downright mean when drunk. None of them generally stopped to learn that she was part of the family that was in charge of the "family-owned-and-operated" resort they were so fond of. Dalton was much better at managing the booze cruisers than she was. That damn smile of his could melt the panties off a corpse.

"Why are you so tense?" Kyle said, coming up behind her. His hands went to her shoulders and he started to massage her tense muscles.

"I'm not. I just hate booze cruises."

"Well, all we have to do is get through a few hours today and then, the next two days is just us."

She sighed, leaning back into him as he continued to knead her muscles. His hands felt so good on her body, it didn't seem to matter where they were.

"Two whole days to do whatever we want on this boat," he said quietly, leaning down so his head was right next to hers.

Drea exhaled loudly, feeling a chill run through her at his sexy words. Good Lord, that man knew what to say to her. "And just what kind of things are you imagining here, sir?"

"Sweetness, if you only knew the things I have thought about doing to you on the trampoline, up in the captain's chair, and on this very bar."

"Hey kids!" Vaughn's voice called out before Drea even had time to fully react to all the things Kyle's words were making her feel. She looked up to see him and Grayson jumping on the boat, feeling Kyle pull away quickly. She felt the loss of his presence way down deep, and she hated it.

"What's up, guys?" Drea asked, returning to the drink mixers on the bar.

"Just out taking a walk, thought we'd say hi," Vaughn answered.

"We just had breakfast together a couple of hours ago, but hi!" she responded, a little confused.

"You can't lie worth shit, Vaughn, 'fess up. We wanted to make sure you were really okay taking the booze cruise out. I know how much you hate them. I can go with Kyle if you prefer," Grayson said, coming around to stand across the bar from her.

She froze. As much as she disliked this part of the job, she didn't want to be away from Kyle. She wanted to hear the rest of what he was saying before her uncles showed up.

"No, it's fine. It's just one of those weeks where you're really ready for the guests to change over. I know you both know how that goes."

Her uncles laughed. They knew exactly how she was feeling in that sense. The beauty of the resort was that no two weeks were alike. Certainly there was the bonfire on Tuesday and nightclub night on Fridays, and certain meals that only showed up on certain evenings, but week in and week out the feel of the resort changed with the waves of guests who came and went. Some weeks you never wanted the guests to leave and others, you'd pack their bags for them if it meant they were gone faster.

"I know you'll be glad when that meathead is gone," Grayson said.

"Oh shit, he's gonna be back on here again today," Kyle grumbled.

"Yup, both Brig and Staci with an i," Drea said, forcing an overly large fake smile and a thumbs-up.

"Don't toss him overboard," Grayson commented, pointing at Kyle with a sarcastic smirk.

"If he hits on Drea again, I make no promises, sir."

"Hits on Drea again? How many times has he hit on you? Does he need to be uninvited?" Vaughn cut in.

"No, Uncle Vaughn, it's fine. Besides, I'm pretty sure Uncle Gray put the fear of God in him the other day."

"Good man," Vaughn said, holding out a fist for Grayson. The brothers bumped knuckles and nodded at each other solemnly.

Her uncles stayed a few more minutes, chatting with Kyle about some logistical things concerning the boat and upcoming schedules. She loved watching him in his element, taking control and ownership of the vessel even though most of those concerns should fall to Grayson. He knew his stuff when it came to the boats and sailing, but it was the business side of things that always managed to surprise her. It shouldn't—he'd been a business major in college and had always talked about one day being his own boss—but seeing that side come through still made her feel all warm and fuzzy.

When her uncles finally made their exit, Drea was more than relieved to see them go. It wouldn't be long before everyone arrived for them to set sail and she wanted some time alone with Kyle.

"Hey," he said, coming up and leaning against the bar next to her. She grabbed the rag that was sitting near the sink and started to wipe down the counters, trying to keep her hands busy.

"Hey back."

"This family dinner invite, you think it's really because he's making roast beef?"

"Yes," she answered, confused.

"Well, he brought it up after the whole 'you're going away together?' thing and after yesterday morning, I just wanted to make sure."

"What does yesterday morning have to do with anything?"

"Well, after my little..."

"Tantrum?"

"I was going to say freak-out, but okay, after my little tantrum, I ended up in the kitchen. And he was there and kinda went all Yoda on me asking if it was about a girl. And I didn't get into specifics, but I told him yes, and so now I wonder if he's on to us."

"Would it be so bad if he was? I mean, I'm not trying to put the cart and horse in the wrong order here or anything and presume..." she started to ramble.

"Presume? I think we're past presuming, sweetness," he said, turning so his right hip rested against the bar, reaching out and pulling her close. He kissed her temple. "You're mine, and I'm yours. If you want to label that, great, if not, that's fine too. But after last night, we are most certainly a thing."

She breathed a sigh of relief, feeling herself relax, not realizing she had tensed up so much. Hearing him say the words made her want to jump up and down then kiss him until neither one could breathe.

"Okay, then, since we're 'a thing' as you put it, would it be so bad if Uncle Miller knew?"

"Yes!" he said emphatically, pulling away from her. "I enjoy being employed, Drea. And I need this job."

"You're not going to get fired over being in a relationship with me," she countered.

"Wanna bet? Your uncles would not handle that well. You know how overprotective they are."

Drea grumbled. He had a point. Her uncles hadn't quite come to terms with the fact that she wasn't a little girl anymore. She loved them more than anything, and loved that they had changed their entire lives after the accident that took the lives of her parents and aunt, but she sometimes wished they would back off now that she was older.

"I just think that Uncle Miller would be a safe choice, that's all."

"Maybe, but for now, will it be a deal breaker to just be our little secret?"

"Um, well, I might have already told Leona," she said, nervously biting her bottom lip.

"I gathered by the look she gave me this morning," he laughed. "I amend my statement to include the best friends then."

"Perfect," she said, grinning brightly at him.

"Yes, you are."

THE GROUP TOUR started out a little rocky, but seemed to have calmed down. According to Brig, all eight of them had met for breakfast and started pre-gaming with mimosas and then moved to tequila sunrises shortly after. Each and every one of them was wasted by the time they got on the boat, and Kyle was sure he and Drea would be power washing puke off the deck later this evening. Thankfully, hitting a couple of large swells just outside the no wake zone scared a couple of them, and their stomachs, into slowing down their intake.

Despite their poor choice in morning activities, they had been a fairly low-key group. They had all taken up residence in the front of the boat, either on the trampolines or the front hulls, and were laughing away, soaking up the tropical sun. Each one of the girls wore an itty-bitty bikini, held together with just a series of strings, while each one of the guys was in short, tight swim trunks that rivaled Speedos with how much they showed off.

A couple of hours into the cruise, once they were well

into their second pitcher of rum punch and were anchored out in open water, one of the guys tugged on the bikini strings of the drunkest blonde and her boobs fell free. Since the week had proven she had few inhibitions sober, they were certainly all gone based on how much booze was coursing through her veins, causing her to grab her top and fling it toward the edge of the boat. Luckily one of the other meatheads caught it midair so no one had to go on a search and rescue expedition.

The cacophony of giggles set off by this little stunt started a ringing in Kyle's ears. How could one group of women be so loud, especially on open water? He would never, ever complain about Drea and Leona laughing too loudly on movie night again. He climbed down from his perch just in time to see all the other blondes following along and removing their tops as well. *Oh boy*, he thought.

"Nudity's not a problem, right, Captain Kyle?" Staci called out.

"Not as long as you're covered up by the time we head back to the resort," he answered. "But if you ladies wanna show 'em off, please, be our guest."

Drea cut her eyes over and glared at him. He shrugged as if to say "what do you want me to say?" She shook her head, obviously not thrilled.

"I didn't realize we suddenly worked at the Playboy Mansion," she mumbled.

He walked up behind her and wrapped his arms around her waist, pulling her up against him. "Is my girl jealous?"

"Yes, I'm jealous," she sniped. "There are four beautiful blondes up there with perfect tits out on display. I can't compete with that!"

"First off, you don't have to compete with anyone, because not a single one of them has anything on you.

Second," he said, sliding his hands from her midsection until they rested on her breasts and leaning down to whisper in her ear, "these are the most stunning tits I have ever seen and I am counting down the hours until I can play with them again."

Drea blushed a little at his words. He liked knowing that he had this kind of effect on her. Even better since every word he said was the truth. She turned around in his grasp so that now those beautiful tits were pressed against his chest. Just the feeling of them against him was starting to make him hard.

"You just want in my pants," she whispered in response.

"I won't lie about that."

"Ahem," a deep voice came from the other side of the bar. Kyle looked up as Drea turned around to find Brig standing there. He pulled his hands away from her body at the same time she quickly pulled away from him, trying to pretend they weren't twelve seconds from a lip lock.

Oh shit, how much did he see? Kyle thought.

"So, we were just wondering if shots were a possibility?" Brig asked, trying not to be awkward about disrupting them.

"Um, yeah, sure," Drea answered. "We have some mini plastic cups, right here." She knelt down to grab something underneath the sink. She stood up with a sleeve of shot-sized red Solo cups in her hand.

"Thanks."

"Do you all want one? I'm not supposed to let you serve yourselves."

The awkwardness was still there, and seemed to be growing by the minute, as the three of them stood there. Brig had clearly gotten an eyeful of his embrace with Drea and didn't know what to say.

"You know what, dude, just take the bottle," Kyle said,

picking up the handle and passing it to Brig. "It's just us out here—we won't tell. Just don't let any of them do anything stupid."

"Sure thing," Brig said, nodding. He turned to walk away and then pivoted back again to face them. "You know, you two could have just said something the other day. I'd never try to cut in on another dude's woman. I don't play that game."

"Oh, no, Brig, it's not what—" Drea started, stopping when Kyle put his arm around her shoulder.

"It's just that we're not really public information yet, and with her uncle on the boat, it wasn't really..." he trailed off, hoping to make his meaning clear.

"I feel ya, dude. Just wanted to make sure there are no hard feelings." He turned away fully this time and walked back toward the rest of the group.

"They're fake, by the way," Kyle said quietly, so only Drea could hear.

"Huh?"

"Staci's 'perfect,' as you called them, boobs. They're fake."

"And you know this how?" Drea asked, skeptically.

"Dalton."

THE REST of the day proceeded without incident and, very thankfully, without puke. Brig seemed to be more than happy to cut off his buddies and the ladies who he felt had partaken enough.

When everyone was finally off the boat, and they had bagged up all the trash and given the deck a basic rinse, Kyle went to join Drea who was sitting on one of the trampolines up front. The wind was calm and the sun not far off from setting, surrounding them with the perfect setting for a moment of quiet before Friday night dinner.

"I'm exhausted," Drea commented.

"That makes two of us, sweetness."

"You ready for your first Friday night dinner?"

"Anything I need to know going in?"

"Not really. It's basically like Wednesday breakfast, except we don't have bets to compare," she shrugged. "Oh! I can promise you they will tell you all about why we have Friday night dinner, so prepare for an embarrassing story about me."

Kyle popped up quickly, and reached his hand out to Drea to help her up. She grabbed it and stood, looking at him skeptically.

"Is the idea of me being embarrassed that exciting?"

"Yes," he answered without hesitation. "Although I'm certain it's actually a super cute story. But if your uncles are going to be in storytelling mode, then this might actually be a good time."

That, and he really, really wanted to see Drea embarrassed.

CHAPTER SIXTEEN

KYLE KNOCKED on Drea's door promptly at seven fifteen, dressed in khaki shorts and a short-sleeved button-down shirt. This was the most dressed up he'd been since the last time he visited his mom a couple of Christmases ago. He wished this was for a real date, just the two of them, without her entire family involved, but he wasn't going to complain about being included in family stuff either. Being invited to this dinner meant that they trusted him on some level, and he hoped he could leverage that into support of him and Drea once he was out on his own.

She opened the door, dressed in a baby-blue, spaghetti-strapped sundress that he was pretty sure forced her to go braless. *Stop thinking about her boobs—you're about to have dinner with her uncles. You can't sport a semi at this meal.*

"Why'd you knock? Why didn't you just come in?" she asked, looking confused but moving out of the way to let him in. He smiled at her and pulled a single lily from behind his back. "What's this for?"

"Hasn't a guy ever brought you flowers on a date?"

"Uncle Miller let me have some extra roses on Valentine's Day when I was like twelve, does that count?"

"No, not even close. I'm happy to be the first, though."

"You've racked up quite a few firsts of mine already," she said coyly, standing up on her toes to kiss him softly.

Kyle groaned as she stepped away to put the flower in some water. He snuck a peek at her ass as she walked away. The top of her dress was fitted, but not overly tight, and the skirt was loose and flowy but only came to just above her knees. It moved easily with her hips as she walked and he couldn't help but wonder what she had on underneath.

"Stop staring at my ass," she said, without looking up from her task.

"Just wondering if there is anything on underneath there."

She walked back over to him, grinning mischievously, and slipped her arms around his neck. He encased her in his arms, placing his hand on her lower back, and pulled her into him. He ran his hand up and down her back, feeling for a bra, and was pleased when he didn't feel one. He started to journey lower, when she wiggled out of his grasp and took a couple of steps back.

"Behave yourself during this dinner, and maybe you'll find out," she winked.

THEY WALKED into the kitchen to find everyone but Vaughn already sitting at the table. Kyle looked at his watch to make sure they weren't late. It was seven thirty on the nose—they were right on time. The kitchen smelled fantastic, like rosemary and garlic, with fresh bread wafting in every couple of breaths. He pulled out a chair for Drea, and then pushed it in slightly as she sat down. He took the seat to her left, as if it was automatically his seat. He could get used to this.

She reached over under the table and snuck her hand into his, just letting them sit there for a moment, holding hands. Her hand fit into his so perfectly, it was like it was made to fit there. The thrill of holding her hand wasn't new —he'd always enjoyed taking her hand in his—but there was some extra excitement in it to be secretly doing it in front of her family, knowing that it wasn't them just being friendly.

"Sorry I'm late," Vaughn said, bursting through the door, carrying four bottles of wine, two in each hand.

"It's seven thirty-two," Simone said, dryly pointing out he wasn't exactly late.

"Yes, but we meet promptly at seven thirty."

"You're the only one in this family who is 'prompt' about anything, man," Grayson said.

"As long as he has the wine, I don't care," Miller added from across the kitchen. "I'm just finishing up—give me five more minutes."

"Yes, would you sit your ass down and open the wine, please? I spent the afternoon with the governor's wife, and well, I just need a drink," Simone said, grabbing for one of the bottles.

Vaughn set the bottles down on the table and pulled a corkscrew from his pocket. He opened the first bottle and poured a larger than average glass for Simone, before pouring himself something normal. Kyle motioned to Drea to see if she wanted some, and she nodded her head slightly. He grabbed two glasses and poured them each a smaller glass, and handed hers to her. She smiled brightly at him, taking a sip.

"So, how'd the cruise go this afternoon? Everyone behave themselves?" Grayson asked. Drea's hand stopped mid sip, and Kyle tensed at the question. Could Brig have said something about what he saw? No, he said he understood that they weren't public yet, so he wouldn't have run off and complained. Although if someone else in the group saw something, there was no telling what the reaction would have been.

"Can I get a definition of 'behaved' please?" Drea said, quickly recovering from her pause. "Because for a moment today I wondered if we had become a charter for the Playboy Mansion."

"What's that supposed to mean?" Miller asked, bringing the first round of food to the table.

"All the girls on the trip ended up taking off their tops and spent the afternoon combating tan lines," Kyle said, trying to hide a grin.

"Maybe I should have sent Dalton," Grayson commented.

"Pretty sure he's already seen what was on display, but he would have still appreciated it more than Drea."

"Were they nice?" Grayson asked.

"Grayson, seriously?" Vaughn asked.

"Kid got an eyeful all day, it's only right to ask the question!"

"You don't have to answer, son," Miller said.

"They were the best money could buy—I'll leave it at that," Kyle commented. The men all chuckled and nodded their heads in understanding. He looked over at Drea who was rolling her eyes. He would bet that if he glanced over at Simone he would see a similar reaction.

"But other than the peep show, everything went fine?" Grayson returned to his original inquiry.

"Yeah, they managed to not actually have sex on the trampolines," Drea said sarcastically. "And despite showing up pretty hammered already, no one puked. So I'll call it a successful day."

"Alrighty, that should be the last of the food," Miller said, bringing over a large platter of sliced beef. "So no more talk about puke. Let Friday night dinner commence."

They all started to pass the food around and served themselves as they went. It was a simple meal of roast beef, with green beans, salad, and Kyle's favorite side dish, au gratin potatoes, and the ever present, freshly house-baked bread. Kyle might have to steal some of that away for later too. It was like Miller had cooked this meal just for him.

"So Kyle," Vaughn started, "do you know why we have Friday night dinner?"

"Vaughn, you promised not to tell this story," Simone said. "Don't embarrass Drea in front of her guest."

"It's just Kyle, and I'm only going to tell the story if he hasn't heard it. He's her best friend, right? He probably already knows it."

Kyle looked to Drea who was keeping her head down looking at her plate. This felt like a trap somehow, but he wasn't sure whether he was supposed to know the story or not. If he did, would that reveal that they were closer than her uncles realized? He decided to err on the side of caution and went with the truth.

"All I know is that it was started when Drea was in junior high, ish? Right?"

"Right, she was twelve," Vaughn started.

"Thirteen. She was thirteen," Miller interjected.

"You sure?" Vaughn asked.

"I raised her, didn't I? Pretty sure I remember the milestones."

"Okay, so she was thirteen. She was totally obsessed with that show, *Gilmore Girls*. You know it?"

"I have been forced to sit through an episode, or twenty," Kyle said, nudging an uncomfortable-looking Drea.

"She wanted to be just like them, and on the show they had Friday night dinners, so she insisted that we do it too."

"There are worse people in the world to want to be when you're thirteen than Rory Gilmore," Drea added. "And in my defense, we didn't have a regularly scheduled family meal then. We could have stopped Friday dinners when we started Wednesday breakfasts."

Kyle could feel the tension in Drea as she defended her teenage thinking. He didn't really think the story was that embarrassing, but he also knew that her uncles had a tendency to treat her like she was still that thirteen-year-old girl, and he understood her frustration with that. He wanted to lean over and kiss her, tell her he saw her for who she was now, a beautiful adult woman with a mind of her own. But he knew that this would be the worst place to do that, so instead he tried to change the subject.

"Miller, the meal is fantastic, as always. Thank you. But I hope you didn't make this just for me."

"This was actually Dave's mom's recipe. I made it the night we celebrated our engagements to the girls, so I felt it was fitting for tonight," he said, raising a glass in the direction of Simone and Vaughn. Simone smiled sappily and raised her glass in return, while Vaughn simply nodded.

"I know you guys were working all day, but have you talked about what you wanna do with your days off?" Simone asked.

"No, but truthfully, I'd be happy if we just anchor out somewhere and then take a long nap in the sun," Drea replied.

"You could do that here," Vaughn said. "If that's your whole plan, then there is no reason to go anywhere."

"That's not the plan—I just said we didn't have a plan. And yes, the whole purpose is to not be on the resort."

"There is nothing wrong with staying on the resort. It's safer here," he said.

"Are you saying my boats are unsafe?" Grayson asked from around a bite of bread.

"No, but you never know what could happen."

"Drea and Kyle are both excellent sailors, which, you know, is why we trust them with our guests every day!" Grayson spat out.

"We're right here," Drea said.

Kyle wanted to jump into the conversation and defend their getaway, but was afraid to say the wrong thing. The tension he was feeling off Drea was only escalating as her uncles went back and forth, so he reached back under the table and lightly ran his hand up and down her thigh. She turned and smiled at him tensely.

"We get it, Vaughn, you don't like the idea of her going away, but let the kids do what they want," Miller said.

"They can relax here just as easily as they can on the boat. And we were all just in San Juan a couple of months ago. Why go back so soon?"

"Get the sand out of your vagina, man!" Grayson barked. "Just let them go. No one questions what you do with your days off."

"Sorry I brought it up," Simone said quietly, looking at Drea. Drea simply shrugged in response.

"No one questions because I'm an adult and—"

"So is she!" Simone interjected. "She's twenty-six, he's twenty-seven. Well over the adult age line!"

"The next words out of your mouth best not be that you're the boss," Miller stated. "Because we are all equal in this."

"And I'm Kyle's boss," Grayson said. "And I'm the one giving him the keys."

"Still here," Drea said, louder this time.

"Well, if you two really think it's best to just let her run off with some boy—"

Drea stood, stopping Vaughn midsentence. Everyone turned to look at her.

"Okay, as much fun as this has been—enough. We're taking a weekend off. We're going sailing, not to the moon. And he is not just 'some boy,' he's Kyle! Who has worked here for five years! You know him, he shows up to breakfast most mornings. Yesterday he was 'part of the family.' So now if you'll excuse me, I'm done with dinner. I don't need dessert." She turned around and huffed out of the kitchen.

They all sat there for a brief moment in silence. When Vaughn went to open his mouth to say something, Simone put her hand on his arm and Kyle was pretty sure he heard her whisper "just stop." He pushed back from the table and stood up, placing his napkin on top of his dinner plate.

"If you'll excuse me as well, I think I'll go after her," he said solemnly.

"Good idea, son," Miller said.

He turned to go and made it halfway to the kitchen doors before he heard Miller shout, "Wait!" He turned back around to see the older gentleman rushing toward him with a small bread basket he covered with a cloth napkin.

"I know she said she doesn't want dessert, but a man knows his little girl. Even if she thinks she doesn't want it now, she will later," he said, handing Kyle the basket. "Save you some trouble from having to sneak back in here." He whispered this last part so only Kyle could hear, adding a wink at the end.

Kyle simply nodded his thanks and turned to go.

Drea swung in the hammock that was a few steps from her back porch on Big House Beach. It had always been her favorite place to come and read while listening to the waves. There had always been something kind of romantic about it in her mind, even though she was the only one who ever used it.

She heard Kyle round the house as he approached the side of her porch and slipped off his shoes. She looked over to watch him and saw him place a bread basket next to his shoes before he strode the couple of steps toward her. Without saying a word, he grabbed the side of the hammock, making her slow swing come to a halt as he climbed in. The movement of his body joining her was enough to set the netting back in motion as he snuggled her into him. Pulling her close so she was lying with half of her front side on his, he wrapped his arms fully around her and kissed the top of her head. They lay there for a moment just like that, swinging back and forth, before he finally broke the silence.

"You okay, sweetness?" he asked. She nodded, without looking up at him. "You can tell me if you're not. I got you either way."

"No, I am. I'm just really tired and Uncle Vaughn being in that mood just pushed some buttons."

"Tired, huh? Someone keep you up all night?" He tickled her lightly, making her squirm.

"Yeah, just *some boy*," she said, emphasizing the phrase her uncle used earlier. She couldn't believe that her uncle had had such a strong reaction to the two of them going sailing. She told herself that it was the wedding making him act this way—after all, he'd always seemed to like Kyle. All of her uncles liked him. He'd engrained himself not only in her heart, but in her family as well. "Maybe if we told them that you're my...whatever, he'd stop flipping out."

"Your whatever? By 'whatever,' do you mean boyfriend?" he asked.

"Um, yes?"

"You questioning that because you don't know where we stand or because you don't like the term boyfriend?"

"I guess that depends on you. Do you like the term boyfriend?"

"I told you this morning, sweetness," he answered, kissing the top of her head again. "You're mine, and I'm yours. If you want labels, great. If not, then we'll just have to figure out how we're referring to ourselves."

"Okay then, boyfriend," she said, smiling. She flipped herself over so she was fully on top of him now, her breasts pushing against his hard chest. "I don't want to talk about my crazy family anymore."

"Then what do you want, beautiful?"

She blushed slightly at him calling her that. She loved all the little things he'd started calling her since they kissed for the first time the other night. They made her feel so special, all warm and fuzzy inside.

"I want to just lie here with you, kissing and snuggling and listening to the ocean until I forget I have a crazy family."

She wiggled her hips slightly against his, eliciting a dark, intense look in his eyes. His hands slid down her back, over her ass and thighs, finding the hem of her sundress. As he moved them back up her thighs, this time underneath her skirt, he leaned in, touching his lips to hers. When his hands found her bare ass cheeks, courtesy of the tiny thong she was wearing, he groaned into the kiss, slipping his tongue past her lips. He kissed her long and hard. With his mouth and hands on her like this she felt like she was flying and would do whatever it took to make sure it didn't stop. Still kneading her ass, he pulled back slightly and looked deep into her eyes.

"As you wish, sweetness."

CHAPTER SEVENTEEN

DREA WOKE up to the sounds of someone rummaging through her kitchen. *Not just someone. Kyle,* she thought. They'd spent the rest of the evening wrapped up in each other in the hammock, cuddling and kissing, with little bouts of talking in between kisses. If she had ever imagined the perfect evening, that would have been right up there. Just the two of them, curled up together on the beach, doing nothing. Part of her had wondered briefly if one of her uncles or Simone would try to come find her after they all finished eating, and how exactly she would explain being caught mid-kiss, but he had done exactly what she had asked of him, and kissed her until she lost track of all thoughts.

She must have nodded off at some point while they were out there, since she didn't remember making it to bed last night. Her heart swelled with the idea that Kyle had carried her to bed and tucked her in. She wondered if he had slept here last night and made another early morning exit, only to come back and rummage through her kitchen.

She swung her legs out of bed, realizing that she only assumed it was Kyle in her kitchen and should probably make sure. For all she knew, Vaughn had let himself in and had decided to rearrange her whole cottage.

Padding slowly into the kitchen, she smiled when she found Kyle standing at the counter pouring coffee into two mugs. She looked over to find a duffle bag sitting by her front door, packed and ready to go.

"I'm very glad it's you I'm finding in my kitchen this morning," she said, walking up to him.

"Just who did you think would be in your kitchen at this hour?" he asked, turning to embrace her. He leaned down and kissed her good morning. She moaned softly in response.

"For all I knew it was one of my uncles."

"I really hope you're not greeting your uncles in just your thong like that," he said, laughing.

She pulled away from him slightly and looked down. She was indeed in just the tiny scrap of lace she'd worn under her sundress last night. She giggled and looked back up at him with a wicked little smile on her face.

"I don't know that any of them have put me to bed in just my underwear, at least not as an adult."

"Touché," he said, leaning in to kiss her again. "Well, I grabbed some coffee on my way back from grabbing a few things for this weekend. And for breakfast, we have these."

He produced a plate with two large, gooey-looking brownies on them. Her eyes went wide, as she realized in that moment how hungry she was.

"How did you manage to find those in the kitchen at this time of day?"

"I didn't. Miller sent me home with them last night. He said he knew you'd be sad you missed them."

She grabbed one off the plate and took a bite, letting the flavors melt on her tongue. She closed her eyes and let out an over-exaggerated moan, licking her lips to make sure she got all the chocolate. Looking up at Kyle as she licked her lips, she watched him just shake his head laughing. He reached for a little brown bag that was sitting on the counter next to the bread basket the brownies must have been sent home in.

"This, was also on the door handle," he said, holding up the bag by the little paper handles. She put the plate down and went to grab it, but he grinned and pulled it away too quickly. "Now, who exactly would be leaving little gifts on your door, huh?"

She stood on her tiptoes, jumping a little, and grabbed it out of his hands. He laughed as she took the bag and playfully glared at him. Peeking into the bag, Drea scowled a little, just before throwing her head back and laughing hysterically. She pulled out a little note and read it out loud.

"May the remake be a little more hands-on, winky face, D." She laughed again, handing the note to Kyle. He looked down at it, perplexed, until she reached into the bag and pulled out a ruby-red string bikini and held it up for him to see.

"What the hell?" he spit out, laughing. "I have so many questions, but I'll start with, how does Dalton know what size you wear?" he eyed her suspiciously.

"That is apparently one of the great mysteries of life," she replied, giggling hysterically. She put the top back in the bag and grabbed her brownie, taking another bite. "I guess I should go throw some things in a bag so we can hit the water." She turned away from him and started to head toward her bedroom.

"I'd like to request you pack only that," he said, pointing to the bag.

She turned around, winking at him and blowing him a kiss before she headed back to her room.

IF SOMEONE HAD ASKED Drea to describe her perfect day, one of the first things that would always come to mind was being out on the water with Kyle. She'd always loved being out on the boat, even as a little girl. The first time they had gone out as a family, Drea had been so excited to feel the wind on her face and smell the ocean that she ran around the catamaran from side to side so she could take everything in. All three of her uncles had about had a heart attack when she leaned over the side to try and touch the water as they skimmed along the top.

When she was a little older and Grayson agreed to teach her how to sail, she took every opportunity to be out there with him, learning everything she could. She'd spent hours and hours shadowing her uncle, going out on guest tours with him and even sneaking in a few solo trips here and there when she could convince her uncles it would be fine. When she was eighteen and Grayson had asked her if she wanted to work with him on the boats full time, it was an easy answer. Only briefly did she feel bad that she didn't want to follow in Miller's culinary footsteps. But he understood that she didn't share the same passion for food that he did, and he didn't want anyone running his kitchen who wasn't going to treat it like it was anything other than a sacred place.

She stood by the portside railing watching the coastline of the island as they cruised along, soaking in the sun. It not only felt fantastic to be up on this deck hanging onto the railing, rather than down at the bar, but the quiet that came from it just being the two of them was relaxing in itself. She turned to look up at Kyle who was concentrating fully on driving the boat to whatever destination he had in mind. She hadn't questioned him this morning after they got everything ready and headed out of the marina—she truly didn't care where they ended up. She was so excited to have time to themselves without the watchful eyes of her family or even the curious gazes of their friends on them.

Weekends were a weird time at the resort. Most guests either arrived or departed on Saturday or Sunday, so there was lots of coming and going. It could be a bit of organized chaos trying to get guests out of rooms in time for them to be flipped for whoever was to occupy them next. But there was always a small contingent who was there just for the week-end, so they still ran a limited number of excursions, only adding to the logistical nightmare. Leona never failed to have some kind of story during the changeover about rooms getting mixed up or items left behind (it was a top *ten* list for a reason) and Drea looked forward to hearing all about it Monday. But right now all that mattered was being alone with Kyle.

She looked up at him again and her insides got all squishy. She thought about all the times she'd watched him up there piloting the boat, and all the times she'd wished that it could be just the two of them. On the occasions they did get to go out by themselves, whether it just be over to Turtle Cove or on a longer trip, how she'd dreamt of him kissing her, holding her in his arms as they felt the waves move under them. She had even let her mind wander further down the rabbit hole, picturing the two of them splayed out on the trampolines exploring each other's bodies. It had always been a fantasy, something that was so far out of reach it was all she could do to hold on to the idea. At least until today. Today she was hoping to make some of those fantasies come true.

She walked up to the very front of the catamaran and pulled off her sundress. She was wearing the bikini that Dalton had left for her this morning, and she felt incredibly sexy. Normally something this flimsy would have made her feel so self-conscious that she wouldn't have dreamed of wearing it alone in her cottage, much less out on the boat, but watching Kyle's eyes darken this morning when she'd held it up for him gave her the courage to put it on and try to flaunt it for him. She couldn't deny that the top made her breasts look fantastic, even if the tiny triangles didn't fully cover them. One tug of the strings that tied up at the base of her neck or behind her back would have sent the top wayward, easily revealing herself. Just as the two strings on either hip would easily reveal south of the border should they meet the same fate.

Yet somehow, the idea of this happening lit a fire in her. She wanted to show off for Kyle. Wanted to feel his gaze on her and know that she lit him up the same way he did her. They had the friendship part of this whole relationship thing down—they'd been close since he agreed to come work for her uncles. But it was the "more" part of it she wanted to make sure she got right. To finally experience all those feelings she had read about, and to act on so many of her fantasies.

Folding up a towel to use as a pillow, she lay down on the trampoline and got herself comfortable. The warm sun felt so good on her exposed skin, she thought that maybe she should consider wearing a bikini to work more often—just maybe one with a little support to it. She grabbed her book, opened it up to where she had dog-eared the page, and held it up to start reading. There wasn't anything particularly sexy about this pose, but she figured as long as he was driving, he wasn't going to be paying much attention to her anyway.

KYLE LOOKED down from the captain's chair to find Drea sprawled out on the trampoline reading a book. She looked stunning just lying there, relaxed, focused on whatever was happening on those pages. She had no idea just how damn sexy she was when she was just being herself. That little itty-bitty bikini wasn't hurting the situation either.

Kyle wasn't sure if he wanted to smack Dalton upside the head or buy him a beer for leaving such a thing on her door. After Thursday morning in the alleyway, Dalton had helped Kyle figure out how to apologize to Drea so that she would hear him out and not tell him to go fuck off after what a jackass he'd been. He'd known exactly what Drea needed to hear and made sure that Kyle was prepped with a couple of different layers of apologies in case she wasn't having it. Thankfully for Kyle, Drea listened the first time and he didn't need everything his first mate had equipped him with.

He shouldn't have been surprised that Dalton had more tricks up his sleeves other than groveling, or that he had Kyle's back in all this. Kyle should have known better than to think that story of the blondes going au naturel on the booze cruise, and how said event left Drea feeling a little self-conscious, wouldn't inspire him to try and play fairy godfather behind the scenes. What he didn't quite understand was how he had obtained a string bikini so quickly, or known exactly what would fit Drea. Either way, he was incredibly grateful in this moment.

He killed the engine and let the boat slow down on its own until they were simply moving along with the water and not in any specific direction. He slowly made his way down to the deck Drea was lying on, trying to be as quiet as possible to not disturb her. She looked so relaxed, and it made him smile. After last night's family dinner had gone a little sideways, he just wanted to make sure she was happy and not focused on all the stress that came with working for the family business. An overwhelming urge to protect her and keep her safe was growing inside him, leaving him wondering if this was how her uncles felt. The only difference was that *they* were the ones he wanted to stand up to in her defense, not just the outside world.

Watching her like this was almost enough to make him forget that he had a personal mission—that he was saving so that one day he could be his own boss, own his own boat, and maybe find a way to provide for her the way the three men he admired so much had all these years. He also had his mom and her medical concerns to think about. How he'd find a way to support both women, at least initially, was beyond him, but he couldn't worry about that right now. The much more pressing concern was the next two days with the beauty before him in a red string bikini.

"Hello, beautiful," he said in a low, husky voice, strolling over to the end of the trampoline. She put her book down and raised her arm to shield her eyes from the sun as she looked over to him.

"You're not so bad-looking yourself, you know," she responded, smiling.

"Is that so?"

She nodded quickly, watching as he approached and

sat down next to her. He leaned down and kissed her, lightly at first, then deepening the kiss after a moment. She wrapped her arms around him and he shifted so he was all but on top of her. Kyle could feel his dick hardening every time she swiped her tongue across his, and it was all he could do not to strip her down right there. He eventually pulled back, eliciting an unhappy grumble from Drea.

"You keep that up and we won't make it off this boat," he said playfully.

"Would that be so bad?"

He let out a low groan before replying, "It would kinda ruin what I have planned."

She sat up and turned so she was facing him head-on. "Where are we headed?"

"Well, first stop, Old San Juan to hit up our favorite street vendor, and then I figured we could pop over to Fortaleza Street to see the umbrellas."

"I love the umbrellas!" she squealed, throwing her arms around his neck and pulling him close.

"I know you do, sweetness," he laughed, rubbing his hand up and down her back, toying with the bikini's strings. "I figured you'd kill me if we stopped in San Juan and didn't go see them."

"I wouldn't kill you, but I probably would have pouted." She looked at him and pulled her lips downward into a frown to show off how she thinks she would have looked.

"No pouting allowed on this trip. After the umbrellas, we can just stroll around and do whatever, and then, I have a surprise for you."

"Oh, what is it?"

"Then it wouldn't be a surprise."

"Fine, be that way," she said, putting on the frown

again. Kyle laughed at her playful reaction and leaned in to kiss her.

"Sorry, sweetness, I'm keeping this to myself until it's time." He closed his mouth and pretended to lock it with a key. "But I promise, it'll rock your world."

CHAPTER EIGHTEEN

ONCE THEY HAD DOCKED and secured the boat, and Drea had slipped on something a little more substantial than the little red number she'd been sporting all morning, they headed into Old San Juan. They wasted no time, heading straight for the little street vendor who made the empanadas they loved so much.

The vendor was the same gentleman that Drea remembered from her childhood, and he smiled at her in a way that made her think he recognized her on some level as well. They'd stopped here every time they were in this city, and allegedly, all three of her uncles, as well as her father, had been sent on errands over here just to fetch some for Drea's mother when she was pregnant. Time and time again Miller had tried to reproduce the little meat pies, but they just weren't the same.

They found a little bench overlooking part of Plaza Colón, with a direct view of the massive Christopher Columbus statue that stood prominently in the middle. Drea took a big bite out of the empanada she was holding, sighing in contentment as she chewed.

"I'm not sure I fully understand why there is a statue to a man who isn't from Puerto Rico in this plaza," Kyle said in between bites.

"Because he got off the boat here," Drea answered.

"So, because he made a pit stop here before continuing on to, arguably, commit genocide and be responsible for the death of millions, they built him a statue?"

"Yes," Drea answered with a nod of her head. Kyle glared at her skeptically. "Okay, truth be told, I have no idea. Admittedly, I should know my Puerto Rican history better since I am half Puerto Rican, but history was never my best subject."

Kyle laughed. "Do you remember anything about the history of the island?"

"I know why there are so many cats."

"Okay, so why are there so many cats?"

"Because there once was an old cat lady who, as she got older, was worried that her cats would be lonesome when she passed away. So she married them off and encouraged them to have lots and lots of baby cats so they would never, ever be lonely," she responded, as if the answer was completely obvious.

Kyle burst out in a roaring laugh, almost knocking the food out of his lap and his drink off the bench. Every time he thought he'd caught his breath, he'd look over at Drea, who was looking at him very seriously, and he'd lose it again.

"There is no way that is the real story!" he said, trying to catch his breath.

"No, it's not, but it's the story Uncle Miller used to tell me when I was a little girl and asked about the cats, and I always really liked it so I've always just stuck with it."

"Oh, sweetness, you're too cute."

They returned to eating, this time in silence, even

though every now and again Kyle let out another little laugh. Drea assumed it was because he was still thinking about the old lady and the cats. When they were all finished eating, Drea cleared their trash.

"Can I show you something?" she asked Kyle.

"Anything."

She grabbed his hand and took him up the hill headed inland from the plaza. After walking a couple of blocks, she stopped them in an open space in between an old church and a Burger King.

"I am aware of the sordid history of that BK, Drea. I hope you don't think that I'm that much of a horndog that you had to show me a fast food joint that used to be a brothel back in the day."

Drea looked at him incredulously. "No, the Church. Iglesia San Francisco. Can we go in?"

"Sure, if that's what you wanna do," he said, confused.

They walked into the church and took a moment to look around, making sure they weren't disturbing Mass or confession. When they saw that no one was in the sanctuary, they went inside and sat down in the very last pew.

"This is where my parents got married," she said quietly. "Uncle Miller and Aunt Marta too."

"I thought they got married on the beach?"

"No, they met on the beach. They got married in the church. Although, only because my grandparents insisted. After all, if they were going to marry gringos, they were at least going to do it in front of God." She giggled, thinking about the story Uncle Miller had always told her.

After the rushed courtship and less-than-traditional proposal, her grandparents on her mother's side weren't entirely thrilled with the way their daughters were willing to just up and marry the first strangers to come along. But

Miller and her father had won them over quickly enough, and agreed to the church wedding if that's what the girls' parents really wanted. So the priest was called, and three weeks later the two couples were married. Three months after that, Drea's mother woke up sick to her stomach and a doctor's visit soon confirmed that she would be doing something major not in tandem with her sister since they first met their husbands.

"Were they buried here too?" Kyle asked cautiously.

"No, there wasn't enough left to bury."

"Can I ask what happened? All I know is there was a kitchen fire."

"A kitchen fire is putting it nicely," Drea smiled sadly. "The resort had always been a dream of my uncles and my dad. I don't fully understand how they came to own the property—something about an old man their grandfather used to know or something. Well, when their dad passed from cancer, they bought the resort from this guy and they, along with my dad, started to fix it up. So, everything is going along like it should and Miller is getting his ultimate kitchen, complete with some top of the line industrial stove. Install day comes and they are all so excited, because the oven that had been in there was sketchy at best. Well, short story long, the gas didn't get shut off properly when switching out the equipment, so gas had been leaking into the kitchen the whole time."

She paused, taking a long, slow breath. It had been a long time since she'd even thought about this story. She just wanted to get through it without crying. She told herself that she could cry afterward, once he knew the whole story. He reached over and grabbed her hand, squeezing it lightly in support. She took a deep breath to start again.

"Once it was totally installed, they went to turn on the

gas range to make sure it all worked. Well, the kitchen had been filling with gas the whole time, so when they turned it on, the whole place just went whoosh," she said, making an exploding motion with her free hand. "Everything went up in flames."

"Where were you?" Kyle asked, squeezing her hand again.

"With Uncle Vaughn. It was during my naptime. I was only six months old, so I was old enough to be rolling around and sitting up but not quite old enough to crawl, and my Mom had worried that even napping I'd find a way to get myself into trouble. Sometimes I think that's why he's always so serious about me being safe, because in a way, he's literally the reason I'm alive." She sniffed, still trying to fight back the tears. "Uncle Miller had stepped out to grab some champagne he had squirrelled away in another refrigerator. He stepped back into the kitchen right as it exploded. He was far enough away that he only suffered some burns, whereas everyone else was so close that they were just gone. But that's why he doesn't ever wear short sleeves, even in the summer. His arms are all scars."

With that last sentence, she lost all her resolve. She let out a quiet sob and the tears broke through. Kyle reached an arm around her, pulling her into him. She nuzzled her head into the crook of his neck, continuing to cry and sob. She couldn't help herself. She wasn't sure if it was the church, or being with Kyle, or just that she hadn't taken the chance to miss them recently, but her emotions took over. Most days she was fine with the hand that she'd been dealt. It's not as if she'd been unloved or had no family at all. It was a weird dynamic with her uncles, but they were still a family and made it work.

"I'm so, so sorry Drea. I don't remember all that much of

my dad, but I do still have a few memories. I can't imagine what it must be like to have never known them."

"Some days it's fine. Others I feel cheated." She sat back up and wiped furiously at her tears. She hated that she was bawling like this in front of Kyle. This hadn't been her intent, to take this serious and dark turn; she had simply wanted to show him some place that made her feel close to her parents. "I'm a mess. I'm sorry, this wasn't why I brought you here."

"You're a beautiful mess," he said, bringing a hand to her face to wipe away her tears. "And I'll gladly listen to you tell me whatever stories you want, happy or sad. And if they're sad, I'll sit here and hold you while you cry. I want all of you, Drea, that includes the tears."

She laughed lightly at his perfect-boyfriend answer. She thought about giving him a hard time about it, asking if he'd read that line in one of her books or something, but then she thought better of it. She knew that it was just Kyle and that he'd always been there to support her through everything, even when they were just friends. She considered pinching herself to make sure it was all real, but his hand that had moved to squeezing her knee let her know it was.

"Can we go do something happy now?"

"Umbrellas?" he asked, optimistically.

"Yes, please."

THEIR VISIT to the church had taken up more time than Kyle had expected, but they still had enough time to hit up Fortaleza Street before they needed to head to his surprise location. He hadn't meant to open a can of worms by asking Drea about her parents, and part of him felt guilty for it. But he had meant what he told her while they were sitting there —he wanted all of her, and that included getting to know all the parts she didn't like to show. Wiping away her tears was a small price to pay for being able to hold her in his arms and having her open up to him.

The walk to Fortaleza Street was mostly uphill from the church and Drea grumbled a number of times along the way. Kyle had offered to give her a piggyback ride, and each time had been met with the response of "but I'm in a sundress," not that he had any clue what difference that made. All he knew was that once they did make it up there, her reaction would have been worth every step.

As they rounded the corner and the brightly colored umbrellas came into view, it was all Kyle could do to not let Drea's giggle go straight to his groin. She grabbed his hand and pulled him the rest of the way to the street corner, moving faster than he'd seen her move in awhile. She hopped up and down, giggling as she did so, looking up wide-eyed at the rows and rows of an everyday item that had been repurposed to create something spectacular. While it didn't bring quite the same level of joy to him as it did Drea, Kyle did have to admit it was cool looking. Watching Drea get as excited as a small child on Christmas over something so simple was easily going to be a highlight in his mind for a very long time. Her giggle rang out, echoing off the buildings in the alleyway, making it that much more potent.

She pulled him close and made him take a selfie (or twenty) with her. At first it seemed stupid—they could just hand the phone to one of the dozen other people milling about taking pictures—but as she continued he got caught up in her antics and started to make silly faces right along with her. He loved seeing this side of her return. Her smile and giggle were some of his favorite parts of her. But to know she was able to recover so quickly, having just been sobbing not all that long ago in the church, showed a resilience that he didn't know she possessed until today. All combined, it made him respect her even more.

"We came, we saw, we conquered the umbrellas," Kyle said, when he thought Drea might finally be done with the selfies.

"How does one conquer an umbrella? Especially ones elevated three stories up as a work of art?" she giggled.

"Umm, I'm gonna have to think on that," he replied. She giggled again, throwing her arms around him and kissing him. The stirring in his pants was starting to get borderline uncomfortable. He needed to figure out how to control his dick around her when she kissed him like that. Going through life with a constant hard-on was not something he looked forward to. "Ready for my surprise stop?"

"I totally forgot! How could I forget?"

"The magic of umbrellas, I suppose." She giggled once more and Kyle had to stop to shift himself in his pants, hoping she didn't notice.

"Well, lead the way, good sir."

WHAT SHOULD HAVE BEEN a fifteen-minute walk from the umbrella street to the beach took them closer to a half hour, due to stopping to peer into shops and taking selfies along the way. The couple of stops he made just to kiss her didn't exactly speed up the trip either. Not that he had been in any kind of hurry to get there. He was enjoying being able to be with Drea as her boyfriend, open and out in public, not having to worry about who might see them. It hadn't even been a full day, but he already knew it would be a rough adjustment once they were back on the resort and had to hide things again.

They reached Playa Peña Beach just as the sun was starting to set, and Kyle was all of a sudden more than a little nervous. He hadn't expected the emotional moment earlier today in the church when he planned this little stop. He hoped that after the afternoon they'd had she would see it as an attempt to be romantic and not him stirring up the memory pot all over again.

"We're at Playa Peña," Drea commented, taking in her surroundings. Her eyes started to get that glassy look again, and her voice got small as she said, "this is where my parents met."

Kyle stopped in his tracks, taking her in. She was taking in slow, heavy breaths, trying to fight back some of the tears he could see forming in her eyes. He should have developed a plan B after her breakdown earlier. He should have just found a nice place to have dinner, or something, anything other than taking her to a place that was tied to painful memories.

"I know, sweetness. I thought it would be nice to sit and watch the sunset here, just like they did on their first date." He sighed, taking her hands in his, looking her in the eyes. "But I didn't stop to rethink that after everything you shared while we were in the church. So if this is too painful, then we can go anywhere else."

"No," she answered, shaking her head. A tear slipped out, and she wiped it away. "This is perfect. It's just, how did you know?"

"Know what?" he asked. He was confused by her question. He thought everyone who worked at the Indigo Royal knew that Playa Peña was where Miller and his best friend met their wives. Wasn't that why the little wedding chapel on site was named Playa Peña? Or maybe he only knew because he was close with Drea. Maybe now he looked like some weird stalker knowing this tidbit.

"Know that I've always wanted someone to bring me here for the sunset. And, I mean a romantic someone, not my family. I've dreamed about it since I was a little girl, being able to have a moment on this beach just like they did." She sniffed, wiping another escaped tear from her cheek. "I've never told anyone."

"Anyone? Even Leona?"

"Even Lee. I might have written it in a diary when I was little, but that's as close as I've ever come to voicing it."

"Well, I promise I wasn't reading your childhood diary. I know this place was something that was theirs and I thought maybe it was something that could be ours too." He leaned down and kissed her forehead gently. It was as if he could hear the smile spread across her face as he did so, and that let a flood of emotions loose in him.

Taking her hand, he led her farther down the beach and found an outcropping of rocks in a little alcove that seemed like the perfect place for them to sit. The beach was relatively quiet, since the majority of locals and tourists would be heading to dinner at about this time, but the alcove still provided an extra level of privacy for the two of them. Kyle brushed off the top of the large flat rock, that was the perfect chair height, and sat down, scooting back with his legs spread so he could pull Drea in between them and hold her in his arms. She settled into the spot he made for her easily, resting her head back so it lay on the front part of his shoulder. Wrapping his arms around her, he intertwined his fingers with hers, tightened his arms around her, and kissed the top of her head.

They sat there, curled up in each other, not saying

anything for a long time, just watching the ocean. It was almost completely dark now, and they hadn't seen another person on the beach for quite awhile. Kyle reached up and started to massage Drea's shoulders, figuring after the sentimental afternoon they'd had, she was probably carrying a little bit of tension there. She mewed and moaned lightly as his fingers kneaded her flesh and she tilted her head exposing her neck.

Leaning in, he pulled her hair back and placed a trail of soft kisses along her neck as she did so, causing her moans to take on a different shape. She moved her body from side to side against his, causing the erection he'd been managing to keep under control all evening to swell back to life. He moved his hands from her shoulders to back down around her waist, slowing creeping up toward her chest. When his palms reached the undersides of her breasts, she let out another little noise, egging him on more.

He loved the feel of her breasts in his hands. To him, they really were the most perfect set he'd ever seen. They fit so perfectly in his grip and the feel of their smoothness against his calloused hands gave him goosebumps. Her nipples responded to his touch like they were created to be touched by only him, and he loved every little reaction they elicited from her. Sweeping his thumbs over them now he could feel them pebble under the fabric of her dress. This caused her to wiggle some more, turning his cock rock-hard underneath her.

She turned about ninety degrees in her seat, so that both her legs were draped over his left one, and placed her hands on his chest. Tilting her head back, Kyle leaned down and captured her mouth in his, tasting that sweet, unique taste he'd come to associate with her. He was pretty sure he could get drunk off her kiss alone. Kissing her like this had turned an already amazing night up a couple of notches. Everything she did was just perfection and for the life of him, he couldn't figure out what on earth he had done to deserve the angel that was currently in his lap.

Sucking on his bottom lip, Drea stood up in the sand and turned to face him. She reached for the button of the khaki shorts he'd changed into after they docked, undoing it and slipping her hand down in between his shorts and his briefs. She slowly palmed his cock while continuing to nibble on his lip, and Kyle thought for a second he might just come right then and there. When she reached into his briefs and pulled out his rock-hard length and dropped to her knees, Kyle was so taken aback he couldn't move.

"What are you doing?" he asked, unable to hide the surprise in his voice.

"You gave me something special, and I want to give you a special memory in return," she answered, with a wicked little grin on her face. She gripped his cock firmly, and slowly started gliding her hand up and down.

"Sweetness, you don't have to—" He was cut off by the feel of her tongue circling the tip of his dick. "Oh, God...."

"It's not about having to," she answered with another lick, this time from base to tip. "It's about *wanting* to."

With those last words, she knelt down, wrapped her whole mouth around him, and sucked. A wave of lust shot through Kyle at the feeling of her warm, wet mouth taking him in. She bobbed her head up and down slowly, using her tongue on the underside of his shaft on every upward motion. Kyle couldn't believe the sensations he was feeling. She sucked cock like a goddess and there was no way he was going to last if he let her continue like this. He needed to be inside her and now.

He managed to somehow straighten himself up,

unaware he'd even leaned back, and reached down to lift her up from her knees. Pulling her into him, he claimed her mouth, kissing her hard, his tongue dancing with hers in long, sweeping strokes.

"Did I do something wrong? I've never...so, I'm sorry if it was bad..." she whispered, looking away from him as she broke the kiss.

"You did everything right, sweetness. Maybe a little too right," he said with a low laugh. "But as amazing as your mouth feels, I know that your pussy feels even better and that's the only place my dick wants to be."

He reached up her skirt, running his hand up the inside of her thigh, slowly moving toward her heat. When he finally reached his destination, he found her already wet, the little thong she had on soaked through. He ran his hand back and forth over the soaking fabric, getting her even more worked up.

"I like when you say things like that," she murmured through her heavy breaths. She ground her hips against his hand, trying to create more friction.

"Yeah? You like when I talk dirty?"

She nodded, unable to form words as he continued to rub her. Taking his time, he moved the little bit of lace covering her sex to the side, finally making skin-to-skin contact. She let out a sound that was a cross between a moan and a whimper, and it made him even harder in the process. He slowly inserted two of his fingers into her, and damn, was she tight. Her knees went weak when he entered her that way, and she had to grab ahold of his shoulders so she didn't collapse.

"That's my girl," he rasped, continuing to massage her insides.

When her knees quivered again, he gently pulled his

fingers out and raised them to his lips. He took his fingers into his mouth and sucked her arousal off of them. She looked at him with wide, shocked eyes as he did so.

"You taste amazing," he growled. "One more reason to call you sweetness."

Kyle could see the blush creeping up her face in the moonlight. Reaching into his pocket, he found the condom that he'd grabbed before heading to shore, ripped it open, and rolled it down his cock.

"Come here, baby." He grabbed her hips and pulled her into his lap, so she was straddling him. She positioned herself over him, and he slowly lowered her down his length. He let out a groan as he felt her tightness take hold of him.

They both remained still for a moment, taking in the feel of them coming together. She kissed him, in little tiny kisses, one right after the other. He shifted his hips to start grinding against her, but she slowed him down by taking on a tempo of her own. He was lost in the feeling of her moving up and down, back and forth on his shaft as she rode him. The look on her face told him she was just as lost in the moment as he was. Making love on the beach in the moonlight hadn't ever been something he'd thought about, but damn if they weren't going to have to try for a repeat performance at home.

Drea reached down between them, finding her clit with her middle finger, and started to rub furiously. Her whimpers and whines were becoming louder, but they were both so into the moment neither was concerned with who might hear.

"Yeah, baby, come for me," Kyle growled in her ear. Apparently those little words were all she needed. She exploded on him, her whimpers becoming silent as she fell apart in his arms. The feel of her pussy gripping him even tighter as she continued to move was pushing him over the edge too. He could feel his own orgasm building, and with a few last thrusts he came, hot and hard.

Coming down from her high, Drea collapsed against him, still straddling his lap. Her breath was labored, and he could feel her heart racing as she rested her forehead on his shoulder. He wrapped his arms around her tighter, letting her know that he was here, and he wasn't letting go.

CHAPTER NINETEEN

THEIR IMPROMPTU BEACH tryst had left both of them wiped, but in a good way. After they'd righted themselves, they walked along the shore. The beach was still mostly quiet, with only a few other couples out and about, looking for the same kind of quiet, alone time that Drea and Kyle had been. The coolness of the ocean felt good against Drea's ankles—her whole body still felt like it was on fire after what she'd just done. Hardly believing she'd been so bold, she was having a hard time keeping all of her feelings in check.

She thought about her parents, and how they had met right here twenty-seven years earlier. One of the few items she had from her mother was the journal Sofia had kept around the time of meeting Drea's father. Miller had given it to her for her sixteenth birthday, holding back the tears as he watched her flip through it for the first time. It had quickly become one of her most cherished possessions, having spent hours and hours poring over the pages until she had almost memorized some of the entries.

Her parents had fallen for each other hard and fast, but

it was obvious from reading her mother's words that what they felt for each other was deep and true. The passion was clear to Drea, even all those years later, and for the first time in her life she'd felt a real connection to them. The journal entries chronicled all the major events of those months, from the night the guys met them on the beach, to Sofia's confusion about whether Dave was serious about his proposal, to the magic that was their wedding day. The very last entry in the journal ended with Sofia revealing that she felt that she and Dave were "about to set out on our greatest adventure yet." Taped just below it was a printed photograph of a positive pregnancy test.

Her favorite entry, the one she'd read over and over again, had been the one where Sofia had detailed their "first date." It was the evening after the young men had crashed the party the sisters were at, having convinced them to give them a chance. The four of them had started out together, hanging out and window shopping in Old San Juan, and stopping at a street vendor for food. In her mind, Drea always assumed it was the empanada cart. After they had finished dinner, Dave had stolen Sofia away, giving his best friend a moment alone with her sister. They'd headed to Raíces Fountain, which had long been referred to as the most romantic place in the city. Although Drea had never understood what was so romantic about the fountain—she'd much preferred the whimsy of the umbrellas—she could appreciate that there had been something about it that had enchanted her mother. Their first kiss was in front of the fountain, and they had even taken a picture of themselves kissing. Sofia and Dave's selfie skills with the old school film camera hadn't been spectacular, so the photo was at a weird angle, but that only served to make the happiness and excitement all the more palpable.

After the fountain, they had apparently made their way back to the beach where they had met the night before, settling in the sand and watching the sun going down over the ocean. Sofia said in her journal entry that she knew then that Dave was her forever. Sofia hadn't held back in her journal entries, and chronicled—in a little too much detail for a teenage Drea—just how she'd given herself wholly to Dave that night on the beach and never looked back. It was something that had weirded Drea out at first, reading about her parents doing such a thing, but as she got older she viewed it like she did any of the other books she read—two people who loved each other so much they just couldn't hold back.

It wasn't lost on Drea now that Kyle had unknowingly recreated her parents' first date for them. It was part of what helped her let go and take the risk of seducing him in such a public venue. She'd felt so connected to her parents and their love in that moment she had to find a way to express it, and while she knew what she felt for Kyle was just as real as what her mother had felt for her father, she wasn't quite ready to put it into words.

She wondered what Kyle was feeling in all this. She knew that this wasn't a fling to him—he'd said as much a couple of different times now. But she'd been so far gone even before he kissed her that it hadn't taken much to push her over the edge. She looked at him like Sofia had looked at Dave in all the photos in the journal, with stars in her eyes and the smile of a woman who had given her heart away.

Kyle's voice startled her from her thoughts and brought her back to the moment.

"What?" she asked.

"I said how does some gelato sound? And then we can head back to the boat and curl up under the stars?"

"That sounds perfect. Are you sure you didn't read my childhood diary?" she giggled.

He lifted the pair of their hands that was intertwined and brought hers to his lips. Kissing it lightly, he smiled at her, his eyes lighting up brightly as he held his lips against her skin for a long moment.

"I promise, sweetness. But I'm glad I'm knocking it out of the park."

There was a little gelato shop right at the edge of the beach, and they stopped inside, taking turns trying all the flavors. The older lady behind the counter was more than happy to indulge them with a myriad of samples, some flavors over and over again, as they compared and contrasted, feeding each other with the little sample spoons. When they finally made their choices and ordered their cones, the older lady insisted the order was on the house.

"No, no, we'll pay," Kyle said, trying to hand some cash to the woman.

She shook her head passionately. She said something in Spanish so quickly that Drea couldn't translate it, then walked away into the back room, ending the conversation. Kyle looked at Drea with a guilty look on his face before slipping the cash onto the counter by the register.

"I need to tell you something," Drea said when they were about halfway to the dock, breaking the silence they had maintained since the gelato place. Kyle stopped in his tracks, looking at her with concern.

"What's wrong, sweetness?"

"Nothing, absolutely nothing. Tonight has been a dream come true. I just need you to know how much of one."

"I'm happy to hear you say that. The look on your face has told me all night how happy you are."

"I don't think it really does," she sighed. "I have my mom's journal from when she met my dad. She dedicated multiple pages to talking about their amazing first date and all the things they did. Ever since Uncle Miller gave me the journal, I've dreamed of going on a date as magical and romantic as the one she described on those pages. And you...you pretty much recreated the whole date. You gave me my own magical evening." She blinked rapidly, trying to hold back the happy tears she could feel springing to life.

"Stop for stop?" he asked, looking a little perplexed.

"Well, we went to the umbrellas instead of the fountain, but my favorite place versus her favorite place, so yeah, pretty much," she shrugged.

"Wow."

"I know."

"I didn't mean to, had I known..." he trailed off.

"No, it means more because you didn't know. I meant it, it was magical. You gave me something that I can't even begin to put into words—you gave me a connection to them."

She saw the proud smile pull on the corner of his lips as he took in her words. She meant them. He gave her something she'd thought she'd never be able to find. For years she wondered what it would feel like to fall like this and experience something as powerful as her mother described. Kyle had made it happen.

"For you, sweetness, I'd do anything."

It had been quite the day, with emotions all over the place. Now, curled up on the trampoline on the front hull of the *Runnin' Down a Dream,* the highlight reel kept flashing through Kyle's mind, preventing him from sleeping. When he came up with the idea of a day in Old San Juan he hadn't had much of an agenda other than to have fun and make Drea smile. The city had been a familiar one, but he had hoped that would lead to a relaxed feeling and would ease expectations that they were doing anything other than enjoying each other's company. Overall, it had been more of a success than he could have ever imagined.

The sounds of Drea's giggles tangled with those of her sobs in his head, pulling on his heart strings. Nothing would ever take away the pain of never knowing her parents, he knew that. But he would do everything in his power to not ever have to hear her cry like that again.

When she asked if she could show him something, he had been immediately excited. The look on her face had shown so much—happiness, excitement, nervousness. He knew whatever it was would be something incredibly special to her and he felt honored that she wanted to show him. The church itself was beautiful. For all the times he had passed it, he'd never been inside. Sitting inside, listening to her talk about her parents' whirlwind engagement and their wedding day, he couldn't help but picture Drea as a bride. He wondered if she would want a church wedding just like they had, or if she would prefer a low-key affair like Vaughn and Simone were planning. He knew he should be freaked out about thinking about her walking down the aisle, but somehow the thoughts didn't seem out of place.

However, when the conversation turned to the loss of her parents and aunt, he saw the pain she hid away come through and it sliced straight through him. He had known there had been an accident when they were rehabbing the resort that resulted in their deaths—it was part of the resort history each new employee learned when they started working there. The brothers made sure that every employee knew that "safety first" was a lifestyle, not some cute motto to be floated around and that if someone did something that didn't have the safety of the guests and other employees as the primary focus, then it was a terminable offense. He hadn't realized that Miller had been so close to losing his life, and had essentially watched his wife, best friend, and sister-in-law lose theirs right in front of his eyes. He also had no idea about the scars the man apparently bore as a daily reminder.

Kyle felt like he'd been given a decoder ring for so much of the Quinlan/Miller family dynamics with this. Why Miller insisted on taking custody of Drea and why the brothers had changed around so much of the plans for the resort to accommodate this new lifestyle. It explained on some level why Vaughn was so over-the-top about safety overall, but Drea's in particular, and why she gave him so much leeway with his overprotectiveness. Prior to this afternoon, he'd thought he'd known pretty much every side of the angelic woman who was lying beside him wrapped up in a blanket, but now he wondered what else there was to discover.

The magic of the day hadn't been lost on him. He'd felt how special it had been every second of the way. But when she dropped the bomb on him that he'd somehow duplicated the events from a date twenty-seven years earlier, it had knocked the wind out of him. It had really been sheer dumb luck on his part that it happened this way, but he didn't want to take away from what she was feeling. Maybe somehow the late Mr. and Mrs. Miller were looking down on them. Whatever it was, he was thrilled he could give Drea that connection to them.

The connection she was feeling with her family was something Kyle had wished he felt toward his own dad. He had so few memories of the man apart from the stories his mother would tell him. Tom Egan had managed a weird schedule, often working nights and weekends. Being a drug interdiction officer for the Coast Guard meant that you spent little time behind a desk and a fair amount of time out and about doing search and seizures. As a child, Kyle hadn't thought much about it. Sure, his dad wasn't home a lot, but when he was home, he was certainly an involved and present parent. He attended soccer games and school concerts, and they'd even gone camping once, just the two of them. But then one morning when Kyle got up he found his mother in tears in the kitchen. When he asked what was wrong, she simply told his six-year-old self that Daddy had been in an accident and wouldn't be coming home.

Kyle remembered the funeral, all the men in the Coast Guard dress uniforms telling him he was "the man of the house now." He remembered being handed the flag while at the gravesite and wondering what he was supposed to do with it. But more than anything, what he remembered was watching his mother cry and knowing then that it was up to him to take care of her.

His mother had done an excellent job raising him by herself, and he knew that she missed her husband. More than anything, what Kyle missed was the idea of his dad. It was the loss of having someone to do all the things a boy should do with his dad that Kyle felt most of all. It had been his mom who had taught him to tie a tie, lectured him after his first fight, explained the birds and bees, and who had enlisted a neighbor to help teach Kyle all about boat mechanics after seeing him express interest. It had been his mom who shoved condoms in his pocket before his senior prom, telling him that this is where his father would be reminding him to "wrap it up or else." She'd been trying to do what she felt was best and he owed her everything for that.

It was for this reason he'd been so focused since moving down here. He'd gotten so lucky meeting Grayson that day and being offered a job at the Indigo Royal. The job paid enough, on top of covering most living expenses, that he could save to one day start his own company and still send money home to help his mom. He was so close to having enough saved. If the math he ran in his head most days stayed true, he only needed to hold out another six months or so. He'd broken every rule he'd made for himself by falling for Drea, and then broke the rewritten rules when he kissed her the other day.

But after today—sharing stories of her family, her giggles under the umbrellas, the look in her eyes while they made love on the beach, and her happy tears when she told him that he had made a secret dream come true—he couldn't bring himself to regret any of it. The lack of regret did nothing to ease his worry about coming clean to her uncles though. The insight provided as to why they were the way they were only made him realize that he'd not only be risking his current job, but also their support in getting his own business off the ground if they were to find out. Asking Drea to keep this a secret for another six months wasn't fair, however, and he couldn't do that to her. There just wasn't a good option.

She stirred next to him and he glanced over to make sure that he hadn't somehow woken her up. She'd been out the second her head hit the little travel pillow that he'd brought with them, not even waiting for him to lie down. Leaning over, he brushed some of her hair from her face and kissed her cheek. He loved the peaceful look she had on her face, and he wanted to freeze this moment in his memory. Now that she was really his, he needed to figure out all the details.

And since it was her happiness at stake, he would have to find a way.

CHAPTER TWENTY

THE SUN WAS RELATIVELY high in the sky when Drea finally woke up the next morning. Finding a wadded up blanket next to her, she assumed Kyle had draped it over her at some point during the night. The fabric of her sundress was all twisted around her waist, causing her to have to sit up in order to straighten it out. After fixing her dress, she ran her fingers through her hair, realizing in the process of doing so that they were moving. She looked up to find the sails raised and full of wind.

Looking around some more, she found Kyle up in the captain's chair, gently steering the boat, letting the wind do most of the work. His dark brown hair was waving in the wind and he had a little bit of stubble on his normally smooth face. His focus was out at sea, not realizing she was awake, so she took this moment to simply drink him in. At some point between arriving back last night and now, he'd changed back into his board shorts and a long sleeve T-shirt which, based on its current position of being draped across the back of the chair he was leaning against, he seemed to have since shed as well. His upper body was incredibly well-defined, his broad shoulders showing off some serious muscles. She loved watching those muscles work as he was dealing with the rigging and sails. He hated the gym as much as she did, but unlike her, he was obviously getting enough of a workout via the job to compensate for never going.

His good looks had stood out to her the second her Uncle Gray pointed him out on his follow-up trip to the marina. Grayson had gone on and on the night before at dinner about the smart, fun kid he'd come across at the marina and how helpful he'd been. Grayson had been so impressed with this normal kid—who obviously had no idea that his bosses probably would have wanted him to kiss Grayson's ass—and the help that he provided, that he was insistent that when he went back the next day, he was going to make sure this kid got the credit. He had insisted that Drea accompany him to see the kid in action, despite the fact that she would have rather done anything else other than go with him. She'd only tagged along on the trip as a way to get off the island and away from the resort for a couple of days. But one look at Kyle as they approached had made giving up a day of shopping worth it.

She had been taken by his looks from the moment he looked at her. However, it had been who he was as a person that truly won her over. They'd hit it off from pretty much the moment Grayson had introduced them, and he had hung back with her as his coworker caused a scene over who got the credit for the sale of the boat. When Kyle had tried to intervene to mediate the altercation, she saw that he was just as much of a good human as he was good-looking.

As she stood there on the boat watching him, it occurred to her that, if possible, he'd gotten better-looking in the years he'd been at the resort. Either way you looked at it, the guy was hot.

He looked down and caught her staring at him. He smiled widely, and blew her a kiss. Her left hand shot up and grabbed the imaginary kiss from the air and shoved it in the pocket of her dress, before bringing that hand to her lip and returning the action.

"Give me five minutes to get us to a place we can anchor and I'll be down," he called out to her.

"Sounds good, I'm gonna change out of this," she replied, motioning up and down to her clothes from the day before.

For a moment, Drea considered putting on the purple suit that Dalton had given her a few days ago, instead of the red one that she'd worn the day before. However, she just couldn't bring herself to do it. She had felt so damn good in that little red one, and loved how Kyle looked at her while she was wearing it. She made sure to loosely tie the top into place, so if it just so happened that it came undone, oh well.

Reemerging from below deck, she could hear the little electric kettle working its magic to heat up some water and found Kyle standing behind the bar. It was not a place she usually found him, unless he was there hanging out with her, so she welcomed the sight. In fact, pairing this image with the one of him in her kitchen yesterday morning, he was starting to look downright domestic.

"Instant coffee coming right up," he smirked. He poured some water from the kettle into a camping mug and handed it to her. She took a quick sip, smiling over the mug at him.

"Thanks. What time is it?"

"A little after ten."

"Oh my God, how long did I sleep?"

"You needed it. Yesterday turned out to be a big

emotional day," he said, coming around the bar and placing his hands on her hips. "Your cute little body needed the rest."

She took another sip of the coffee, letting the taste flood her mouth. Instant coffee was certainly not the best thing out there, but it was better than no coffee.

"I'm sorry I unloaded on you yesterday. I just wanted to be able to share them with you."

"I like that you did. I know how much it weighs on you, and I'm happy to share some of that."

There he went with the perfect-boyfriend answers again, making her insides swoon. As much as she loved the answer, she knew that if she wasn't careful, she would blurt out a response that might be too much too soon.

"Is there a plan for today?"

"Unless you want to do something different, my idea had been to just hang. We can just lie in the sun, maybe go for a swim, play truth or dare, whatever you want."

"Truth or dare?" she asked, laughing. "Just what kind of dares are we gonna do on the boat, just us?"

He stood there with a puzzled look on his face, obviously having not thought this part out.

"Well, I had been joking, but give me time and I'll figure it out!"

"Will you now?" she said, mischievously. "Then truth or dare is most certainly on the to-do list."

THE MORNING HAD BEEN peaceful and warm, just the way Kyle felt it should always be in the islands. He'd finally gotten a little bit of sleep, somehow letting his worries about how to make everything work take a back seat in his brain for a bit. However, when the sun came up, so was he, unable to force his body to rest any more. He hadn't wanted to wake Drea—she needed the rest. She felt so damn perfect curled up next to him, making him wonder again what he did to deserve having someone like her. The little cooing noises she made in her sleep made her that much more endearing, and it wasn't just his morning wood that stirred.

His heart felt like it could explode every time he looked at her, and he wondered how he got here so quickly. There had always been a deep connection between them, and from the moment he arrived in St. Thomas they had been a pair. Drea pulled him into her circle and they had built their friendship on the basis of laughter, trust, and a love of sailing. But now, it went so much deeper than that friendship. He craved her. It wasn't just the sex, although being with her physically was a mind-blowing experience, and he looked forward to giving her a number of other firsts. But it didn't seem to matter *what* they were doing, he wanted to be with her. He wanted to be able to hold her hand, make her laugh, and most importantly, make her feel safe and loved.

As he had gotten the sails ready this morning and navigated them back in the direction of St. Thomas, he tried to make sense of all his feelings. If he knew anything, it was that he'd never felt this way before about another human being, and he couldn't exactly put his finger on what it was. He felt like they had been together forever, not just a few days, although the five years of friendship they had under their belts might have contributed to that feeling. He just knew that the idea of a life without Drea made him want to throw up.

A distraction was desperately needed, but he didn't know how to take his mind off of all of it. Usually one of the things he loved the most about being out on the water was that he was alone with his thoughts and the open air helped clear his head. Not today, though. Today the open air only filled his head with thoughts of Drea. Thoughts of a life with her, the two of them holing up in that little cottage of hers, making it theirs, of her in a white dress on the beach, her wild curls waving in the sea breeze, of her tummy prominent and round with their baby, of growing old and gray with her. These were the thoughts that would get him in even more trouble though. He needed to try to focus on something more superficial, like how just the thought of her amazing curves made him instantly hard.

They'd already checked off a number of things he'd imagined doing with her, and all of them had been better than he had ever thought possible. He'd never been like Dalton where sex was just another physical activity—he'd always had to have some kind of connection to the other person. But the last couple of days had been something else. Everything about Drea set his nerve endings on fire and even something as simple as feeling her lips against his had sent all the blood in his body rushing to his dick. Yet there was still so much more he wanted to do with her, both in bed and out. He wanted to give her the world.

She was back up at the front of the boat, wearing that itty-bitty red bikini again. When he had said that it was all he wanted her to pack, he was only kidding, but he loved that even if she had packed another suit, she'd chosen to only wear this. He loved seeing her this comfortable, not only in her own body, but in their relationship. It had to be a good sign that she was back in that suit. Maybe he would get to recreate the action from the booze cruise after all.

After dropping the anchor and lowering the sails, he moved to the front of the boat to join her.

"Ready for truth or dare?" he asked as he sat down next to her on the trampoline.

She put her book down and looked at him skeptically. "Did you figure out how dares are gonna work?"

"No," he admitted. "I thought about truth or shots, but we should probably be responsible sailors and not get wasted." She nodded. "So, then I thought truth or strip."

"Truth or strip? So if I don't want to answer something, I have to take off a piece of clothing?"

"That had been the idea until I thought it through a little more and realized we're both in swimsuits."

"Good call." She winked.

"Not that I don't want to get you naked," he said, waggling his eyebrows.

"You don't need a teenage game of truth or dare for that!" she laughed, making her boobs jiggle in the process. He watched as they moved freely in the loosely tied bikini top, imagining what he would do if one just popped out.

"Good to know. Anything else I should know?" he winked.

She giggled, shaking her head from side to side, making those wild corkscrew curls of hers go flying. "I'm an open book, you can ask me anything. I don't have anything to hide."

"Me either."

"Good, then you can go first."

CHAPTER TWENTY-ONE

KYLE WASN'T sure what to say. Conversation had always come easy to the two of them, but then again, silence had never been awkward either. Not that it was now, as he sat here trying to rack his brain for something to share. What could he possibly share that she didn't know?

"You're supposed to ask me a question," he said, trying to make up for his lack of prepared topics.

"I was thinking! I was trying to make it really good," she swatted at him. He dodged her contact, but only barely, laughing at her getting all flustered. "Tell me what you remember most about your dad."

"That he was never around?"

She furrowed her brows at him, looking almost disappointed that that had been his answer.

"Seriously, he wasn't around much. He was a drug officer for the Coast Guard, it was a big job, and it kept him away a lot. He was a great dad from what I could tell. He came to my games and school events and stuff. But what I remember most was that it was a big deal that he made it to those. I'd like to think that if he had lived, that he would have been around more as I got older, and that we would have done more father-son stuff, but he was gone just after I turned six so I never got the chance to find out."

"Do you miss him?"

"Yes, but not the same way I think you miss your parents. I can't explain why, but I think that maybe since he wasn't around much before, that it was easier to accept that he wasn't ever going to be around again."

"But don't you feel like you were robbed?"

"Sometimes. But my mom did a great job in making sure that I didn't miss out on anything. We had this old neighbor, Mr. Willett, who had lost his wife a couple of years before my dad died, so my mom used to ask him to do 'man things' with me," he said, using the air quotes around the words man things. "He had this boat that he was constantly fixing up, in fact I'm not entirely sure the thing ever actually worked. But he taught me about boats and mechanics and all that. Mr. Willett passed when I was in college, when he was ninety-three. Losing him was rough."

"I'm sorry," she said. The look of sadness in her eyes consumed Kyle as he took her in. She felt everything so deeply, and even though she'd never met the old man, he knew that she was heartbroken over his death simply because Kyle had been.

"Do you ever wish you'd had a normal childhood?" he asked.

She went to answer and then paused. "You know, I've never really thought about it. Even if my parents hadn't passed, I still would have grown up on the resort. Maybe my mom and aunt would have enforced a little more normal kid stuff, but I don't feel like I ever really missed out. I still had birthday parties, and learned how to ride a bike. Okay, so learning how to cook was on an industrial stove and I have been driving a golf cart since I was seven, but my uncles always took off work for Christmas, so Santa still came to visit. Uncle Miller made sure that my experience was as normal as he thought it could be considering the situation. In his mind, he was a single dad, and he took on the majority of the parenting load. Although Uncle Vaughn and Uncle Gray were always right there to help, so I'm sure that was a relief. But that also meant I had multiple parent-types enforcing the rules. So, I was still forced to do my homework before I could go out and play, and you know that I had a very strictly enforced curfew. I was like pretty much any other kid on the island."

"I guess I just have a hard time imagining growing up on the island."

"I'm sure that growing up in the States is very different. But I think if the only thing that had been different about my situation was that we had been in the States rather than St. Thomas, then not much would have changed. Each one of my uncles would have taken on the same role, it just might have looked a little different. But, really, I loved the childhood I had. I really have nothing to complain about."

"Other than maybe that curfew," Kyle laughed.

"Ugh. Uncle Miller was the one who put it in place, but I don't know that he ever really cared, as long as I was home by a reasonable time and he knew where I was. He knew his kid, and he knew I wasn't going to get into that much trouble. As I'm sure you can imagine, it was Uncle Vaughn who was the stickler about it. One time, knowing that Leona and I were going to be out way later than allowed, I set all the clocks back by like three hours in each one of the big house apartments so that it looked like I came home on time. Next morning I thought I woke up late, because the clock read what I thought was like three hours behind. Turns out, Uncle Gray had gone and changed them all back after I got home so that I wasn't found out."

"I have a new respect for the man."

"Right? Teenage Drea thought about changing them to get away with it, but it never occurred to her that she'd have to change them back." She shook her head, laughing at the memory. "I only found out it was Uncle Gray who did it because after I rushed out to the common room, he was sitting there waiting for me. He just laughed, told me what he did and that it would be our secret. And you know what, now that I think about it, I don't know if he ever told the other two or not."

"He strikes me as the type that would take such a thing to the grave."

"Unless you tickle it out of him. Don't let him know I told you, but tickling is his weakness."

"I'll keep that in mind, should I ever need to tickle my boss."

"He won't be your boss forever, though, right?" she asked, hesitantly. He could tell she didn't want to push the issue.

"That's my plan."

"What makes you want to go out on your own so bad? You don't hate working at the resort, do you?"

"Not at all. Working for your family has been one of the best experiences of my life. But I have always dreamed of being my own boss—making my own schedule and doing things how I want to do them. I have all these ideas, and I want to try to make them into realities."

"Why don't you just talk to Uncle Gray about them? I know he's been looking to have someone take over the marina and boat excursions. You'd be perfect!"

"He offered me that role about three months ago, actually."

"And you turned it down?"

"Not turned it down, per se. Just told him I'd need time to think about it. He told me that he'd give me all the time I needed."

"But the answer is going to be thanks, but no thanks?"

"Unless something changes, yes. One, I don't want to force my ideas on him. It's still his baby. I saw firsthand how that goes at the marina I worked at in Florida. It doesn't end well when they are no longer in control. But I want to be able to work with the cruise ships for day tours, as well as people who are staying on the island at a rental house or something rather than a resort. Maybe even run a discounted tour or two once a month for locals who work in the tourism industry who don't get to do the fun things all these visitors get to."

"That sounds like a great idea. I really think you should talk to Uncle Gray. He values your opinion."

"I know," he sighed. "And I know he wants to expand into more adventure-type things, which is why he needs someone to take over the boats, but I still don't feel that I would be able to do everything I want to. Every idea I have would still be subject to the approval of your uncles."

"That's fair," she said, resigning herself to his answer. "What's number two?"

"You."

"Me?"

"Yes, you. If I'm out on my own, we can be together."

"Aren't we together now?"

"I mean really together. Out and proud together. Not *worried Kyle might lose his job* together," he said, referring to himself in the third person. "Our relationship would be one less thing that would be subject to their approval, at least where the resort was concerned."

He knew he sounded like a broken record. But he also knew that regardless of how much her uncles liked him as an employee and her friend, accepting him as her boyfriend would be another thing entirely. It would be an uphill battle all of its own, and one he was only prepared to fight if he had a way to support her that wasn't dependent on the resort.

"I was really a consideration?" she asked. It hadn't been what he expected her to say, so it caught him a little off guard.

"Yes, of course. You have been for a very long time, sweetness. I have wanted you since the moment you showed up at the dock that day in Florida."

DREA COULD FEEL her cheeks blush with his admission. She had no idea that he'd felt those same sparks she had that day. For years now she'd convinced herself that she was imagining it.

Letting his words sink in, she looked out over the deep blue waters that surrounded them. The sun sparkled off the top of the waves as the boat slowly rolled along them. The feel of the boat rocking underneath them was calming, as if lulling them into the deep conversation. A smile crept up her face, even though she was suddenly feeling shy about it. She looked away so Kyle couldn't see her reaction.

"No response?" he asked. "Shy Drea is not one I'm used to."

She turned back so he could see her face and the smile

stretched across it. "Sorry, I just feel a little awkward some-times when you say things like that."

"Like what? That I want you?"

"And other things. I love hearing them, but I don't know how to react to how it makes me feel."

"And just how does it make you feel?" he asked slowly, drawing out the words.

"All mushy inside," she said, as if she were embarrassed by it.

"Kinda like how you feel when you read those smutty books of yours?" he teased.

"Don't you mock my books!" She picked hers up and pretended to hit him with it. "But to answer your question, sorta? The books give me the warm fuzzies and make me all swoony—"

"Swoony? Is that a word?" he asked, cutting her off.

"It is now. So, they make me all swoony, and when you get all perfect-boyfriend-y, it's like that, but, like, times a hundred. My insides kinda melt, and I don't know what to say."

"So I make you melty?"

"Now who's making up words?" she mocked.

He laughed a deep, whole-body laugh that made her tingle inside. It didn't seem to matter what he did, she was a goner. It had started that day in Florida for her as well, and she wanted to tell him that, but she was more than a little afraid she'd come off sounding a little crazy.

"Enough about my melty insides. Next question."

"What do you want to be when you grow up?" he asked her.

The question was simple, and she loved how he had worded it the same way you would ask someone who was five. She didn't know why she thought it was cute when he said it, since had it been her uncles it would have only pissed her off. Maybe it was because she knew that Kyle respected her as a woman who could make her own choices. It was a question she'd been asked a lot as a child. Week after week, guests would come to the resort and see the precious little girl running about, following her uncles around or helping out some of the staff. Some would ask her just the way Kyle just had. Some would change the wording around to ask if she wanted to take over the Indigo Royal, but the focus had been the same. The questions stopped somewhere around high school, about the time she started to blend in and look as if she were just another staff member, rather than a real life Eloise.

"You really want to know?"

"I wouldn't have asked otherwise."

"What I really, really want to do is put a spa into the Indigo Royal."

"We have a spa."

"No, we offer massages and mani/pedis and call it a spa," she corrected him.

"Okay, so, stupid man question—is that not the same?"

She sighed. It was pretty much the exact reaction she was expecting. Not only from him, but from pretty much anyone. The term "spa" had come to have a wide variety of definitions and to many, it often boiled down to a few key treatments being offered some place. But just a few pampering-type options wasn't what Drea had in her head.

"No, not really. I'm talking all out. Different types of massages, nail salon, hair salon, makeup application, body treatments, baths, whirlpools, saunas, steam rooms. Maybe bring in a reflexologist and offer different specialty items. I don't want it to be just something guests do while on vacation. I want the spa to *be* the reason they're on vacation."

"Is that a thing?"

"Absolutely! There is a place in Bora Bora that Simone and I keep talking about going and checking out. Yes, they have all the great things you hear about doing in Bora Bora like boating, snorkeling, etcetera, but their spa—their spa is like the best in the world. People choose this resort to go to this spa. It's not a 'hey, since we're here, let's get a massage.' Certainly, there is some of that, the walk-in traffic. But it's not the only traffic it gets. They have a tea room...*a tea room!* They offer six different types of massages. Different body wraps and scrubs, and they have a custom cool pool and multiple hot tubs that are each a different temperature. Some of their treatment rooms even have a glass floor so you can look into the ocean as you're getting your massage or whatever."

"Wow. Sounds...intense."

"Just think about the potential!" she said, getting animated. "If we invested in creating that kind of atmosphere at the Indigo Royal, and we could make ourselves *the* place on the island to go for these kinds of treatments, it'd be huge. St. Thomas doesn't have anything like that right now. Right now we rely mostly on the people deciding while they're here that it would be nice to get a massage or something. The amount of traffic we could bring in from girls' trips and honeymoons could be massive, not to mention if we open it up to non-guests. It should be fairly easy to fit it into the 'grownup playground' marketing we have going. Indigo Royal, where you go play and relax."

"You've put a lot of thought into this," he commented.

"Yeah, it's been a secret little dream of mine for a while."

"It's not such a little dream, sweetness. But I think it's

something that could be amazing. Why haven't you brought it up to your uncles?"

"Are you kidding me? They'd never hear me out."

"Sure they would. Their world revolves around you and the resort. If you brought them an idea that could be their next big move, then I think they'd be all in."

"Their world revolves around me as if I were still twelve. You know better than anyone how they can be. They would never, ever take my idea seriously. I'm still a little girl in their minds."

"This could be your chance to prove you're not."

"Yeah, right. You see how they talk about me like I'm not even there while we're at dinner. I love them—they are amazing and they have given me everything. But I know how this conversation will go. I'll bring it up, and then they'll proceed to debate it like I'm not even in the room. And if they do even acknowledge my presence, it would be to say that I'd never be able to do it."

"You really think they'd say that?"

"Well, maybe not in so many words, but I think that would be the basis of their thought process."

"I think you need to at least try. I think they believe in you more than realize."

"Make you a deal," she said. "I'll float my spa idea by them, if you tell them we're a couple."

CHAPTER TWENTY-TWO

THE SILENCE that passed between them seemed to skip a beat with each wave that rolled beneath the catamaran. The words still echoed in his head, as if she had thrown down a gauntlet.

"Did you just issue me a challenge?" he said playfully. This was the Drea he was used to, the one who loved to challenge him and never shied from an adventure.

"Not just you, both of us," she answered proudly. "We both apparently have things we want to say to them, but are afraid to do so. Didn't you say that Uncle Gray told you to stop being a chicken?"

"Chickenshit, actually."

"Well, this is our chance. We do this together."

He looked at her face as she finished, seeing in her eyes a brightness that hadn't been there a moment ago. She was making plans for them, and he loved it. For the first time in a while, he was starting to feel optimistic about the whole thing. Maybe it could be as simple as she made it out to be. In all his overthinking and analyzing, he hadn't considered what having her support would actually mean to him. Man, could he be a dumbass.

"Together. I like that," he answered, gazing into her eyes.

"Just you and me against the world," she whispered in response.

"I love that." He leaned in and kissed her, taking her mouth slowly.

She responded by scooting closer to him. Never breaking the kiss, she positioned herself so their bodies were facing each other head-on, her legs spread, draping over each one of his, straddling him. He reached around her body, running his hands up and down her back. As he came upon the little strings, he took them in his hand and played with them for a moment, before tugging on them lightly. He'd been toying with the idea since he saw her come up from below deck this morning wearing this suit, and he figured now was as good a time as any to make his move.

When he tugged with a little more purpose than before, the strings quickly came undone and the suit top went slack around her breasts. He could feel her smile against his lips, and her body shook a little as she giggled. Leaning back, she broke their kiss and looked down at the fabric loosely hanging from her neck. The top fluttered a little bit in the breeze, teasing her nipples and giving Kyle a glimpse of the beautiful breasts that it had barely contained to begin with.

"Oops," he said, shrugging one shoulder, a mischievous smile spread wide across his face. It was taking every bit of restraint he had not to reach up and yank it off her neck.

"Nudity isn't a problem, is it, Captain Kyle?" she replied impishly, mocking Staci's words from the other day.

"Oh, it most certainly is not!"

The laugh she let out filled the open air around them,

sending shock waves through him. It was a big, full sound that packed a serious punch, and he couldn't have hidden his own smile even if he had tried. She grabbed the bikini top and pulled it over her head, getting the strings caught in her mess of curls. Her breasts bounced lightly as she tugged, trying to free the top. The gentlemanly thing to do would have been to help her untangle the strings, but he couldn't tear his eyes away from the beauty that was her cleavage. A couple of seconds later when she had gotten herself fixed, he looked up at her to find her watching him stare at her. He reached out, taking one perfect sphere in each hand.

"I don't know that I can tell you enough just how perfect these are."

"Did Dalton really tell you that Staci's were fake?"

Kyle gently removed his hands from her chest, leaning backward to rest on them, and nodded. He was very curious as to why that's where her mind automatically went.

"Does he tell you about all the chicks he has sex with?" she asked.

"Not all, but I hear about most on some level. It's usually not much more than a confirmation that he got laid the night before. But with Staci, he shared a little more."

"Like her fake boobs?"

"Well, to be fair, one look at them and I could tell they were fake. But yes, it was one of the things he mentioned."

"What else did he tell you?"

"Why are you so curious?"

She shrugged one shoulder trying to act as if it were no big deal, but Kyle could tell otherwise. There was something deep in her eyes that he needed to uncover. The sounds of the water around them filled the silence as he waited for her to answer. He didn't want to push her, but he knew that he needed to understand what was going through her head. When she hadn't answered after another moment, he decided he needed to take action.

Grabbing onto her waist, he quickly brushed his fingers back and forth over her sides, lightly tickling her. The action made her squirm and let out a round of giggles. She continued to squirm under his grasp for a moment, before finally taking in a deep breath.

"Fine, fine," she said, catching her breath. "Because I wanted to know what you two tell each other about girls. So I know how much Dalton is gonna know about at work on Monday."

The thought hadn't occurred to him that she would be worried that he would kiss and tell. In fact, thoughts of what he would share with his buddy hadn't crossed his mind in any way. If she was worried about Dalton looking down on her, she had the situation all wrong. Or maybe she was just worried because she didn't know what to tell Leona and wanted their stories to match. Even though the two acted like they were only friends due to work, Kyle knew Dalton turned to Leona for more than just help getting his bathroom cleaned.

"Pretty sure I could tell him we spent the entire weekend naked on this boat fucking like rabbits and it wouldn't change how he looks at you. This is Dalton—the man views having sex like an extracurricular. Ask him what he did the night before, 'oh, you know, hit up the gym, had a beer, got laid.'"

"Good point."

"I would bet that Leona asks more questions than he does."

"Depends on if she's on or off again with Carlos. If she's on, then I won't be able to get a word in edgewise."

"Carlos? The maintenance guy?"

"Yeah, did you not know that?" she asked. He shook his head in confirmation. "Oh, well, yeah, the two of them have been on and off again fuck buddies for years. Why do you think the 'light bulbs need replacing' all the time?" She used air quotes around Leona's secret code.

"Huh, well, that answers my theory about her and Dalton using each other."

"Just once, when he first joined the staff. I don't remember her reason for not making it an ongoing thing, though."

"Yeah, you and Leona share way more than us guys. Here I thought I was in the know because Dalton slipped in telling me about her thing for Cullen Cruz."

"Everyone knows about that. What everyone doesn't know is that she lost her virginity to him when we were seventeen," she said conspiratorially.

"Leona? Our Leona? Lost her virginity to a sports legend?" Kyle asked, perplexed by what Drea had just told him.

"Well, he was just a regular player then," she answered, shrugging it off as if it was no big deal.

"Cullen Cruz has never been 'just a regular player,' as you put it. He's been a household name basically since he started."

Drea just looked at him like he was making a big deal out of nothing. "Well, when he first came here ten years ago, he was just an everyday football player, or so we thought. We knew he was famous, but he wasn't so famous that he couldn't walk down the street. One or two people recognized him, but he was able to be pretty anonymous, at least for the first couple of years."

"This conversation has been very enlightening," he said, trying to wrap his head around what she just told him. He wasn't even sure how they'd gotten to this point in the conversation, but that was just part of what he loved about her. "Whose turn is it?"

"I've lost track," she giggled.

"Well, I've got something I want to know."

DREA HALFWAY FROZE as the words came out of Kyle's mouth. She could see the sneaky smile sliding across his face and just knew that he was up to no good. But she trusted him, so she just waited.

"You said last night that it was the first blow job you've ever given," he said, matter-of-factly.

"Yes. So?"

"So, what else is on your firsts that we need to cross off?"

It felt like her heart just suddenly stopped beating and as if she'd forgotten how to breathe. She'd gotten so used to her heart speeding up whenever Kyle was around, but those words were like he'd sucked all the air out of the sky.

"You want me to just run down the list of everything I've never done? Or just the sex things?" she asked playfully.

"Let's start with the sex." He winked, leaning in to kiss her.

He pulled her close and she wrapped her arms around his neck. The feel of her nipples brushing up against his skin sent a shiver down her spine, and she arched her back slightly trying to make more contact.

"If we haven't done it, then it's safe to assume that it'd be a first for me."

"Well, then, I'll have to start to come up with some ideas."

"Open to suggestions?"

"Just what did you have in mind?"

"Well, believe it or not, I've never been skinny-dipping, and since I'm already half naked, now seems like the perfect time."

"How have you never been skinny-dipping? That seems like something you and Leona would have done in high school."

"Somehow, it wasn't something we ever thought to do."

"Then I think that sounds like a perfect thing to do."

The squeal that left her seemed to cut straight through the air, as she popped up from his lap. Placing her hands on her hips, she grabbed hold of the little strings tied there. Tugging on both sides at the same time, she let the small piece of fabric covering her fall away. She felt the warm air against her sex and wondered if Kyle could tell how turned on she was. There was no one for miles, but the idea of being totally naked with him out in the open like this got her blood rushing.

Kyle remained sitting, looking up at her, about eye level with her sex. She saw him lightly lick his lips and she swore she could feel herself getting wetter. Putting his hands on her hips, he finally stood. Her hands seemed to have a mind of their own, reaching out and touching his smooth chest, running up and down over the ripples of his muscles. He looked her straight in the eye with a wicked grin and in one swift move, he dropped his shorts, never breaking eye contact.

Excitement pulsed through her veins as she broke away from his grip and headed to the edge of the boat. Without thinking twice, she pushed off from the deck and dove in head first. The cool water encased her quickly as she broke through the surface, instantly cooling her off. It felt so good in contrast with the heat that was still radiating through her. As she broke back through the surface, she opened her eyes to see Kyle still standing on the edge of the catamaran. He looked so good, standing there in the sun, in nothing but his birthday suit. Even from here she could tell his big beautiful cock was hard, but not fully erect, and she wanted to get her hands on it. She pointed at him and then crooked her finger back and forth, enticing him to come join her.

He licked his lips again and leapt in, his feet hitting the water first. He popped up from under the surface right in front of her, spitting some salt water into her face. She couldn't help but let out a giggle and splashed him in return. He reached out and wrapped his arms around her, and she responded by wrapping her legs around him. Her center was still warm as she pressed it against his cool body and she could feel his hardness slide under her ass.

"I think I rather like this," she commented.

"Being naked in the ocean?"

"Yeah. It's freeing to not be constricted by my suit."

"So, all future swimming trips are to be done naked, got it."

A strange feeling hit her then, listening to him talk about the future, even if it was just something as little as going swimming. She'd had to stop herself a number of times these last couple of days from trying to imagine what a future with him could look like. Picturing them trying to cook together in the kitchen, sitting out on the porch watching the sun rise and set over Big House Beach, curled up together at bonfires. She allowed herself a moment to think about how as much as she loved the church parents got married in, she was pretty sure she wouldn't want to get married there herself. She knew that she was getting ahead of herself, but much as her mother had known that night on the beach, Drea knew now, holding on to each other as the clear blue waters of the Caribbean splashed around them, that he was her forever.

They continued to swim and splash around for a while enjoying the warm sun and the cool waters. The weather was perfect, the waves were calm, and other than a couple of other boats that went by, they were all alone. This weekend had been just the break they needed from the resort. Even though they saw each other every day at work, it had been weeks since they'd gotten some real down time. The resort had been booked solid the last couple of months, so that no one had really had time to breathe, much less do anything other than business as usual. Part of her wondered how Vaughn had found time to plan a secret wedding among all the chaos that surrounded them.

Swimming back to the boat, she climbed up the ladder to the deck and looked around for a towel. Before she could reach for one that was sitting on the bench near the bar, she felt Kyle's arms wrap around her from behind, drawing her flush with his body. The coolness of the water droplets on his skin warmed quickly between their two bodies, causing them to feel a little sticky. His hands found her breasts almost right away, flicking her nipples. The giggle that had been about to escape her from the surprise of his presence turned into a soft "mmmmmm" as he continued to play with her body. His lips met her shoulder and he peppered kisses up her neck, moving her hair out of the way as he went.

Feeling like her knees were starting to get a little wobbly, she reached behind her and grabbed on to his torso. He took this as encouragement to continue his assault on her body, turning his kisses into nibbles. Slowly walking her toward the bar, nudging her forward step by step, his attention to her nipples went from playful flicking to long, purposeful pinches and twists. She arched her back and closed her eyes, trying to get more of her into his hands, feeling every little movement he made zing through her body.

After a couple of steps, she reached her hand out, unsure exactly where the bar was and worried they might run into it. As she did so, Kyle grabbed her outstretched hand and used it to spin her around, so she was now facing him. Taking her mouth in his, he continued to walk her the last few steps until her backside hit the bar. No sooner had she made contact than he picked her up by the waist and hoisted her up onto the bar. Standing in between her open legs, he picked up each one and wrapped them around his waist. She couldn't stop a giggle from escaping as he pulled back from their kiss.

"Well, hello, beautiful," he said low and husky.

"Hi," she answered back, a lot more breathy than she had intended.

Capturing her mouth with his again, he kissed her for a moment before starting to work his way down her neck, along her shoulder, and then finally arriving at her breasts, her pert nipples already standing at attention from earlier. He took one in his mouth and swirled his tongue around the sensitive little peak, sending a zing of lust straight to her clit. She grabbed his head and held him close as his hand came up so that her other side didn't feel left out. She closed her eyes, trying to take in every sensation. She loved the feel of his mouth on her, and how it was as if she were the center of his world when they were like this. He stopped suddenly, releasing her nipple with a pop, like one would a lollipop.

"Tell me, sweetness," he growled, his voice somehow even gruffer than before. "If last night was your first time giving, does that mean you've also never received?"

The look on his face was almost predatory as he asked the question, and Drea drew in a quick breath in reaction. She suddenly couldn't speak, the butterflies in her tummy starting to spread to the rest of her. Biting down on her bottom lip, she simply nodded in response.

She was pretty sure she heard him actually let out a low growl as he leaned in to capture the bottom lip she'd been biting in his teeth. He sucked on it hard, making her match the sound he was making. The feel of his hands unwrapping her legs from around him caught her off guard for a moment, until she felt one of those hands find her center and slowly run his fingers through her folds.

"So, you're telling me that no one has ever tasted this beautiful, sweet, bare pussy of yours," he said, continuing to carefully massage her.

Drea let out a little whimper as his finger passed over her clit. She tried to wiggle her hips to find that finger again, but his other hand held her hips firmly in place. Everything he was doing to her was igniting her insides, and she felt like she could burst at any moment. Even the idea that he might replace his fingers with his mouth pushed her close to the edge. She wanted that so badly—those had always been her favorite scenes in her books, after all—but she was too afraid to ask for it.

"Huh? Use your words, sweetness," he encouraged, finding her clit again for a quick second.

"Never," she said in between breaths. "No one, you'd be my first."

The smile that spread across his face at her answer let her know that he liked hearing that confirmation. His hand disappeared from her sex, and she cried out at the loss of contact, until she saw him bring his hand to his mouth and rub his bottom lip, coating it with her arousal.

"Well, I think that's something we need to rectify. Because I've been dying to get my head in between your thighs and show your gorgeous little pussy just what my tongue can do," he said. "What do you say, sweetness, you want me to tongue fuck you?"

CHAPTER TWENTY-THREE

It was official, Drea couldn't breathe. Her eyes went wide and it took all she had to nod under his heated gaze. "Y-y-yes," she finally managed to choke out.

Kyle didn't need any more encouragement from her, apparently, and wasted no time in kissing his way down her body. He pulled her hips forward so she was sitting on the very edge of the bar, and when he got to her belly button, quickly dipped his tongue in and out, tickling her. She squirmed underneath him, enjoying the anticipation that was quickly growing within her. As he reached her hips, his kisses became slower and more drawn out, as he continued to tease her. The feel of his mouth on her was incredible and she felt like she could easily get lost in this feeling. His lips were warm and wet, firm and loving, and each new kiss felt like she was being branded as his.

Slowly coaxing her legs open wider, he knelt down and started to slowly run his hands up and down the insides of her thighs. The anticipation was almost too much, and if Drea had felt like she could burst before it was nothing compared to what she was feeling now. She was breathing harder and swore she could feel her pulse thrum through her entire body as if it were the waves crashing the shore.

Then out of nowhere, she felt it, his tongue against her. It was like nothing else she'd ever felt, and yet it was easily one of the best things she'd ever experienced. With a long, slow deliberateness, he licked her from the very bottom of her slit all the way to the top, just missing her clit. He circled his way back to the bottom down the right side, before repeating the motion, this time circling back down the left. She shuddered at the feeling, unable to hold it in. She shifted, trying to get him to make contact with her clit, just as she had when it was his fingers doing the work. But he was a man with a plan, and teasing her was currently on the docket. He nibbled a little on her folds and she bucked underneath him. He let out a little chuckle and continued to avoid direct contact with her clit.

"Kyle," she moaned out.

"Yes, sweetness?" he asked, somehow not letting up from the activity at hand. She panted in response. "Oh, you like that, huh? You taste so sweet, Dre, I could lick your pussy all day."

Suddenly, she felt his tongue hit her clit and it was like someone turned it up to eleven. Everything in her came alive and everything else around her came to a halt. Flicking it back and forth, up and down he focused solely on the little bundle of nerves for a solid minute. Her hands flew to the back of his head, trying to hold him there. She never wanted this feeling to end, and Kyle didn't show any signs of stopping. He slipped two fingers into her, and formed a suction on her center, sucking on her clit.

"Oh my God, I'm...I'm gonna..." she cried out, wrapping her fingers in his hair.

It was as if her words lit a fire in him, pushing him to go harder, faster. He returned to the flicking motion on her clit and that, paired with the fingers playing inside her, sent her barreling over the edge. Her back arched and her legs went rigid as the orgasm shot through her like a bullet through a gun. Her vision went black, eyes slamming closed, and she saw stars on the back of her eyelids. Kyle continued to love her with his tongue, gentler now, as she thrashed right there on the bar.

He slowly rose to his feet as she finally returned to earth. Her limbs felt like jelly and she wasn't sure she could move. No amount of reading had prepared her for what Kyle had just done to her body. His lips returned to her neck, working their way up to her jaw and then her mouth, as his hands resumed a slow caress of her sides. She sat back upright, cupping her hands around his jaw and pulling him in for a kiss. The slightly tangy taste that clung to his lips and tongue spurred her on, taking the kiss deeper and deeper with each stroke of her tongue. The idea that his tongue had just rocked her world was such a turn-on, one that she hadn't even realized could be. She wanted to return the favor, but right now, just kissing him was so much more important.

"Dre," he moaned into the kiss. "You have no idea what you do to me."

"Same."

Drea reached down between them, leaning forward slightly, finding his rock-hard length standing at attention. She grasped him firmly, slowly twisting her wrist as she moved her hand up and down. He grew harder in her hand, making her feel so powerful and full of life. All the books she'd read hadn't prepared her—she had never, ever dreamed she could feel anything like this.

This wasn't just a physical connection. She felt every-thing right now, and felt it deep into her bones. She wanted to shout out and whisper it all at the same time, feeling the words trying to force their way through the surface. She loved Kyle and there was simply no other way around it. She just hoped that he felt the same way.

"Sweetness, I need to be inside you now," he said through gritted teeth. He pulled back from her embrace, and kissed her on the forehead. "Tell me you need me too."

"Yes, please," she moaned. She hadn't intended for it to come out like she was begging, but she was so needy for him and his touch right now that it didn't seem to matter.

Kyle winked at her as he turned to reach for the bottom drawer on the top right part of the U that the bar created. It was where they kept miscellaneous odds and ends such as scissors, duct tape, rags, and at the very bottom of the drawer, Dalton's not-so-secret stash of condoms. Drea wasn't entirely sure what had prompted him to start keeping some there shortly after he started at the Indigo Royal, but she knew he did actually take advantage of the convenient hiding spot, since the box was regularly replaced.

The view of Kyle's ass as he bent over to rummage through the drawer was fantastic. She'd always liked the view of his backside and looking at it in the buff was no different. Actually, that was a lie—seeing his bare ass was much, much better than staring at it through swim trunks. She smiled to herself, thinking about all the times she'd watched him bend over through the years and how all she had wanted to do was playfully swat his butt. If there was ever a time, now was it.

Quietly slipping off the bar, she took a step or two until

she was just behind him bent over the drawer. Drawing her hand back, she let it go swiftly, her open palm meeting his bare cheek with a reasonably loud smack. He popped up, turning around and glaring at her, his eyes filled with lust rather than anger, and grabbed her by the wrists. Raising them above her head, he shook, making a tsk tsk sound with his tongue.

"Oh sweetness, you wanna play rough? We can play rough," he growled.

"Your butt was just too cute. It was begging for a little love pat," she giggled.

"Cute? Love pat?" He narrowed his eyes at her, stalking a few steps toward her, backing her up until she hit the bar again. "I think you're looking for trouble."

She shrugged, trying to play coy. The butterflies in her tummy returned as he put an arm on either side of her, pinning her in. She couldn't believe how badly she wanted him, needed him in this moment, and the look in his eyes told her that he was feeling much the same.

"Find what you need?" she asked, quirking up a brow.

His shoulders slumped and arms relaxed, as what looked like defeat took over his body. Resting his forehead to hers, he let out a sigh. "No. The box is empty. The one I grabbed for last night was apparently it."

"Oh." The discovery hit her like a brick. She didn't want to stop, she wanted to feel him inside of her, feel his hard body against hers. She'd been on the pill since she was fifteen, thanks to Simone taking over that area of teaching, but she'd never had sex without a condom before. She hadn't wanted to rely on just the pill. Nervousness flushed through her and she thought about the possibility of it now. Kyle was her forever, she was sure of it. She had to tell him.

"Sweetness, I'm so sorry, I was a dumbass for not being better prepared. I shouldn't have relied on that stash."

"I'm on the pill," she whispered.

"What?" he asked, pulling back from her quickly.

"I'm on the pill—we don't have to stop. Make love to me, Kyle."

KYLE'S HEAD SPUN, as if his head were a tether ball and her words had been a kid at recess. He couldn't believe what he was hearing. Was she really asking him to go bareback?

"Dre, are you sure?"

"More than I have ever been about anything," she said softly. "I want you to make love to me until we both can't move."

His heart leapt from his chest as he took her in—standing there, stunning in just her birthday suit, fresh off what seemed to be an earth-shattering orgasm, offering him the ultimate connection of skin-to-skin contact. He wanted to tell her right then and there that he loved her, but knew that now wasn't the time. He needed to tell her when it wouldn't come across as if it was just about sex. Pulling her close again, he wrapped his arms around her waist, until their bodies were flush against each other once again, and held her tight. Forehead to forehead, nose to nose, he breathed in her scent, just wanting to be close to her. She slipped her arms around his waist and lowered her head until it was resting under his chin.

Her forehead was now resting against his breastbone, rising and falling with each breath he took. They stayed there like that for a moment, silent, just taking each other in.

"That is, unless you don't want to," she said, not moving a muscle, so her head was still against his chest.

"I have never wanted anything more in my entire life, sweetness."

Bending slightly at the knees, he scooped her up in one swift motion. Her arms flew around his neck as she giggled again. Damn, he loved her giggles—loved how free and easy she was in letting them go, loved how the sound lit up places in him he didn't realize could light up, but more than anything he loved being the reason for the noise. Stepping into the sunlight, he made his way to the front of the boat and onto the trampoline. The bouncy surface was warm to the touch on the bottoms of his feet, so he flattened the blanket that was still there with his foot before laying Drea down on it. The blanket was warm as well, but it would be better than the trampoline fibers on her back. He wanted this moment to be perfect for her.

Once she was settled on the blanket, he lay down on his left side next to her, and began stroking her again. She reached up and cupped his face with one of her hands, grazing his cheek with her thumb. The words were bubbling up again, and he pushed them down, making himself focus on something else, anything else.

"I'm clean, I promise," he said, rushed.

"I know. I trust you," she replied. "I'm clean too."

"I've never done this," he said.

"Me either. It's a first for both of us," she smiled.

A first for both of them. The thought made his heart skip a beat. He wanted to give her the world, to make sure she was happy for the rest of time. This moment seemed like the first step in that direction.

He lowered his mouth to hers, swiping his tongue across her lower lip before taking her in a slow, sensual kiss. The hand that had been caressing up and down her side slid up to her breast and started playing with her nipples again. They pebbled under his touch, not wasting any time. She arched her back, responding to his touch. Her response fueled his semi into a now raging hard-on, as it lay across her thigh.

Drea reached across her body and found his length with her hand, grasping on to it. Jerking him slow and steady, she was making his cock harder than he ever thought possible. As she rolled slightly toward him, he removed his hand from her breast and brought it down between her legs. Still incredibly wet from her earlier orgasm, he quickly found her clit and circled it with his middle finger. She gasped into their kisses the moment he made contact, squirming underneath him. He worked his finger furiously around the bundle of nerves, sending Drea into a frenzy. He could tell the closer she got to her climax, her grip on his shaft tightened. After another moment, she pulled back from the kiss, letting go of him and grabbing onto the blanket as her orgasm overtook her entire body. Coming down from her high, she opened her eyes to find him staring at her, taking her in.

"That's not fair. I've come twice now and you haven't even come once," she said, all breathy.

"You let me worry about fair, sweetness."

Pushing himself up, he rolled over so that he was hovering over her. He nudged her legs open wide and positioned himself in between. Lining up the head of his cock at her entrance, he paused for a moment, silently verifying with her. She nodded slightly, and that was all he needed. He pushed into her, deliberately drawing out the moment of first contact. Inch by inch she took him and it was the most glorious feeling in the world. Her pussy was warm and wet and she was so tight around his cock. Without even knowing, it was like he had waited for this moment his entire life and he had no intention of doing anything but enjoying every last second. Once he was all the way in, he gave Drea a moment to adjust to him. When he was sure that she was ready, he pulled out and drove right back in again. She let out a moan of pleasure and he knew she was feeling the extra connection the lack of condom seemed to provide.

"You feel so fucking good, Drea," he whispered.

"So do you. I feel," she gasped in a breath as he thrust into her, "everything."

"Good, baby, that's exactly what I want."

He thrust into her harder, although keeping his strokes long and slow. Moving her hips as he did, she met him thrust for thrust. Every nerve ending in his body was on fire and his mind was racing with all the things he was feeling in this moment. He was finally understanding why it had been called making love. For as amazing as her insides felt encasing his dick, it was the rest of her, taking over his heart and mind, that he felt more than anything.

When she moaned out his name, breaking him from his haze, he picked up the pace. Driving into her hard and fast, he could feel the muscles of her pussy pulse and release around him, spurring him on. Just as he felt the beginning of his orgasm starting to build, Drea bucked underneath him, her pussy muscles clenching down around him like a vise grip. She screamed his name and held on to his shoulders for dear life as he continued to pound into her. Her insides continued to spasm, pulling his own climax from deep inside him.

He collapsed on top of her, breathing hard. After a while, their breaths slowed and their heart rates returned to normal, the rise and fall of their chests in sync. Ever so slowly, Kyle withdrew from inside Drea and rolled over onto his back, pulling her into his side as he did.

"That was incredible," he said, breaking the silence. "You, Dre, are incredible."

CHAPTER TWENTY-FOUR

THE REST of the afternoon passed quickly, with the two of them lounging around in the sun, making love some more, and just generally enjoying their time alone. Drea had a hard time wrapping her head around how so much had happened in such a short period of time. It felt like they had been away for months, rather than just an overnight. The whole weekend had been a dream come true, but there was still a part of her that was happy to be home. If nothing else, it would be nice not to sleep on the trampoline.

As they docked the boat and made sure they had all their stuff packed up, they heard a familiar voice coming from the pier. Drea looked up over the front of the boat to find Grayson hanging off the back of the *Livin' On A Prayer,* lying on his front, hands covered in grease.

"Hey kids, how was your weekend away?" he asked, wiping his hands on a rag.

"It was fantastic," Drea said, her face lighting up. She tried to keep her smile from taking over her face, but she was pretty sure she was failing.

"It was nice to step away from the resort a bit," Kyle added.

"Good, you guys deserve the break. You'll be happy to know, Dalton didn't burn the place down," he said jokingly. "Drea, Miller was just asking me if I had any idea when you'd be back. I think maybe he was hoping to snag you for dinner."

"Oh, okay, I'll go hunt him down. Night, Uncle Gray!"

They made their way down the pier toward the resort, walking side by side, careful not to touch. Drea wanted to hold on to his hand so badly she could taste it, but she knew that even contact as simple as that wouldn't be enough. She respected Kyle's desire to keep their relationship to just them for the time being, even if she wanted to skip all over the resort and tell everyone.

When they got to her door, she felt a sudden sadness come over her. They hadn't discussed where they would be staying tonight, and while in her mind she had been assuming that they would stay here, it occurred to her at this moment that they hadn't actually had a real conversation about it. She'd gotten so used to him just being right there these last couple of nights that the idea of sleeping without him left her feeling hollow.

"Did you wanna come with me to find Uncle Miller?" she asked, feeling very self-conscious about the whole thing.

"It's Sunday night. I have my call with my mom, which I should probably do from my room," he answered.

"Oh, okay."

"But once that is done, I can come back over if you'd like. I'd invite you to my place, but there are way too many eyes in the staff dorm that could see you leave tomorrow."

She laughed quietly, "Good point, and yes, I would love it if you came over later."

He looked around quickly to make sure no one else was nearby, and when he saw the coast was clear, he leaned in and kissed her. She popped up on her tiptoes, trying to draw in closer to him. Even after spending all weekend kissing him, she hadn't had enough. She doubted that she'd ever get enough of kissing him.

When they finally pulled away, she opened her door and started to walk through, only to turn around to watch him walk away. He blew her a kiss as he approached the trees and then was gone.

KYLE HATED WALKING AWAY from Drea after the amazing weekend they'd had. If anything, what he really wanted to do was drag her out back and curl up with her in the hammock again. It would sound weird to anyone else, he knew that, but he felt the loss of her when she wasn't within a few feet of him. But he needed to grab some food and call his mom, just like he did every Sunday night.

Making his way into the kitchen, he was almost plowed over by a waiter who was struggling with an overfilled tray. He apologized to the kid, hoping that everything on that tray made it to the table in the dining room. Making a mental note to leave via the alleyway, he crossed the kitchen until he was standing next to the family table.

"Kyle, my man! You guys are back," Miller said, walking up and giving him a side hug.

"Yeah, we just got back. Drea should be making her way over in a bit, but I've got my weekly call with my mom, so I was hoping to grab some scraps or something," Kyle said, returning the gesture.

"I'm not feeding you scraps—sit. How about a grilled cheese and some chips?"

"Sure, but please don't go out of your way."

"I'll do what I want, young man, sit," Miller answered, pointing a knife at the chair behind Kyle.

Kyle did as he was told, watching the older man prep two slices of bread and place them on the griddle.

"How'd things turn out with that girl of yours?" Miller asked.

"What?" Kyle asked, caught off guard.

"Last week, you were all tied up in knots. I take it by the smile on your face that things worked themselves out?"

"Indeed they did, sir."

"Good. Well, you continue to put that smile on her face, then I don't know that I'll have much of a job left."

"Come again?" He couldn't believe what he was hearing. Did Miller know? There was no way. Drea had said Miller would be understanding, but she would have said something had she actually told him. Maybe it was just a lucky guess. Or maybe even a stab in the dark. Miller saw all sorts of female employees on a daily basis—maybe someone else had an extra bright smile recently and Miller thought he'd put two and two together.

"I'm not saying things are always gonna be easy, or sunshine and roses, but I can tell that it's a deep down, soul-reaching happiness, and that makes every last bit of it worth it." Miller slid a spatula under the grilled cheese and flipped it into a to-go container.

"I don't know what to say to that," Kyle responded, still confused by Miller's commentary.

"Just promise me you won't be a dumbass and that you'll cherish every moment," he said, handing the to-go container to Kyle. Kyle took the box from him and smiled.

"That I will, Miller. I promise."

THE HEAVY DOOR to his room made a loud bang as it swung open and hit the wall behind it. Kyle hadn't meant to open it with that much force—he just hoped that whoever was currently living next door wasn't home. He threw the duffle he'd been carrying on the bed, before crashing down on it himself.

He thought about his conversation with Miller as he bit into the sandwich he brought back. The warm cheese oozed out from the bread, requiring him to take another quick bite to avoid a mess. *Kind of like how Miller just oozes wisdom sometimes*, Kyle thought. He laughed at the thought, but was thankful for the words and sentiment that Miller passed his way earlier. Regardless of whether he actually knew the woman in question was Drea or if he was just speaking in general, it was a comforting feeling to know that someone other than his mother had his best interests at heart.

He hadn't felt this kind of connection with another man since losing Mr. Willett when he was in college. Even in his late forties, Miller was significantly younger than Mr. Willett had been when he and Kyle started hanging out, but the two men still shared the same innate ability to see right through to what other people were feeling. Neither man had a problem calling people out on it either, but managed to do it in a gentle way that left you feeling cared about in the end.

Finishing up his sandwich, he looked down at his phone. It was eight twenty, a full five minutes after his mother was supposed to call. She always managed to call at eight fifteen, seven fifteen her time, right on the dot, every

Sunday. Worried something was wrong, he pulled up her contact info and hit the call button. The phone rang a couple of times before a tired sounding voice answered.

"Hi, baby. To what do I owe the honor?"

"It's Sunday night, Mom."

"Oh goodness, it is! Is it that late already? Oh my, where did the day go?"

"Is everything okay, Mom?"

"Of course it is! I just lost track of time, that's all. How are you, Kyle?"

"I'm good. Just got back from San Juan with Drea."

"Oh, did you guys have a weekend off? That must have been nice. What'd you do while you were there?"

"It was great—it was really nice to just get away from the resort for a bit, actually. The guests were crazy last week, so when Grayson offered us the cat for the weekend, we took it. We didn't really go with an agenda in mind," he answered, trying to figure out where the line was in sharing with his mom. "But we walked around a bunch. Drea showed me the church where her parents got married."

"Wow. That must have been very special."

"It was."

"Kyle, you know I try very hard to just let you live your life without commentary from your mother, but," she said, pausing and taking a deep breath, "if a woman is showing you a piece of her history like this, she is trying to tell you something."

Kyle rolled his eyes and let out a little laugh. She had a point—she was pretty good at letting him live his own life. She'd helped him along the way when he asked for her opinion, like in choosing a college, but overall she stayed out of it. When he'd come home with the job offer from Grayson and told her he was thinking of accepting, the only response she had given him was "when can I come visit?" For her to be slipping in her opinion now meant something; it also meant she'd been thinking about it for a long time.

"Just how long have you been holding back an opinion about me and Drea?" he asked her.

"Since just about my first visit down there," she said with a yawn. "The two of you look at each other like Romeo and Juliet."

"Mom, are you okay? You sound off."

"I'm fine, just a little tired," she answered, dismissing his concern. "Now, are you going to officially confirm my suspicions?"

"We're," he paused. Was it fair to tell his mom when he had asked Drea to keep it from her uncles? "We're testing the waters."

"Well, fine, be coy," she yawned again,

"Really, Mom, are you sure you're okay?"

"Yes, yes. Really, I'm just tired, I promise."

"You'd tell me if something were wrong though, right? You're taking your meds and all that?"

"Kyle, who is the parent here? I told you I'm fine. Now, if you just got home you must be exhausted, and I could certainly use a good night's sleep. So, how about we just catch up later this week?"

"Sounds good, Mom," he said. "Love you."

"Love you, too, baby,"

He ended the call and slumped back on the bed. It concerned him to hear her sound so tired, but he trusted that she knew herself well enough to know that she just needed some extra sleep. She'd never been one to not take care of herself, so maybe his concern was for naught.

Grabbing his phone again he sent a text to Drea saying to let him know when she wanted him to head that way. He wanted to make sure she had enough time with her uncle. After hearing more of the family history this weekend he realized just what role each one of them played in her life and he wouldn't dare take away from that.

Her reply came almost instantly, telling him she was heading to see Miller, and that she needed to find Simone about wedding stuff, but she should be home in about an hour and she'd see him then. He felt like this could be the longest sixty minutes of his life.

AFTER DROPPING her stuff off inside the cottage, taking a quick rinse-off shower, and changing into a clean sundress, Drea made her way to the resort's kitchen. She opted for what she considered the long route, walking through the main lobby of the resort, stopping for a moment to take in the space. In her head, she could see it all so clearly, how they could redesign the lobby to house an entrance to the spa. It would lead off the little hallway that currently led to the office, but instead it would just veer to the right, before it reached the employees-only area.

The long hall entrance would be dimly lit, with soft lights highlighting the jewel-toned walls, and the sounds of a water feature luring guests toward the spa desk. Once checked in, they would be led to locker rooms where they could change before stepping into the luxury waiting room, complete with plush couches and instrumental music. She could see the treatment rooms, saunas, and pools all mapped out as well. It was easy to picture guests lounging about, relaxing and taking in the beauty of the view from the resort.

She loved the idea of creating a menu of services and

finding the best staff to come and make this dream of hers a reality. It would do so much for the resort to offer something like this, not only for their guests, but if it were open to the public they could take advantage of some of the vacation rental traffic as well. The increase of vacation rentals had been a major topic of conversation between her uncles and Simone the last couple of years, and while Vaughn wasn't sure it was hurting their bottom line too badly, Drea knew that something like the spa could really go a long way to opening up new lines of revenue.

Finally tearing herself away from the lobby, she made her way through the dining room and into the kitchen. True to form, Miller was flitting about the kitchen, throwing things in pots and pans, oblivious to the world around him. One of his kitchen assistants caught her eye as he dodged her uncle, just trying to keep up with his erratic movements. She shook her head, laughing to herself as she watched the scene. She felt bad for the kid on some level, but on another, she was aware that Miller knew himself and his behaviors well enough that the position of kitchen assistant paid accordingly. Another moment or so later, Miller looked up to find her standing there.

"Hey there, baby girl. I just made Kyle a grilled cheese to go. You want one too?" Miller asked.

"I'd love one, but mine can be for here."

"You want the works?"

"Yes, please."

"Just the way your mom and aunt would have liked it! One grilled cheese with bacon and tomato coming right up!" he said, reaching for a loaf of bread.

The kitchen assistant who had been scurrying around Miller a moment ago appeared by her side with a small basket of Miller's hand-cut kettle chips. Just the sight of them made Drea's stomach growl—she was hungrier than she realized. Grabbing the basket from him, she thanked the kid and made her way over to the family table, turning in the chair to still face her uncle.

"Wow, kettle chips? You went all out for Kyle," she remarked sarcastically.

"Not really, I was teaching Mikey here how to make them," he said, indicating the kid who had given them to her with a tilt of his head. "So naturally, we were left with a whole bunch."

"Job well done, Mikey," she said, holding up a chip.

The young kid blushed slightly at the attention, quickly scampering away as soon as he had the chance. She snacked away at the chips, watching her uncle work his magic with the griddle.

"Uncle Miller, can I ask you something?"

"Of course, baby girl."

"How did you know Aunt Marta was the one?"

Miller looked up from the griddle, sighing. "I'm gonna guess that 'I just knew' isn't really going to be an acceptable answer, huh?"

"I mean, if that's the answer," she paused. "Do you remember the moment you just knew?"

"Now that," he said, pointing the spatula he was using at her, "is a much easier answer."

He flipped the sandwich a couple of times and grabbed a plate and slid the sandwich onto it. Bringing it over to the table, he set it before her. He grabbed the chair next to her and flipped it around, straddling the back.

"It was the day after we crashed that party where we met Marta and Sofia. We were in Old San Juan, and your dad and mom had run away to go spend time alone, which was more than okay by us. We walked down to the big gate and walked along the shore there. Marta found a coin on the ground, a penny or something, and she held it up, told me to kiss it and make a wish. I thought she was insane. I was not kissing money, which is dirty to begin with, much less money that had been on the ground and stepped on by God knows who. But she was the prettiest damn thing I had ever seen, and please remember I was twenty-one; I was not always the most gentlemanly, so I was thinking about getting laid. So I kissed the penny, made a wish, and she tossed it into the water."

"What did you wish for?" Drea asked, taking a bite of her grilled cheese.

"That I would get in her pants."

"Uncle Miller, you did not!"

"I did. I told you I was not the gentleman I am now," he fessed up, holding his hands up in surrender.

"So, then what happened?"

"It was a magical moment, she said so herself, so I took it upon myself to up the magic and went in for a kiss. Except somehow I slipped on the rock I was standing on, and fell into the water," he said, pausing for dramatic effect. Drea burst out laughing, and Miller just shook his head. "That right there is pretty much the exact reaction Marta had. She pulled me out, and for some reason happened to have a pair of sweatpants in her backpack, so I swapped out my very wet shorts for those. After I changed, she looked at me and said, 'You know, Miller, if you wanted into my pants so bad, you could have just asked.'"

Drea stopped midbite, not believing what she was hearing. "Seriously?"

"Seriously. Your aunt had the most amazing sense of humor, kiddo. And that was it, that was when I knew."

"Because she made a bad joke?"

"No one said love was always sparkles and glitter, baby girl. There are those moments—watching Marta walk down that aisle toward me was certainly one of them—but most of the time it's bad jokes, grilled cheese sandwiches, and just being content in one another. And when you find the person you want to spend your life making bad jokes with, or whatever your thing is, it's like life takes on a whole new meaning."

Drea just nodded her response. She thought about the weekend she'd just had with Kyle, and how much she loved being out on the water with him. They'd always had the view of 'life's an adventure' in common, whether it was the adventure of the open waters, trying a new food, or even just making it through a tour with a set of guests that were a little unruly. There was no one else she wanted to go through an adventure with other than him.

"What makes you ask, baby girl?" Miller inquired.

"I took Kyle to Iglesia San Francisco while we were in San Juan this weekend, and told him the story of the weddings. I knew Mom's side of things from her journal, but started to wonder about yours."

"Well, if Kyle doesn't think we're a family of nutters after all that, then he's more of a keeper than I realized."

CHAPTER TWENTY-FIVE

The next two days went by without any major fanfare or incident. Monday morning met them the same way it always did, completely oblivious to the perfect little world they'd been in, and full of real-life responsibilities. The resort was sold out again this week, and there had been enough interest in sailing tours that they were scheduled for doubleheaders on both Monday and Tuesday, keeping everyone moving at light speed.

As much as Drea loved being busy, two tours a day meant that there was no breathing room, much less time to do anything more than steal a glance or two at Kyle as they moved around the boat helping guests. There were so many moments when Drea wanted to kiss him as they passed, or reach out and squeeze his hand, but she stopped herself, trying not to call attention to them.

When Tuesday evening finally arrived, she was so tired it was all she could do not to collapse on the boat. Walking to the front of the boat, she found Kyle and Dalton sitting on the trampoline, each one with a beer in hand.

"Where did you find those?" she asked, sitting down

next to Kyle. He handed her his and she took a sip. It had started to warm from being in his hand, but still tasted okay.

"Down in the backup fridge on the lower deck. I'll go grab you one if you want," Dalton answered.

"No, I'm good," she said, taking one more sip of Kyle's before handing it back to him. She lay down and rested her head in his lap, before curling up like she was going to take a nap.

"Tired there, sweetness?"

"Exhausted. I could go to sleep right here."

"Nope, not allowed," Dalton said, popping up and heading toward the bar. "It's bonfire night!"

"What has you all excited about the bonfire?" Kyle asked.

"For your information, there was a fiery little redhead from this morning's tour I'd like to track down," he called out.

Kyle rolled his eyes, looking down at Drea, and she just giggled in return. Some things never changed. They heard the opening and closing of drawers, and Dalton suddenly appeared from around the bar.

"You two got something you want to tell me?"

Drea sat up quickly and looked at Kyle with wide eyes. It hadn't occurred to her that they would need to replenish the stash. Panic must have been written all over her face, because Kyle just smiled at her, raising one finger to his lips vertically, telling her not to say anything, before leaning in and kissing her. His lips felt so good against hers, and if she hadn't known any better she would have thought it'd been days since they kissed rather than just this morning.

"Sorry, dude, I owe you," Kyle said, pulling away from Drea. "I do need to know one thing, though."

"No, I've never actually screwed anyone on the boat.

CAN'T FIGHT THIS FEELING   241

Which is apparently more than you two can say," he called out jokingly as he walked closer to them, adding a wink in. "The boathouse, however..."

"Not where I was going with this, but that's good to know. What I do want to know is, just how do you know my girlfriend's size?"

Drea blushed hearing Kyle use the term girlfriend. She liked the way it sounded on his lips and really liked knowing it was referring to her. It felt good to be open about it, even if it was just Dalton they were talking to.

"Oh, that's easy. Leona."

THEY WALKED through the woods toward the lobby to meet her family about as close as they could without touching. Every couple of steps or so, the backs of their hands would brush against each other and the slight contact sent a zing of excitement through Drea. She was already more excited than she figured she should be for Kyle to join in on the bets tonight, but attempting to keep a secret from her family had her buzzing.

Miller was leaning against the same pillar as always waiting for everyone else to arrive. He was always the first one there, no matter what. It was one of the things Drea had come to count on—didn't matter how early she was, he'd be standing there waiting on her on Tuesday nights. The smile that spread across his face when he saw the two of them approaching warmed her heart. That wasn't just any smile, that was his 'everything is right in this moment' smile.

"You ready for this, Kyle?" Miller asked, turning toward them.

"I think so."

"Drea prepped you on how it works?"

"Yup, and I think I know what I'm going with."

"Man comes prepared," Miller remarked, turning toward Drea. "Think he has what it takes to avoid the shirt?"

"He won't tell me his guess, so I guess we'll see," she said, shrugging.

"Who won't tell?" Grayson asked, coming up behind them.

"Well, look who showed up on time!" Miller roared.

"Shut it," Grayson responded, flipping his brother the bird.

Just as Miller was blowing Grayson a kiss in response, Vaughn and Simone came rushing up to the group. Simone was straightening out her skirt, and her lipstick was slightly smeared. Drea managed to catch her eye and motion to her to wipe her lip. Simone quickly did so, mouthing "thanks" to Drea in response.

"Too busy snogging in your office?" Grayson snarked.

"Please, our niece is present," Vaughn said.

"Vaughn, she knows what snogging is. She doesn't live under a rock," Miller interjected.

"And she was the one just now to let Simone know her lipstick was smudged," Grayson added. "You're still wearing some of that lovely color yourself." He reached over to jokingly try and rub it off his brother's face.

"Still, no need to be uncouth," he replied, swatting his brother's arm away.

Drea turned to Kyle and rolled her eyes. This is exactly what she had been talking about on the boat. It didn't matter how old she got, she was to remain under the impression that her uncles were monks. Maybe someday she'd let Vaughn know that most of what she'd learned about sex as a teenager had come from his bride-to-be.

"Anyway," Vaughn said, desperately trying to change the subject. "Everyone ready?"

The group nodded, but no one spoke up with their contribution.

"Age before beauty, so Vaughn, you're up!" Grayson said.

"Fine. The old guy in room 531, you'll know him by his ill-fitting toupee and blindingly bright tropical-themed shirt, will manage to hit on everyone here under the age of thirty by nine pm. So Drea, watch out."

"Should I see him coming, I'll just start making out with Kyle," Drea said, trying to make it sound like a joke.

"No!" Vaughn shouted right as Grayson turned to high-five Kyle. "Don't encourage that," he threw in, glaring at Grayson.

"Give it a rest, Vaughn, she was making a joke," Simone said, before turning to Drea. "Although at this point I'll give you fifty bucks to do it if you see your uncle coming, just to give him a heart attack." She reached out and high-fived Drea.

"Continuing on, Grayson?" Vaughn said, trying to change the subject again.

"I'm sticking with a staff hookup. May have failed me last week, but not two weeks in a row."

"How very original!" Simone said sarcastically. "My money's on the elderly lady with the knitting needles following Dalton around all night trying to see if she can stick him with one of those needles."

"The little redhead that is here celebrating her twenty-first with her parents? She can't hold her booze as well as she thinks she can, so I say we're gonna have a puker on our hands," Drea added.

"Well, before she pukes, her dad is going to try to give a

really embarrassing birthday speech, not that anyone around will pay him any attention," Miller threw out there. "Kyle, you're up, son."

"Well, for my first submission, I contend that at least one of the women here for the divorce party will strip down to nothing and run for the water. But I'm pretty sure once one does it, they'll all follow suit."

"Good one," Grayson said, high-fiving Kyle again. "You're a natural already!"

"Great, then we'll see everyone for breakfast!" Simone called out, pulling Vaughn away, back toward his office.

Drea shook her head, laughing at Simone, understanding exactly how she was feeling. It was taking everything in her not to do the same with Kyle. If it wasn't for the fact that she'd promised Leona they'd all hang out together at the bonfire, she'd be tempted to try it. She waited until the rest of her family walked away before turning to him, squinting her eyes in curiosity.

"Skinny-dipping, huh?" she asked, walking up to him until their bodies were all but touching.

"What can I say? I had a fantastic muse this past weekend," he answered, winking at her.

SOMEHOW THE BONFIRE seemed bigger tonight. Kyle knew that wasn't possible, yet the more and more he looked at it, the bigger and brighter it seemed. Maybe it was just that all was right with the world as he and Drea made their way to find their friends at the weekly event. They weaved in and out of the crowd of guests, stopping briefly at the bar, before finally finding Leona and Dalton on the far side of the bonfire patio. The two of them were sitting in the new sling beach chairs that Drea and Simone picked out earlier this year, sipping bushwackers.

"Oh, gimme," Drea said, reaching out for Leona's drink.

Leona handed it to her, swapping it out for the margarita that Drea was holding. Looking around, Kyle found a chaise lounge and pulled it up so it was in line with the beach chairs their friends were sitting in. Plopping down with a thud, he sat all the way back, with the lounger's back mostly upright, before pulling Drea down to sit in his lap. She let out a little noise as he grabbed her by the hips, trying to make sure not to spill the drink in her hand.

"Are we not hiding from the uncles tonight?" Leona asked, watching Drea as she settled in on the lounger.

"I'm protecting her from the creeper in 531," Kyle answered.

"There's a creeper in 531?" Leona followed up.

"According to Uncle Vaughn there is," Drea told her. "He bet on this dude hitting on all of us tonight, so if you see someone in a bad toupee, grab on to Carlos or someone."

"Ugh, Carlos can kiss my ass."

"I'm pretty sure he got tired of that, Lee," Dalton interjected.

"Bite me, Dalton."

"Memory recalls you really enjoyed when I did that."

Kyle just about spit out the beer he'd been sipping on. Ever since Drea confirmed these two had actually hooked up, and that Dalton's comments like this weren't conjecture, he found the level of cheek between the two of them even funnier.

"Do I dare ask what Carlos did now?" Drea asked.

"So, I got a list of demands, I mean, 'requests,' from my favorite guest for his stay in a couple of months," Leona started. "And I made a comment about how that's my least favorite two weeks of the year, because nothing is *ever* good enough for that man. And Carlos has the balls to go and say he is one of the best players to ever play the game."

"That's because Cullen Cruz *is* one of the best players to ever play the game," Kyle said. Drea jabbed her elbow back quickly, nailing him right in the rib. "Ow."

"Whatever, he's not Ronald or whatever his name is."

"Ronaldo," Dalton and Kyle said in unison.

"Now he's pretty," Drea said, tipping her drink toward Leona.

"I'm going to pretend you didn't just call arguably the greatest footballer of all time 'pretty.' And by the way, Lee, arguments against CR7 being the best ever usually involve your boy toy, Cruz," Dalton threw out. "Now, if you'll excuse me, there is a birthday girl over there who I'd like to offer my birthday suit to."

"Whatever, and he's not my boy toy. He can 'bugger off' as he would say," Leona said, trying to mimic a British accent, as Dalton got up and walked toward the redhead he mentioned earlier. "So, you two—happy as clams?"

"For as happy as shellfish can be," Drea said laughing. "That phrase has never made any sense to me."

"That's because it got shortened. The whole thing is 'happy as a clam at high tide,' which is when clams would be protected from predators, so naturally, a happy time for them," Kyle answered.

"How do you know that?" Drea asked, turning slightly in his lap to look at him.

"Mr. Willett, of course. He was a very wise old man."

"You sound like Miller," Leona said. "Speaking of which, there were some lightbulbs out in the kitchen. I should go see if those got replaced. See you tomorrow?" She pushed herself out of the chair and Drea nodded to her that they'd meet up after breakfast.

"Didn't she just say she was mad at him?" Kyle asked, watching her round the bonfire heading toward the lobby.

"According to Leona, angry sex is the best sex," Drea answered, taking Kyle's arms and wrapping them around her, allowing her to snuggle into him.

"I'll file that away under things I never needed to know."

SHORTLY AFTER LEONA went to tend to her concern over light bulbs, the father of the redheaded object of Dalton's attention stood, tapped on his glass, and tried to get the attention of those around him. While he managed to get a couple of glances, most of those around him paid him no mind. This, however, did not stop the man from trying to hold court and perform what seemed to be a rehearsed monologue. The redhead had been chugging something that appeared fruity and tropical since they arrived and about what Kyle assumed was halfway through her dad's "speech," started to wretch and ran off.

"Looks like you don't have to wear the shirt tomorrow," Kyle commented, whispering into Drea's ear.

"Yes!" she whispered in return, shaking her fist in triumph.

They sat in silence for a long while, just the two of them curled up, watching the fire and the party that surrounded it. Kyle was a little surprised that no one bothered them over the course of the evening. In fact, they hadn't so much as seen a glimpse of her uncles. Part of him thought maybe that should worry him, but a much bigger part was enjoying the freedom even more.

Right before Kyle was about to suggest they head in for the night, they heard a female voice yell "yee-haw!" Looking over toward the beach, they found the divorce party, circled around the guest of honor as she stripped down and started to twerk. No sooner had she returned to a fully upright position than she was taking off for the water. All but one of her friends joined in, slipping out of their shirts and shorts with ease and making a run for it. The one left behind just shook her head and started to pick up the clothing left behind.

"He shoots, he scores!" Kyle said, squeezing Drea in closer.

Drea giggled as he did so and Kyle's insides lit up at the sound. Seriously, it was the greatest thing he'd ever heard. Trying to keep it from stopping, he reached down and tickled her sides lightly. Her reaction was exactly what he had hoped for, a burst of more giggles and some squirming from her, which set him off laughing as well.

"You did that on purpose," she said in between gasps of air.

"Sure did, sweetness. Your giggle is easily the best sound there is. I could listen to it all day."

"You could not."

"Could too. 'With mirth and laughter, let old wrinkles come,'" he recited.

"Wow, that's poetic."

Kyle laughed. "Should be, it's Shakespeare. Kinda what he was known for."

"You just happen to have random Shakespeare passages floating around in your head?"

He knew the quote like the back of his hand, since his mother had a framed art print of it hanging in the living room at home. He hadn't counted on Drea not recognizing it—he'd always just assumed it was a quote that everyone knew. "Mom has that hanging in the living room, so I saw it every day of my life. But I did have to memorize a sonnet in twelfth grade English," he noted.

"Yeah? Do you still remember it?" she asked.

Kyle froze. He did still remember it. Filed away in his head, like old song lyrics, he still knew every word to sonnet number twenty-three, like he'd had to recite it to the class only yesterday. He remembered why he chose it too. Mr. Willet had helped him pick it out and helped him rehearse it, telling him stories about how he understood exactly what Shakespeare was talking about. That when he'd met his wife he was so taken with her that he had frozen, just like an actor who had forgotten his lines. Kyle remembered wondering if he'd ever find a woman who did that to him. Giving Drea a little squeeze, he realized he *had* found a woman who did that to him. A woman he loved like that. But he couldn't bust out that sonnet right now, confess such an emotion. He'd tell her soon. This just was not the time and place to say those words for the first time.

"Shall I compare thee to a summer's day..." he said, jokingly.

"You did not choose that one. I know you better than that!"

"No, but it was a good line. I thought I could try it out, be romantic."

"Awww, you succeeded," she said, turning and kissing him on the cheek. "I think I could get used to this, just me and you, curled up at the bonfire."

"Me too, sweetness, me too."

CHAPTER TWENTY-SIX

THE SOUND of water running greeted Kyle as he rolled over in Drea's bed, finding her side empty. A quick look at the little clock she kept on her nightstand let him know that it was late enough that she'd already been for her run and was getting ready for the day. A feeling of contentment washed over him as he lay there, listening to the sounds that wafted out of the bathroom. Last night could not have been better had he scripted it. They'd been left alone by pretty much everyone, staff and guests alike. Even the rest of her family hadn't made an appearance after the bets were taken. After the divorce party decided to go for a late-night dip au naturel, and Dalton had nearly been puked on, Kyle and Drea had snuck away, back to her cottage. Despite her protestations that she'd gotten a second wind, Drea had fallen asleep the moment her head hit the pillow.

Her bed was incredibly soft and comfortable, the kind of place you could easily cocoon yourself in for days. However, the idea of joining her in the shower beat out thoughts of falling back asleep. Throwing the covers off himself, Kyle got out of bed and slipped into the bathroom as quietly as he could. Knowing Drea wouldn't expect him up quite yet, he undressed and slowly pulled back the shower curtain just enough to slip into the shower with her. She let out a little yelp of surprise as he did so, turning around so the water cascaded onto her back and her front pressed up against his.

Her warm, wet skin felt good against his, and he could feel her nipples reacting to the chill from no longer being under the warm water, sending all the blood rushing to his groin. He could feel himself getting harder by the second, and he was sure she could too. By the looks of her wide eyes growing dark and the mischievous grin on her face, she could more than feel it.

"Well, hello there," she said, reaching down in between them, grasping onto his shaft.

"Good morning, sweetness," he responded, leaning down, capturing her lips in his for a kiss. "Need help soaping up?"

Spinning back around, facing into the water, she wiggled her hips toward him. "My back could use some attention."

The shower gel she had in there smelled of citrus, matching her shampoo, as he squeezed some out onto his hands, lathering up. He massaged some into her back briefly, before bringing his hands around to her front, finding her breasts, and pinching her nipples. She let out a moan as he continued. Reaching behind her, she found his cock again, stroking it long and slow.

"Like what you found?" he asked, low and husky.

"Very, very much."

They spent the rest of their morning shower stroking and caressing, until they both were in a state that required them to shower for real. Each taking a turn under the hot water and trying to not freeze while it was the other's turn, they laughed and joked about all the things that happened at the bonfire. When they finally got out of the shower, one look at the clock told them they needed to speed up their routine if they were going to make breakfast on time.

Rushing through the lobby, Kyle held on to Drea's hand tightly, leading the way around guests and staff members. A couple of dirty looks from wait staff in the dining room later, they made their way into the kitchen, both laughing from the wild ride of a morning.

Everyone but Grayson was in the kitchen, sitting down at the table. Vaughn and Simone were both focused on their phones, while Miller sat hiding behind the morning paper. Kyle knew it was him simply by the weird way he folded it. They grabbed the two seats in between Miller and Simone, grabbing cups for coffee as Grayson slid in the back door from the alley.

"Gray, you'll be happy to hear that some light bulbs seem to have been replaced in the kitchen last night. So, you appear to be saved from the shirt," Miller said, putting the paper down and passing a coffee mug to his brother.

"Am I the only one who was in the dark about that reference?" Kyle asked Drea. "Pun not intended."

"I think so," she answered.

"Kyle, congrats, my man, you nailed the skinny-dipping divorcées," Grayson said, holding out a fist to Kyle. Kyle reached out and bumped, feeling pretty proud of himself.

"Excuse you, I called the puker!" Drea exhaled.

"Yes, you did, baby girl," Miller said. "And she puked during her dad's attempt at a speech if I'm correct."

"She sure did," Grayson muttered, shivering from the thought of the amount of vomit the moment resulted in.

"Speaking of, whoever had the distinct pleasure of cleaning that up deserves a bonus this month."

"So, it comes down to knitting needles and the creeper in 531," Miller said.

"I saw Mr. 531 making his rounds, and I did not see a single knitting needle," Vaughn interjected.

"But you said he'd hit on everyone under thirty, and he did not make it to every last person under the age of thirty. Drea, did you encounter 531?" Simone asked.

"Nope, he didn't say a single word to me all night."

"Me either," Kyle interjected. This was met with another fist bump from Grayson.

"But there were no knitting needles either, so some encounters overrules no needles," Vaughn argued.

"Does not!" Simone argued back.

"Well, Simone, consider it an early wedding gift," Grayson said, digging into his pocket for a moment before pulling out his cell phone. "But I texted Dalton and asked if he happened to see grandma last night, and sure enough." He held out his phone to show her and Vaughn.

Grayson: Hey, did you happen to see that older lady with the knitting needles at the bonfire last night?
Dalton: Sure did man! As I was making my exit from that redhead who was puking her guts up, she stabbed me with one of those things! Fucking thing hurt like a bitch...
Dalton: Why, was there an issue?
Grayson: Nope, just wondering. Thanks man.

"YES!" Simone shouted. She did a little dance in her chair, only annoying her fiancé further.

"You paid him to say that, didn't you?" Vaughn asked.

"How would I have done that? You can see the trail of texts!"

"You sure?"

"You want to text him to ask?"

"Damn it!" Vaughn smacked the table.

"Don't worry, bro, I washed it for you," Grayson said, rubbing it in.

"Sorry, Uncle Vaughn," Drea commented.

Vaughn continued to grumble about having to wear the shirt as they all dug into breakfast. This was the most food Kyle had ever seen at breakfast. Maybe it was because of the extra body, or maybe Kyle had just never attended a full Wednesday breakfast to know how much food they started out with. The only thing that seemed to be missing was Miller's infamous magic muffins, and Kyle would bet that if he asked, some could make an appearance.

Other than Vaughn's protestations that the text shouldn't count as proof, the conversation flowed easily, the uncles treating Kyle as if he'd always participated in this ritual, and no one seemed to be any the wiser to what he and Drea were hiding. It was a relief to not feel on edge about their secret, and he wondered if Drea was feeling the same way. She was much more relaxed than she had been the last time they were at this table for a family meal, which was a huge relief.

"Oh, before I forget," Vaughn said. "The lawyer will be here Friday morning to add Simone's name to all the Indigo Royal paperwork. Don't worry, it's only my portion she'll have access to, we're not dividing it into fifths all of a sudden. Drea, I assume you won't have any tours Friday? So you can be here to meet with the lawyer at ten?"

"Why do I have to be there?" Drea asked, confused.

The conversation came to a halt and silence filled the

table. The only noise that seemed to penetrate the silence was Grayson slowly putting his coffee mug back down on the table. The kitchen staff buzzed around them, yet nobody at the table moved. Kyle slid his gaze between each one of the men sitting at the table. All three had unreadable expressions on their faces, yet seemed to know exactly what the others were thinking.

"Miller, did you not tell her?" Vaughn asked sternly.

"May have slipped my mind."

"How have you not told her?" Grayson asked.

"We agreed you'd tell her when she turned twenty-one," Vaughn added.

"And I guess I forgot," Miller responded.

"Tell me what?" Drea asked, confused, looking between each uncle for some kind of answer.

"So all this time she's been working for me on the boats, she's had no idea?" Grayson clarified.

"Forgot? That's not something you just forget," Vaughn ground out. "Five years, man. It's been five years. You mean to tell me it hasn't come up once?"

"Miller, you promised!" Simone interjected. "Right after we fixed up the cottage for her. That was part of the point of giving her the cottage!"

"Tell me what?!" Drea asked again.

Her question was met with more silence and uncomfortable glances between her uncles.

"Tell her," Simone said through gritted teeth. "Or I will. And it needs to come from you three."

"We're all equal partners in this resort," Vaughn said.

"Right, the three of you," Drea said.

"No, kiddo, the ownership of the Indigo Royal Resort is in four parts," Grayson added. There was silence for a moment, all of them letting the weight of those words sink in.

Miller finally broke the silence. "You're the fourth owner, baby girl."

DREA'S HEAD WAS SPINNING. No, maybe that was the room. Either way, she suddenly felt dizzy and like everything around her was chaos. She couldn't have heard him correctly. The Indigo Royal was divided into fourths? She was the fourth partner? The only way that could have been was if she'd inherited it when her parents passed, but they didn't have a financial interest in the resort. She knew the story of the resort; her uncles bought it from a friend of their grandfather after their father passed away from cancer, using the money they had inherited from his estate. Her dad was just along for the ride as Miller's best friend, helping them with the restoration.

"What? I'm what?" she sputtered out.

"You're the fourth partner in the Indigo Royal Resort," Vaughn said calmly.

"How? I don't understand. It's a Quinlan Family Resort. I'm not a Quinlan, I'm a Miller."

"You'll actually find that all the legal paperwork says Quinlan-Miller Investments, LLC, dba Quinlan-Miller Family Properties. But we left that off the marketing material since you were underage and we were trying to protect your interests."

"What? How?" she sputtered again. She felt like a broken record, just repeating the same words over and over, but every one of their answers only confused her more. She reached under the table and grabbed Kyle's hand. "You three bought the resort with your inheritance, didn't you?"

"But how do you think we could afford to renovate it?" Grayson asked.

Drea just looked back and forth between them all. She still didn't understand, but didn't want to ask the same two one-word questions again. Nothing was making sense.

"Drea, look at me, baby girl," Miller said, his voice cracking a bit. "I should have done this a long, long time ago. But I guess that I had a hard time accepting you were all grown up, and this was my way of keeping you little. Because if you didn't know the full story, you weren't fully grown."

He took a long, deep breath and sighed before taking a big gulp from his coffee mug. She could tell whatever he was about to say was hard for him, but she was dying to know the truth. She squeezed Kyle's hand underneath the table. Her heart was racing, but the little squeeze he gave her in return was a big comfort.

"Yes, the story we've told you since you were little is true. We used to vacation here, or well, the former version of here, when we were kids. The property had belonged to a friend of our grandfather's. It'd been in his family for years, originally starting as a family retreat and then someone decided to turn it into a hotel-type thing. It wasn't really successful for them as a hotel, so they shut it down and were looking to off-load it. When we were kids, we'd loved it down here and often tossed around the idea of someday running our own hotel." He paused to take another drink of his coffee.

"So, when our dad passed, we approached Mr. Redford and he sold it to us. However, our inheritance really only covered the cost of purchasing the property. In comes your dad, who had his own family money from the life insurance payouts from his parents' deaths, and he offered to invest in the renovations if we split the ownership four ways and went into business together. We all agreed, and the Indigo Royal was born."

"Wow," Drea muttered. It was all she could manage to get out. Blinking rapidly, she tried to clear her head and wrap her mind around all he was telling her. It was just so much to take in at once. "Why didn't you ever tell me?"

"After the accident, we decided that it was best if publicly it just seemed that we own the resort," Miller stated.

"The lawyers all told us that it was the best way to protect you and your interests if no one knew that you had inherited so much at six months old," Vaughn added.

"Your dad was nothing if not overprepared, so he had a will created right after you were born, leaving everything to you and leaving you to either me or your grandparents. They were too devastated by the loss of both of their daughters to take you in, so I convinced these two, and your life as you know it was formed."

"It didn't take a whole lot of convincing, mind you," Grayson added with a smile.

"Technically, you've had an equal vote in everything since you were eighteen. But we opted to wait until you were twenty-one, in case you had wanted to go to college. I should have told you years ago, baby girl, but I've been selfish in wanting to keep you here. Can you forgive me?"

"Keep me here? Where would I go?"

"Per the lawyers, we are supposed to offer you a buy-out option. In case what you want is the money, rather than an equal interest in the resort. Grayson and I have been under the impression you knew about this and opted to stay, rather than the three of us buy you out," Vaughn stated.

"Buy me out? No, this resort is my life. I'm the family part of Quinlan Family Resorts!" she said, raising her voice on the last part.

"I like hearing that. Although technically you're the Miller in Quinlan-Miller," Grayson laughed.

She stood up from the table and started to pace slightly behind her chair. This was massive news. Suddenly, things started to make more sense. Why Grayson took her on the trip to Florida to look at the boat and why he asked for her opinion on hiring Kyle. Why Vaughn had included her on the discussion before bringing on Dalton and promoting Leona. Why Miller insisted she sit in on his choosing of the new silverware and linens, even though the idea of looking at another colored napkin made her want to cry. These weren't them just asking their niece, they were asking their business partner.

"So I have an equal say in things?" she asked, stopping her pacing. "So if there is something I want to do with the resort, I can do it?"

"Well, we have to discuss and vote," Vaughn said, pointing out proper business etiquette. "But yes, if there are changes you'd like to make or something you want to improve, you get as much of a say as any of us."

"Do you know what this means?" she excitedly asked Kyle, who had been sitting quietly at the table the whole time.

"You get your spa?" he answered, standing up from the table, holding his arms out.

"Yes!" she said, leaping into his open arms. He caught her almost instinctively, picking her up and twirling her around. When he put her feet back on the ground, she immediately popped up to her tiptoes and kissed him.

She was so excited about what her uncles just told her that she didn't stop to think that they were all watching her now as she wrapped her arms around Kyle and continued to kiss him. He didn't seem to be thinking much about that either, returning her kiss full force, sweeping his tongue lightly across hers. She pulled away from his lips, giggling, and looked into his eyes. She could see the same happiness she was feeling reflected back and it made her heart skip a beat. That was, until she heard her uncle's voice.

"What the fuck is going on?!"

CHAPTER TWENTY-SEVEN

Kyle's heart leapt into his throat and his stomach dropped as he heard Vaughn's booming voice from next to them. He'd gotten so lost in the excitement radiating off Drea that he'd totally spaced that they were at breakfast with her family. Her family that didn't know they were together. Not to mention that they'd just dropped a major bomb about the resort.

"Get your hands off of her," Vaughn growled.

"Vaughn!" Simone chastised. He glared at her before standing up.

"I'm going to ask again, what the fuck?"

"Uncle Vaughn, I can explain," Drea started, pulling away from Kyle.

"You don't owe anyone an explanation, baby girl," Miller said.

"Is this why you took her away for the weekend? To seduce her? You used our property to try and take advantage of our innocent niece?"

"No, sir," Kyle started. "Please sit and let Drea and I tell you our story. I promise it's not what you think."

Shit, Kyle thought. He knew this moment wouldn't go well. He'd imagined it in his mind hundreds of times and every time it ended with a different one of her uncles, if not all three, being very, very upset. He drew in a deep breath as he sat back down, hoping to convince Vaughn to do the same.

"No, I will not sit down. And I'm sure it's exactly what I think. You don't get to decide you love her now that you know she has money. If you didn't love her before, you don't now."

"But I did," Kyle shouted, standing back up. "I do. I do love her."

He heard Drea's sharp intake of breath as he said the words. He hadn't meant for them to come out like this, but here they were. But just as he was turning to address Drea, Vaughn cut in.

"I'm sure you do. Because you just heard all about how she owns a quarter of the Indigo Royal."

"Give it a rest, Vaughn, and stop accusing our employee of being a gold digger!" Grayson said.

"Prove to me that he's not and I'll consider rescinding my accusation."

"Consider?" Drea chirped.

"Vaughn, have you watched these two, like, ever? They've been circling each other like animals in heat for years. It was about time something happened," Miller claimed.

"I'm just glad he decided to shit rather than get off the pot," Grayson added, looking over at Miller.

"Me too," Simone stage whispered.

"So you all have known about this? And you're okay with her being with...him?" Vaughn said, gesturing toward Kyle.

The statement was a punch to the gut, and Kyle couldn't believe what he was hearing. Is this really what they thought of him? Some money-hungry lowlife who would prey on Drea to get what he wants? He'd worked here for five years, poured his heart into this place, and this was the reaction he got.

"You really think so little of me, sir?" Kyle asked.

Vaughn just shrugged.

"Uncle Vaughn, you can't be serious!" Drea exclaimed.

"He only wants you for your money, Drea."

"Vaughn, stop being ridiculous," Miller interjected. "And yes, I knew, I have eyes. He looks at her like I looked at Marta."

Kyle looked over at Miller. He was still sitting at the table, but where he'd been relaxed and almost slumped in his chair before, he was now sitting upright, with both arms resting on the table. Knowing that Miller thought that Kyle looked at Drea the same way he had looked at his own wife meant something to him. The love that radiated off Miller when he talked about her was something Kyle envied and something he knew Drea had always idolized. His statement also meant that Drea was right—Miller was defending them and their relationship, even though they hadn't been entirely honest with him.

"What about you," Vaughn said, turning to Grayson. "Do you know about this too?"

"Well, I didn't realize he'd sealed the deal, but I might have been encouraging it," he answered, looking over at Kyle and giving the 'well done, buddy' nod. Kyle nodded back his thanks.

"Vaughn, for the last time, knock it off," Simone finally said.

"You too?"

"Yes, me too. She's had a crush on him since the moment he got here. You know that," Simone answered him. "So when I saw him kiss her the other night—"

"What?" Vaughn cut her off.

"Uncle Vaughn, if you'd let us explain. We've been dating—" Drea started.

"Dating? Drea, he's been leading you on for years. So I'm sorry if you thought there was more to your friendship and I'm sorry that these two have been indulging your fantasies about it," he said, gesturing at his brothers.

"Vaughn, she has not been imagining that there is more to our friendship. We're together, we just chose to keep it to ourselves—"

"Because it's against the terms of your employment contract?" Vaughn said, cutting him off.

"What?" Kyle asked.

"Even if you aren't after her money, which I don't believe for one second, it's still against resort policy for staff to be romantically involved with each other. You're fired."

The words rang in Kyle's ears. He shouldn't have been surprised to hear them. He knew they were coming. It was what he'd been afraid of since day one of this, what he'd been telling Drea would happen. Deep down he'd always known it, but when Miller and Grayson had started to defend him, there had been a glimmer of hope that maybe the outcome would be different.

"You can't fire him!" Drea called out, moving in between him and her uncle.

"Oh, but I can."

"He's my employee, Vaughn," Grayson added in.

"Don't we all get a vote?" Drea asked, panicked.

"He might report to you, Grayson, but as Executive

Director of the resort I get final say over employment. Kyle, get out, you're fired."

It was as if the earth underneath him turned to quicksand. He couldn't breathe as the room spun. He looked to Drea, who was fighting back tears.

"No, no, no," she said.

"Vaughn, don't be an ass," Miller said, standing up. "You are not firing the kid because he is involved with Drea. By that logic you're going to have to find a new housekeeping manager and a maintenance tech."

"I have no idea what you're talking about, but my decision is final. Get out."

He didn't need to be told again. He wanted to scream and throw up, but knew that no matter what he did, he wasn't going to change the man's mind. He looked at Drea, whose tears had started to fall. Reaching out, he squeezed her hand before turning to her uncles.

"Grayson, Miller, it's been an honor."

With those final words, he walked out of the kitchen.

He heard Drea yell his name as he walked away, but he kept walking. He wanted to turn around so badly, but none of it mattered anymore. Everything he'd worked the last five years for was out the window, all because he'd kissed her at breakfast. All his hard work, all the money he'd saved up, meant nothing. He hadn't saved quite enough to try and make it stretch to get his business up and running, and he certainly couldn't also help cover his mom's medical costs.

If he'd only had more self-control, more discipline, he could have held out a little longer. Six more months would have been all he'd needed to have enough saved, and he could have done this properly. Given his notice, gone out on his own, and asked her uncles' permission to pursue her. But it was all over now.

As he made it to the lobby he felt his phone vibrate in his pocket. He pulled it out to find a text from a number he didn't recognize.

Unknown number: Hi Kyle, this is Claudia Maury, I live across the street from your mother. She gave me your number in case there was ever an emergency. Not that there is one now, but I haven't seen her around for a couple days and she's not answering her phone, so I just wanted to check in to make sure everything is OK. Have you heard from her?

Shit, Kyle thought. He knew she'd sounded off the other night when they talked. But he'd been so focused on getting back to Drea he accepted her answer of "tired" and didn't push any further. He should have known better. All sorts of worst-case scenarios flew through his mind as he rushed back to his dorm. He had to get back to Florida.

Drea watched as Kyle just walked out of the kitchen, ignoring her pleas for him to come back. Her heart sank, why would he just keep walking? Her uncle's words echoed in her head, *he's been leading you on for years...sorry if you thought there was more to your friendship.* Vaughn was wrong, he had to be. He hadn't been there this morning in the shower as Kyle told her how amazing she was, or this past weekend in San Juan as he told her how much she meant to him and how she could cry to him whenever she needed to. If he'd known about those moments, he wouldn't have accused Kyle the way he did.

"Vaughn, have you lost your fucking mind?" Miller asked.

"You do realize I was about to promote him to Marina Manager, right? Who am I gonna get to do that now? Much less actually do the tours on the *Runnin'*?" Grayson tacked on.

They continued to argue, but Drea could barely hear them. She slumped down into her chair, just staring into space. She couldn't believe what just happened. How had the conversation gone from being one of the best moments of her life to blowing up in her face? Oh, that's right, her family. She felt something on her arm and looked over to find that Simone had moved and was now sitting in the chair Kyle had been in.

"Drea," she said softly. "Drea, honey, talk to me."

"Simone, not now," Vaughn cut in.

"Shut it, Vaughn, you have done more than enough this morning," she shot back.

That was all it took to snap Drea out of her pity party. She shot up from her chair and slammed both her palms on the table, making the dishes still sitting there rattle.

"Stop!" she shouted. "All of you just stop!"

Everyone in the kitchen stopped moving, even the staff who had been milling about and working like nothing was happening over at the family table.

"Not you," she said, turning around, addressing the staff. "You all can keep doing whatever you were doing."

"Drea—" Grayson started.

"NO!" she shouted again.

Her family all looked at her wide-eyed. She never lost her temper. Anger was not an emotion Drea had very often. She was smiles and giggles and hugs. But in this moment, something snapped.

"I can't believe you. I can't believe you just fucking did that!"

"Drea, he's been leading you on for years. We just have your best interest at heart,"

Vaughn replied.

"We? You're the one who just fucking fired my best employee!" Grayson snarked.

"Enough!" She said, banging her fists on the table. "You do not have *my* best interest at heart. You were thinking about what's best for *you*! All three of you talk about me like I'm not here, when I'm sitting two chairs away. You ignore me when I ask questions. You treat me like I'm still eight. Then this morning, I find out you've been hiding something from me all my life. And not something little, like, oh hey, your birth name is Gabriella and we just decided to call you Andrea. No, you've been hiding something major! Which, by the way, for people who were operating under the idea that I was an equal partner, you certainly weren't acting like it a lot of the time. You couldn't have been too worried about whether or not Miller had told me, since the rest of you certainly weren't bringing it up!"

The words rushed out of her mouth faster than she had intended. But she was pissed and all the anger had her worked up. She couldn't believe them. Couldn't believe they had lied to her for this long and then decided to take it out on Kyle.

"And apparently I can't be trusted with my own heart either. I'm sorry that for whatever reason you don't think Kyle is good enough, but too bad. He's amazing, and he treats me like I walk on water. We just had the most amazing weekend together. Which was not spent with him "taking advantage of me" as you so obnoxiously put it! You don't get to decide who I have sex with! I get to decide that!"

All three of her uncles winced at the mention of her

having sex, but she didn't really care whom she was making uncomfortable at the moment. In fact, the more uncomfortable they were, the better. Maybe that would help get the message across to them.

"We haven't been public about our relationship, but that doesn't mean it wasn't a relationship. In fact, one of the biggest reasons we kept it from you was exactly what happened this morning. Kyle was afraid that you all would lose your shit and would fire him. And me, well, I was naive enough to believe that it wasn't true. I thought that you all would respect my choice of boyfriend and you would accept him into our family the same way everyone accepted Simone. But I guess I was really, really fucking wrong on that one, wasn't I?" She threw up her arms in exasperation. She knew she was ranting but she couldn't stop.

"You know what?" she asked, glancing between all three of them. "I take it back. I take it all back. I don't want to be here. I no longer want to be the family in Quinlan Family Resorts."

"Drea, you don't mean that," Miller said.

"I do," she paused. "I do. Buy me out. When the lawyer is here on Friday, tell him to draw up the papers and buy me out."

"And just what are you gonna do?" Vaughn asked.

"None of your fucking business, now is it?"

CHAPTER TWENTY-EIGHT

KYLE WAS SHOVING clothes into his duffle as fast as he could, not paying much attention to what was really being packed or how unorganized he was being in the process. At the rate he was going, he was just going to make the noon flight out of the airport over in Charlotte Amalie. He'd worry about getting the rest of his stuff packed up later. The staff dorms weren't completely full, so it's not like they would need the room tomorrow. Certainly he could convince Dalton to throw his stuff into boxes and ship it all back to Florida for him.

Back to Clearwater, Florida. Not something he had really pictured in a long time. His sights had been set on St. Thomas since he had arrived and his dream revolved around the port in Charlotte Amalie, right by where all the cruise boats came in. If he closed his eyes, he could still see it, his own catamaran sitting there in the dock, bobbing up and down with the waves. While he'd always liked how Grayson had named all his boats after songs, there was only one thing he'd ever considered naming his: Brave Beauty. It was an easy decision—after all, Andrea meant brave in

French, or so some French tourist had told them one day when they were on a tour.

He hadn't told her this part of the plan. He had wanted it to be a surprise for after he'd gotten up on his feet and secured the boat. The moment was all planned out in his head—walking her down to the pier, showing her the boat, and then revealing the name. In his head, she had cried some happy tears and leapt into his arms, kissing him, owning him in front of anyone and everyone who happened to be around. Next they would have set sail for an overnight, where he would have packed a picnic, complete with her favorite potstickers, and a bottle of champagne. In some versions of his fantasy he proposed, but in most, he simply told her how much he loved her and how this was the beginning of the rest of their lives.

But after this morning, that was all gone. It didn't matter whether or not he went with the proposal, with or without a ring, because there would be no boat, no charter business. All of it was down the drain, at least as far as St. Thomas was concerned. Moving back in with his mother in Florida would allow him to not only save money again, but to help her with her dialysis. Provided he could find a job. If he groveled enough, they'd probably take him back at the marina where Grayson had found him. Or maybe there was a hotel who needed a boat captain.

The door to his room flew open, hitting the door stopper on the wall with a crash. Drea came rushing in, her tear-soaked cheeks breaking his heart even more as soon as he saw them.

"What are you doing?" she asked.

"Packing."

"Why?"

"I'm heading back to Florida."

"Why?" she said, choking back a cry.

"Do you remember what just happened in the kitchen? I got fired. Just like I told you I would," he snapped.

"That doesn't mean you have to go back to Florida! You can stay here, we can figure this out!"

"There is nothing to figure out!" he said, raising his voice. "I'm now jobless, homeless, and the dream I was saving up for is gone! I don't have enough money to start my own business, much less also cover living expenses. No one will hire me once they find out I got fired from the Indigo Royal. My only option is to go back to Florida!"

"No, it's not, I've got the money covered. We can start the charter business together."

"Drea, I can't take your savings."

"I asked my uncles to buy me out."

"You what?" he shouted. "Why the fuck would you do that?"

"Because I love you! And I don't want to be a part of the Indigo Royal if you're not here. My uncles don't treat me like a partner anyway, so it shouldn't matter. I will take my share, and we can go do our own thing."

"No, Drea, we can't," he said simply. "You can't just quit your family for me."

The words hurt to say, especially after hearing her say the one thing he'd waited to hear for years. She loved him. But he loved her too much in return to let her do this. The hurt on her face was obvious, which made the words hurt even more. He hated the idea of hurting her, but he knew this was for the best. He couldn't stay and he wouldn't string her along by giving her the impression they could do long distance. No matter what her uncle seemed to think of him, he wasn't that kind of guy. He was also not the kind of guy to let her give up on her dream, and her dream was the resort spa.

"I can do what I want. And what I want is to be with you, Kyle. I asked them to buy me out, and the lawyer will take care of the paperwork on Friday. I'm not saying it's ideal, but we can make it work."

"No. You can't let them buy you out. This resort is your life. You said so while we were on the boat. You have dreamed of that spa for years. Don't walk away from that."

"And your dream is a charter company. You can't tell me not to walk away from my dream while you're doing the exact same thing!"

"Not all dreams come true, Drea. Mine isn't going to happen, yours is. Florida is my only option. Besides, I haven't heard from mom in a couple of days, and I need to get home to see her."

It was a lame excuse. He knew it, and she knew it. He felt like shit for using it. But she wasn't listening and he didn't know how to make it any clearer to her.

"Drea, I get that you think you have the answer, but you don't. This was great while it lasted, but it's obviously not meant to be," he said, wanting to puke as soon as the words left his mouth.

"You can't be serious," she said, the tears starting to fall again. "Kyle, I love you. You're my forever."

"Don't say that, Drea."

"Why not? It's true. You are my forever. I know it like my mother knew it. And I've known it since that night on Playa Peña."

"It doesn't matter, Drea. It doesn't matter."

"How can you say it doesn't matter?" She walked up to him until there was only a couple of inches in between them. "Are you telling me that you don't love me? Because you just told my uncles you do."

"How I feel doesn't matter. Whether or not I love you isn't going to change things. You need to go back to your uncles, tell them you overreacted and that you don't want them to buy you out, you want to open a spa." He pulled her in close, wrapping his arms around her and holding her tight. He could feel her heart pounding and he had to fight back the tears. He was dying inside. It was taking all he had not to shout back 'I love you too!', but he knew that it would only make things harder. He needed to focus, finishing packing, and get to the airport.

She shoved at him violently, screaming as she did so. "I can't believe you. You're just like them, telling me what I can and can't do! And yes, how you feel does matter, because I just gave you my fucking heart, Kyle. All of it!"

"Drea, listen—" he began, but she cut him off.

"No, you fucking listen. I love you. I *love* you. And back there in the kitchen, you told my uncles that you love me! So either you do love me, too, and we figure out a way to make this work, or you lied, and are exactly what Uncle Vaughn said you are. And I refuse to believe that."

Kyle took a deep breath, closing his eyes, trying to avoid the painful expression he knew was written on her face. He didn't want to do it this way. He didn't want her to believe that he didn't love her with everything he had. But sometimes love just wasn't enough, and this was one of those times.

He grabbed his duffle bag and zipped it closed. There were so many things he was probably forgetting, but he could get any immediate needs in Clearwater. He needed to get out of this room, away from this resort, to a place where he could be alone with his feelings. More importantly, he needed to give Drea the space she would need to move on from him.

"I have a flight to catch. I have enjoyed every moment with you, Drea, but all good things must come to an end. Have a good life."

He kissed her softly on the cheek and headed out the door. Halfway down the hall, he heard her let out a sob that nearly had him running back to her. But he couldn't go, he couldn't let her believe in him anymore. He'd already hurt her too much.

THE SAND on Big House Beach was warm from the sun and felt nice against her legs, but wasn't doing much to fix her mood. Usually the sun and surf were enough to lift her spirits when she was feeling down, but the events of the morning had dragged her down to a new level. She'd finally broken down and put on sunglasses after her eyes, swollen from crying so much, had started to burn when looking out over the waves.

Trying to keep her breathing steady, she breathed in and out with the waves. In, out, in out, over and over again. It wasn't working. No matter how hard she tried, her pulse still raced and her breathing was still ragged. She felt like she could throw up at any moment. She didn't think she had any tears left in her, but that didn't stop a sob from escaping here and there. Worst of all was the empty feeling in her chest. While she could still feel it beating, her heart felt like it had been torn into pieces and scattered all over.

She had never realized that it could feel this awful. This must be what real heartbreak is. She'd thought she'd been heartbroken before, in high school when the kid she'd had a crush on didn't return her affections. But that felt nothing like this. In fact, she'd give anything to feel that disappointment all over again instead of this now. If this is what Uncle Miller had felt when he lost Marta, Drea was starting to get an idea of why he had never dated again.

Her phone dinged again, indicating a new text. She'd gotten a text from pretty much everyone over the last couple of hours, not that she'd read any. Everyone but Kyle. Picking up her phone, she opened it to her messages to check the damage.

Simone: Drea, I know this morning was rough, but I'm here when you're ready to talk. Love you.

Grayson: Kiddo, I'm sorry we lost our cool this morning. I hope you know how much we love you.

Vaughn: Drea, we both said some things this morning I think we didn't really mean. Me more than anyone. I hope you will accept my apology. If you're serious about the buy out, we can proceed, but your uncles and I really hope that you're not. We, I, want you here. Love you.

Dalton: Heard what happened darlin. Heartbreak boozin is on me. Let me know the time and place.

Miller: Baby girl, I'm so so sorry. Please call me.

The latest one was from Leona. She'd been surprised when she wasn't the first one to reach out and that her best friend hadn't already found her on the beach. But maybe the gossip mill hadn't moved quite as fast as she had assumed.

Leona: Ok, so since I'm apparently not gonna hear from you, this must be worse than I thought. I'm sorry girl, but seriously, fuck him. If he's not willing to fight for you, he's not worth your tears. You know where to find me.

Leona: PS> All three of your uncles are moping around here like someone died. So, there's that...

It did make Drea feel a little better that all three of them felt like crap as well. She hadn't meant to unload quite as much as she did this morning, but once she started she just couldn't hold back anymore. She'd wanted to tell them to treat her like an adult for so long, but never was able to find a time to do it. *Better late than never*, she thought.

The jangle of his keys gave him away long before she could actually hear his footsteps approaching in the sand. By the time Miller sat down to her left, she'd blinked back the newest batch of tears and dried her face as much as she could. They both just sat there quietly for a long moment, before he finally broke the silence.

"The day you were born, as we were standing there holding you in the hospital, your Aunt Marta said to me, 'we should have one.' At first, I thought she was kidding," he said, laughing. "You were the most perfect thing I had ever seen, Drea. The idea of Marta and I having one scared the shit out of me. I was sure that I would be a horrible, horrible father."

"Why?" she asked, still looking out over the water.

"Because I had no idea what to do with a baby. But Marta was persistent and I couldn't say no to that woman.

Two days before the accident, she told me she thought she was pregnant, so I said that weekend we'd head into town to grab a test. Not a day has gone by that I don't wish we had dropped everything to go get one right then. I know it wouldn't have changed what happened with the stove that day, but at least I wouldn't have spent the last twenty-five years wondering."

"Uncle Miller, I had no idea."

"No one does, baby girl. Not my brothers, not your grandparents when they were still alive. You are the first person I've ever told," he paused, sniffing a bit. "But after everything happened, I knew that I had to figure out how to be a dad, to be your dad. I really had no idea what I was doing, but what I didn't realize was that no one knew how to be a parent automatically. It's a *figure it out as you go* kind of thing."

"You did a great job, Uncle Miller."

"Thank you, baby girl. Sometimes I look at you and am just in awe that I was the one to raise you to be this amazing young woman. You're smart, caring, have a great head on your shoulders, and have an incredible sense of adventure. Just like your mother." Drea laughed. "But other days, I think about all the mistakes I made and I think it's a wonder that you turned out this good despite all the fuck-ups I had on my part. Like not telling you about your part in the resort."

"I still don't understand why you didn't tell me," she said, finally looking over at her uncle.

"I had it in my head that if you knew, you would leave. The resort was our dream, and you just happened to be sucked into that by circumstance. I didn't do a good enough job in knowing you to know that you felt like this place was your life too. So I thought that if I didn't tell you that you'd just stay, because, well, obligation I guess."

"Why would I want to leave?"

"It's that sense of adventure of yours, baby girl. I always knew there were big dreams in that head of yours. Dreams that I assumed meant you wanted more than our little resort," he answered with a small shrug.

"Why didn't you just ask?"

"Because it seemed like asking would have been a way to push you further into what I assumed was already a desire to run away," he shrugged again. "I can't really explain it, Drea, and I know it doesn't make sense. But not much about how a parent loves their child ever does. And I know I'm not actually your dad, just the guy who raised you, and I don't ever want to take anything away from Dave. But you will always be my child, baby girl."

"You're not just the guy who raised me. You are so much more than that. I hate that you felt that you couldn't tell me. But at the same time, being lied to like that really, really hurts," she admitted, holding back more tears.

"I know, and that's on me. I'm so, so sorry, baby girl. It was so incredibly selfish. But you were all I had, Drea. After the accident, I felt like the only thing I had left in life was you. You became my reason for living. I know it sounds cliché, but you have been my everything ever since Vaughn walked out of his office holding you, still sound asleep, as the rest of the world shifted beneath my feet."

"Uncle Miller," Drea said, exhaling, reaching out for his hand. He took hers in his and squeezed.

"It's a stupid excuse, I know. But as misguided as it was, it was because I love you. Can you forgive an old man?"

He reached an arm around her and gave her a hug. She

let him hold her like that for a long moment before pulling away, fighting off tears yet again. She loved him so much, and knew that he really only ever did what he thought was best for her. It was impossible to stay mad at him for too long.

"I won't lie," she said, pulling away slightly. "It still hurts that you didn't trust me with that information and I'm still pissed. But...but I get it. I get that you just didn't want to lose me like you lost Aunt Marta and my parents. So, I guess you are forgiven."

He wrapped his arm around her again, pulling her close and kissing the top of her head. Into her hair he said, "Thank you, baby girl."

"I'm not so sure I'm ready to forgive the other two, though."

"This is my apology. They are on the hook for their own," he said, smiling a little. "Now, not to rub salt or anything, but I know I am not the only one who hurt you today, and if I were a betting man, I would wager that the pain I caused is nothing compared to what happened after you left the kitchen."

Drea let out a sob, and crumpled into her uncle's arms. Part of her felt so stupid, crying to him like she was a little kid who fell off her bike. But at the same time, it was incredibly comforting to have him here.

"It's okay, baby girl, let it out. Let it out..."

CHAPTER TWENTY-NINE

GRAYSON'S APOLOGY had come the next morning, by way of Leona. Miller had told her before he left her on the beach the evening before that he would send meals over so that she could do her own thing and take as long as she needed. He'd seen her sulk enough as a moody teenager to know exactly what she needed, and was more than prepared with the skills and ingredients to help her eat her feelings.

Dinner had shown up just as the sun was starting to set, hand delivered by Dalton, who also happened to be carrying a handle of rum, another of tequila, and two short tumbler glasses he'd obviously commandeered from the dining room. He didn't speak at all as he laid out the food on the little table on her porch, and he continued to let them eat in silence. It wasn't until after they had food in them that he'd grabbed the two handles, held up each one, and finally asked, "A or B?" She'd opted for the tequila, and they'd spent the night in silence, every now and again taking a shot.

The next morning, complete with what her Uncle Gray would have referred to as "a dehydration headache" rather than a hangover, she found Leona in her kitchen with a basket of magic muffins and Grayson's go-to hangover cure —a bottle of Coke.

"He also gave me this," Leona said, handing her a laminated five by seven piece of cardstock.

Drea took it from her best friend and looked at it. She recognized it immediately and couldn't help but laugh out loud. It was bright yellow and had a winged version of Mr. Monopoly in his tuxedo flying out of an open birdcage on it, reading "Get out of jail free." She'd given him the actual card from the family's set of the board game when she was thirteen and had accidentally ripped a sail on one of the boats, hoping that it would buy her some grace with her uncle. He, too, had laughed when she gave it to him, and told her that it was an acceptable use of the card, and to expect that someday he would return the gesture. She flipped over the card and found his handwriting on the back.

My turn to cash in? Groveling and begging shall commence once coupon is accepted.

-G

Drea sighed and shook her head. Sometimes it was really difficult having family members who could charm the pants off anyone. Just like Miller's apology yesterday, it did little to temper her anger at this moment, but overall it softened her resolve. He wasn't really the one she was incensed with. Was she mad that he kept the secret? Yes. But he'd never been the type to stick himself into other people's business, so she knew that if Miller had said he told her, Grayson would have trusted that and let it drop. He'd also come to her and Kyle's defense. That had to count for something.

OVER THE NEXT FEW DAYS, Vaughn had tried to seek her out a number of different times. Each time she either zagged when he zigged or she flat-out excused herself from the conversation. She had no desire to cause a scene in front of guests, so she kept herself as scarce as possible if she knew he'd be around. Other than Friday morning, when they met with the lawyer to officially add Simone as the fifth owner to the resort paperwork, and the same evening at the rehearsal, Drea had managed to only have to be in his company a couple of times since that breakfast. Simone had told her that if she didn't feel comfortable being her maid of honor because of what happened, she'd understand. Drea had considered the offer, but she knew how much it meant to Simone to have her in that role, so she opted to stay.

"I just don't make any promises to be entirely nice to the groom," Drea told her.

"I think that's perfectly acceptable," Simone had responded.

THE WHOLE RESORT was abuzz with wedding prep come Saturday morning, on top of all the normal weekend chaos. Everyone around her was smiling and laughing, so excited for the happy couple, but it was really all she could do not to act like a zombie. Having been in the guest service industry her entire life, she could fake a smile like no one else, but today it was draining her faster than she thought she could ever replenish.

The nail salon on site was quiet, other than the sound of the faucet dripping in the little sink not far from the pedicure chairs. It wasn't quite the water feature Drea had in mind, and was actually starting to annoy her. With Simone to her right and Leona to her left, along with Simone's mom, sister, and aunts over at the manicure tables, Drea knew she should be a lot more relaxed than she was.

Her tears seemed to have dried up yesterday afternoon, although that might just be from sheer dehydration. Because she certainly still felt like crying. Every time she thought about how just a week ago they'd been exploring the streets of Old San Juan, she wanted to curl up in a little ball and die. In her mind, that day seemed like yesterday and forever ago, all at the same time.

Kyle's words still rang out in her head. *Have a good life.* How could he be so cold? He'd been so sweet and loving just a couple of hours earlier in the shower. Had she known that would be the last time they were together, she would have made the moment last. She certainly wouldn't have rushed them to get dressed when she saw what time it was, or told him that he was a bad influence on her punctuality. Thinking back on it, she hated herself for saying that and wished like hell she could take it back.

"So, how exciting will it be to have a proper spa? I think we definitely need to take that trip to Bora Bora now to check out the Thalasso," Simone said, cutting into Drea's internal pity party.

"Um, yeah," Drea agreed, half-heartedly.

"A spa?" Leona asked. "Why didn't you say anything?"

"Oh, um, I guess I didn't realize it was a go," Drea answered.

"Vaughn told me the other night that if that's what you

want—to create and manage a spa at the Indigo Royal—that he's absolutely in support of that."

"I'm sure he is," Drea said sarcastically. "Trying to buy my affections."

"There are worse ways to do it than a spa," Leona muttered.

Tears pricked her eyes and started to fall before she ever realized what was happening. She sniffed loudly and wiped away at them, trying to collect herself, but it was no use. Thinking about the spa—creating it, running it, and building it into the mini empire she'd dreamed it could be— would never *not* be tied to Kyle now. She'd been so self-conscious in telling him as they were sitting sharing secrets in the sun, but not only did he not laugh, he encouraged her. She pictured him in there with her, picking her up after work or the two of them sneaking off into one of the treatment rooms for some alone time. But now it all just seemed so hollow, like his ghost would forever haunt something that had been her dream.

"Sorry," she sniffed. "I don't mean to ruin your day." She wiped away more tears with the back of her hand.

"Oh honey," Simone said, reaching out her hand. "Don't be sorry. You're heartbroken. It's okay, you're allowed to be upset."

"I guess I was just being a stupid girl, but I really thought we had something."

"You did, honey. If it hadn't been real, he wouldn't have celebrated with you the way he did in the moment at breakfast."

"She's right, Drea," Leona added. "He could have just been talking out his ass that morning before he left. He was upset about your uncles, and Dalton said he got a text about his mom being sick, so he was probably just stressed."

"He told me to have a nice life! That's not talking out your ass!" Drea exploded.

"Girl, I don't know if you've figured this out yet, being raised by three men and all, but guys are dumbasses. Not some of them—all of them. Some more so than others, but they are all dumbasses on some level or another. Sometimes they come to the realization of their dumbassery on their own, other times they need help realizing it. Have faith he'll come around."

"It's over. He won't 'come around.' He's gone back to Florida, for crying out loud. I wasn't important enough to fight for. I was just a convenient fuck."

"You were not!" Leona exclaimed. "Sweetie, I know it sucks because you pined after him forever, but you can't seriously think that's all you were."

"Well, it doesn't matter now, does it? Besides, today is Simone's day, and I'm going to smile and be happy if it fucking kills me."

"I can't believe he actually booked you guys the honeymoon suite," Leona said to Simone, as she wrapped her hair around a curling iron.

It had taken Leona almost forty-five minutes to get Drea's hair straightened with the little flatiron, and then another thirty to recurl and pin into an updo. Her head ached a little from all the pulling and the scraping of the bobby pins against her scalp, but even she had to admit she looked pretty good. If someone looked at her and didn't know she felt half dead inside, they would think she was the picture-perfect maid of honor.

"Only for the night," Simone clarified. "Actual guests have it booked starting tomorrow."

"Still, it's romantic."

Drea turned away so no one could see her roll her eyes. It wasn't exactly the pinnacle of romance that the man booked a hotel room in a resort he owned. Even if he had planned the whole thing months in advance, blocking off the night so guests could book up until the Friday before, and then again the Sunday after. *Damn it*, she thought, *maybe it was romantic.*

"Believe it or not, not only does the man have non-jackass moments, but he can actually be wonderfully sweet at times. You just have to get past the gruff exterior."

"Or not be his niece," Drea threw out. She knew she wasn't being fair to him, but she couldn't bring herself to care. Overall he was a kind and generous person. She knew firsthand just how wonderful he could be, and how much he cared about those around him. He considered every person who worked for the Indigo Royal a member of the family, and there wasn't much he wouldn't do for them. But when it came to his actual family, he sometimes had a funny way of showing it. A way that, this time, had pushed too far.

AFTER THEIR HAIR and makeup was complete, everyone other than Simone left the room and Drea slipped into her dress. She'd always loved this dress, as it had always made her feel beautiful. It was a deep charcoal. The top was fitted and had little spaghetti straps, while the A-line skirt hit her hips perfectly, fanning out just enough before ending a little above her knees. The sweetheart neckline hugged her breasts perfectly, showing off just a hint of cleavage. She wondered what Kyle would have thought about her in this dress. Racking her brain, she tried to think about whether or not she'd ever worn it in front of him and she couldn't remember.

When she had decided this would be the dress she wore for the wedding, she thought about how the neckline would drive him insane. She thought about how he wouldn't be able to take his eyes off of her in this dress, whispering in her ear about how he couldn't wait to take it off of her. Her imagination had run wild with thoughts of him staring at her cleavage all night, about him slipping his hand up her skirt to see if she was wearing any panties. The thought had occurred to her that she could get away with not wearing any under this dress and no one would know—that was until Kyle discovered it for himself.

Thoughts of them dancing the night away, him spinning her around and the skirt on the dress billowing out slightly as she twirled had also crossed her mind. She'd pictured them sitting at dinner, picking off each other's plates, sipping from each other's drinks. In her mind, they had been doing all the things that happy couples do together at weddings and celebrating love. But now that was all gone.

"Oh, Drea, you're a vision!" Simone exclaimed, starting to tear up.

"Don't cry, don't cry!" Drea said. "You'll mess up your makeup and then I'm going to have to get Leona back in here to fix it."

"I'm fine, I'm fine," she said, waving her hands frantically in front of her eyes trying to dry them. "You just look so perfect. I know that today is a little weird and that you're not really feeling it, but thank you for still being my maid of honor. Being a part of your life these last twenty-one years has been one of my greatest joys, and I know that sounds cheesy, but really, I mean it. I have loved every second of being your aunt, and I couldn't imagine anyone else standing next to me today."

"I love you too, *Aunt* Simone," Drea said, fighting back her own tears now.

"Oh, don't start that! I'll never make it out of here in one piece!"

There was suddenly a heavy knock on the door and Drea and Simone looked at each other, confused. They still had almost an hour until the ceremony, and they weren't expecting anyone prior to the photographer who had told them to be ready forty-five minutes before the ceremony time.

"Who is it?" Drea asked.

"Vaughn."

"No, you can't see me before the wedding! It's bad luck!" Simone exclaimed, looking around for a place to hide.

The door opened and Vaughn stepped in, his right hand clasped tightly over his eyes. He stood just inside the doorway, looking very dapper in his light gray suit. There was an off-white pocket square peeking out from his breast pocket and his silver hair seemed to have some sort of product in it. He looked like he belonged in a magazine.

"That's okay, I'm not here to see you. I'm here for Drea."

"I don't have anything to say to you."

"Drea, please, just five minutes. Please," he begged.

Drea looked over at Simone, who was standing half hidden behind a chair in her white silk robe. Simone shrugged as if to say "your choice."

"Hear him out. If you don't like what he has to say, you have my permission to tell him to fuck off."

CHAPTER THIRTY

Drea stood there for a moment, trying to decide what to do. She really wanted to tell him to fuck off now. She was pretty sure there was nothing he could say that would make any of this better. Looking over at Simone in her robe, with her hair and makeup all done for her wedding, her heart softened a little. She'd given Miller and Grayson a chance to say their piece; she figured it was only fair that she did the same for Vaughn.

"Fine," she said, shrugging. "You wanna go hide in the bedroom?"

Simone nodded, coming out from behind the chair. "Just, go gentle on him. I would prefer he be in one piece for our wedding."

She squeezed Drea's hand lightly and went into the bedroom, closing the door behind her. When Drea heard the little lock click into place, she turned to her uncle who was still standing just inside the door with his hand covering his eyes.

"I guess you can come sit," Drea finally said.

Vaughn removed his hand from his face and looked

around the room, making sure they were alone. He crossed the room and picked the chair closest to the door to take a seat in. He motioned for her to sit too, but she hesitated. She didn't want him to get the idea that they were just going to have a nice little chat, but she also didn't want to be too hostile to him. It was his wedding day. She finally sat down in an armchair that was about as far from Vaughn as she could be while still being in the little sitting area of the suite.

"I'm sorry to interrupt, but you've been avoiding me all week and I figured this was the best way to make sure you couldn't escape," he said, laughing lightly.

"I really don't have anything to say to you."

"That's okay, because I have more than enough to say for both of us," he paused. "I'm sorry, Drea. I am really fucking sorry, and I can't get married today knowing that you are still not speaking to me. I can't go through with the biggest day of my life knowing that my little girl hates me."

"I'm not your little girl," she corrected.

"You're right, you're not. Although I'm not sure how I feel knowing that is the part of my statement you feel the need to correct me on."

"Hate is a pretty appropriate word right now."

Vaughn flinched at her statement. "That's fair. That's more than fair. I deserve that. I acted like a first-rate asshole at breakfast the other day. There is no excuse for the way I acted. I could drone on about how it's hard to admit that you're all grown up and that you're your own person now, and it is. It's hard to accept that the itty-bitty baby who used to nap in my office, or the little girl who used to sing everywhere she went, including while in the bathroom, is an adult, making her own choices. But you are. And despite the fact that you were raised by three bachelors making it up as they went, you turned into one hell of an amazing young woman."

"Thanks."

"And I shouldn't have been as taken aback about you and Kyle as I was that morning. I knew how you felt about him. Simone has droned on and on for what feels like forever about how cute the two of you are together. Not that any parent type wants to think about their kid that way. And Miller was right—anyone could see watching the two of you that there was something there, and really, we were rooting for you too. Maybe rooting is the wrong word. Well, my brothers were all about it—I was maybe a little less enthused. But, believe me, I do want you to be happy and to find your person. Would I have preferred he come to us prior to just sweeping you away, sure. But I also realize this isn't eighteen fifty-two and no one needs permission to date you. I like Kyle, I do. He's a great kid, Drea, and he's a hard worker and I know that he wouldn't set out to hurt you. He's exactly the kind of guy you want to date your kid. That's why I invited him to join us for our pre-bonfire rituals. He has become part of this family."

"And yet you said exactly the opposite to us at breakfast."

"I did. How did Simone put it? Oh, I 'lost my shit.' I became a fucking lunatic."

"You weren't very nice last week, either, before we went away for the weekend."

"I know. I have no idea why the idea of you two taking a weekend for yourselves bothered me, but it did. It shouldn't have—it's not like it's something you two haven't done a dozen times before. But somehow, this time seemed different. Oddly enough, that seems to have been exactly what your Uncle Grayson was pushing for, but still, it struck a chord. I felt the need to protect you and so that's what I tried to do."

"You don't need to protect me!" she exclaimed. "I am not a child! I'm twenty-six—I can take care of myself."

"I know. I know," he sighed. He paused for a moment before speaking again. "Your mom went into labor while your dad and I were meeting with the pool diggers. We were standing out there, watching them dig away when she waddled out saying she needed to talk to your dad. I told her 'not now, we're working.' She just looked at me and goes 'okay, then I'll tell the baby now isn't a good time. Should I check your calendar to find out when would be better?' Sofia had no problem sticking it to any of us." He laughed at the memory.

"Miller will wax on about how you were just perfect from the moment you showed up, and yes, you were cute as a baby. But you were just a baby to me. Until one day Sofia sticks her head in my office as I was trying to figure out this booking software that we had just bought. She was just going to leave you in there with me because you were sleeping and she wanted to go see the new stove be installed. She was gone just as quickly as she appeared. About an hour later there was the loudest noise that I've ever heard, still to this day. I went running, and it wasn't until Grayson looked at Miller and me and went 'where's the baby?' that I remembered you were on the floor in my office."

He leaned forward, resting his forearms on his knees, hanging his head. "When I got back, you were still asleep. I picked you up, and there you were in my arms, so small and helpless, and I knew it was my job to protect you from then on."

"Why are you telling me this?" Drea asked, confused.

"Because in that moment, when you were asleep in my arms as an inferno raged in our brand-new kitchen, I felt so fucking useless. I yelled and screamed and threatened to sue anyone who had ever touched that stove. And the only time I have ever felt like that since then was the moment that Kyle kissed you the other day. I can't explain why, but I did. And my knee-jerk reaction was the same then as it had been—to yell and scream and lose my shit. It was a shitty thing to do, but what's done is done. And I'm sorry, Drea."

"You had no right. You are not my father. You were not even my legal guardian," she ground out.

"I know. I know that I'm not even really your uncle. Believe it or not, it was a title I fought at first, but your mom still referred to me as 'Uncle Vaughn' when she talked to you as a baby. And, yes, Miller was the one who assumed the dad role, but that doesn't mean that Grayson and I don't think that you're ours too. We're a unit, the four of us."

She sighed and stood up from the chair. She walked over to the window that overlooked the guest portion of the beach. It was a beautiful, sunny day with only a few small clouds in the sky, and the beach was full of people soaking it up.

"I love him," she finally said. "But you drove him away."

"I know."

"And he wouldn't even say it to me when he was leaving. I told him I loved him, and he didn't say it back. He told you in the kitchen he did, but...he didn't say it to me. And now...now he's gone," she said, turning around. "He left the island, went back to the States. Said no one would hire him once they learned he'd been fired from the Indigo Royal."

"I've tried calling him a couple of times, sent a few texts, but he won't return my calls."

"Glad to know it's not just me," she muttered, turning back to the window.

"I wish I could take it back, Drea. I'd do pretty much anything to change what happened that morning."

She nodded slowly, still glancing out the window. She hated that she understood where he was coming from, but she did. It would be so much easier to just stay mad at him, to tell him to fuck off and leave her alone, but she knew that she would never be able to hold on to the anger knowing that he reacted out of love. However misguided he was, he had been trying to do right by her. Overprotective had been his go-to since day one, and she knew that she couldn't hold his personality against him for forever.

Without looking away from the window, she responded, "I'm still mad and I'm still really hurt, and I can't promise that will change any time soon."

"But it will change, yes?"

"Eventually," she answered, turning back around to face him again.

"Then I guess that's all I can ask for," he said, standing, holding his arms open wide for a hug.

She crossed the room in only a couple of strides and stepped into his embrace. He wrapped his arms tightly around her and squeezed like he might never let go. When he finally did let go, she took a step back, wiping lightly at her eyes to make sure her makeup was still intact.

"If a spa is what you want, by the way, then I'm all in. I think it's brilliant."

"Really?" she asked skeptically.

He nodded. "Yes, really. We can talk about it next week, okay?"

"Sounds good."

"Good, because now, I have to go find a man about getting married."

Drea laughed as her uncle exited the room, closing the door behind him. When she was sure that he was fully gone and wouldn't bust back into the room, she knocked lightly on the door to the bedroom as she opened it. Simone sat on the bed, playing a game on her phone.

Drea smiled big at the bride-to-be. "So, how about we get you in your dress?"

THE SUNSET CEREMONY had gone down without a hitch. It was everything Drea knew Simone had ever wanted in a wedding and she couldn't have been happier for her. With only their families and a few select guests in attendance, they'd all fit on Big House Beach without any issue. Little paper lanterns formed a small aisleway that Drea and Simone had walked down, both unescorted, with the three Quinlan men waiting for them at the end.

The local minister had been short and sweet with his message, getting right to the vows that Simone and Vaughn had written themselves. Filled with laughter at inside jokes, some happy tears, and beautiful promises for their future together, one could feel the love radiating off of the two of them. When it was finally time to kiss the bride, Vaughn grabbed ahold of Simone like his life depended on it and dipped her like it was a scene in a movie.

A large tent had been set up over by the pool with a long table to accommodate those who had attended the ceremony. When everyone was finally seated and had their food, Grayson stood up, clinking his fork against his glass, trying to gain everyone's attention.

"There are a lot of stories I could tell about this man right here," he said, gesturing toward Vaughn. "Stories of all the fun we had growing up, stories about the trouble we got into, stories about how he would boss Miller and me around. He's the oldest, so apparently that was his birthright or something."

There were some scattered giggles throughout the table, and Grayson continued, "But, of all the stories I want to tell, the one that absolutely must be told here and now is about the day that Simone walked into the Indigo Royal for the first time. You see, here we have this stunning beauty, with her long legs and silky hair and those damn high heels she wears, and then we have my brother. Who, by the way, has been sporting the silver fox look since he was like twenty-six —dude gray'd out super early—so he's looked sixty-five since forever, okay? Only fourteen more years until you look your age, man!" Grayson gestured to his brother with his glass as Vaughn simply scowled at him in return. "Well, so old man over here has his jaw on the ground, eyes popping out of his head, kind of like those cartoons we watched as kids. I looked at Miller and said, 'she'll flirt with him, but only to get what she wants, then she's gone.' Miller, being the hopeless romantic he is, goes, 'naw, I got twenty bucks she lasts.' Well, joke's on me, because guess whose wedding I'm at?"

The table burst out in a roar of laughter as Grayson reached into his back pocket and grabbed his wallet. Turning to Miller, he added, "So I guess I gotta pay up. Can you break a fifty?"

"Nope, consider it interest," Miller said, grabbing the bill out of his hand. The laughter erupted again, and this time even Drea cracked a smile. She couldn't help herself— she loved when her uncles played around like this, showing off who they really were. It happened so little since she mostly saw them in semi-public areas now, but this kind of fun and laughter had been all around the big house when she was growing up.

"I guess it's my turn to speak," Miller said, standing up. "I don't owe anyone money, although I must say I'm really happy to see this cash since I'd written that off as a loss quite some time ago! But, as Grayson mentioned, I am the hopeless romantic of the family. I'm also the middle child, so that probably explains a lot. Anyway, twenty-seven years ago when I got married, Vaughn looked at me and told me that he hoped that laughter would be the soundtrack to our marriage. While I certainly wasn't married for quite the length of time I had planned, laughter was certainly a daily occurrence. It was the best thing anyone could have said to us that day, and I'm here today to return the blessing. May laughter be the soundtrack to your marriage." He lifted his glass to toast the happy couple and everyone else followed suit.

As people were finishing up their food and making their way over to Vaughn and Simone, Drea took the opportunity to slip out from the party. She wandered over to the pool, which was thankfully deserted since the bar that was usually open well into the night had been closed for the party. The towel cart had already been stocked for tomorrow's guests, so Drea grabbed one and placed it on the pool deck to sit on while she let her legs hang into the cool water. The water felt good against her skin, and watching the ripples that came off the movement of her legs gave her a good distraction from the party.

It had been such a long week, to the point where she couldn't believe that with everything that happened, it had only been a week. She missed Kyle fiercely, and there was a part of her that felt so hollow without him here. How had it only been three days? All she wanted was to talk to him, to say she was sorry for accusing him of doing what her uncles had said. To tell him he was right, that she didn't want to be anywhere but here, and to tell him that they were all open to the idea of her building the spa.

Leona tossed a towel next to where Drea was sitting and it hit the pool deck with a plop. Squatting down to line herself up with the towel, she leaned a little too far forward and almost ended up in the pool. She probably would have if Drea hadn't grabbed her arm just in time.

"Hey you," she said, once she was sure she was steady in her seat. "Hiding out?"

"Just needed to get away."

"How ya feeling?" Leona asked, giving her a wary look.

"Little less, 'everyone can fuck off,' but not quite optimistic about anything just yet," she answered honestly. "I'm not quite ready to be done being mad at Uncle Vaughn."

"Well, hey, that's a start. Want a distraction?"

"Please!" she pleaded.

"Lee is finally going to admit that she loves Cullen Cruz and that he was the second best lay she's ever had," Dalton said, appearing out of nowhere and crouching down in between the two girls.

"Fuck you, the only feeling I have for that man is hate," Leona responded.

"Methinks the lady doth protest too much," Dalton said, looking at Drea. Drea didn't need to look over at Leona to know she was rolling her eyes.

"Second best?" Drea asked.

"Yes, after me of course," Dalton said with a smirk as Leona rolled her eyes. He magically produced some cups and a bottle of rum. He handed each girl a cup and then filled each one with a little bit of the slightly amber liquid.

Once they were taken care of, he settled himself in between them, poured himself some rum to match theirs and held up his cup in a toast. "To the losers who've lost you and to the lucky bastards yet to meet you."

"I'm not toasting to that," Drea said.

"You stole that from a movie!" Leona accused.

"My sister's favorite. I can recite the whole fucking thing."

"You have a sister?" Drea asked.

"Yup, bitchy little thing still lives in Atlanta, acting like she owns the place."

"You're from Atlanta?" Leona asked.

"Then where'd you learn to sail?" Drea added in, looked at him perplexed, realizing in this moment just how little she really knew about Dalton.

Dalton brushed off the question with a motion of his hand, as if he were pushing it away. "Enough about me. We're focusing on Leona."

"But I already know all her secrets," Drea said.

"There's not that many to know," Leona added.

"Oh, I think there is plenty to know. Like, just how excited are you about Cruz's visit in a couple of months?"

"I am not discussing Voldemort with you," she said pointedly, refusing to give in to Dalton's taunts. "So back to you, sir. Tell us about your sister."

"So, how 'bout them Braves?" he asked, gulping down the rest of what was in his glass.

"They're baseball, right?" asked Drea.

He looked over at her, a little surprised. "You surprise me sometimes, darlin'."

"We went to a game once," she shrugged. "We had gone up to Boston because Uncle Vaughn insisted that we go see some of the Revolutionary War stuff. I think he must have just read a book on it or something. But while we were there, Uncle Gray insisted we go to Fenway to see the Red Sox play, so we did."

They sat there in silence for a while, sipping on the rum, Dalton refilling their cups every time someone was empty. They watched as the party continued, with everyone laughing and sharing stories. At one point, Grayson brought out a small speaker and coerced the newlyweds into a first dance. Drea could see their smiles from where she sat and a pang of jealousy overwhelmed her. She knew what they were feeling—she'd felt it just a week ago on the beach in San Juan. The feeling had over-whelmed her that evening, but in a good way. In a way she had never, ever wanted to end. More than anything she wished it were Kyle sitting next to her right now, feet dangling in the pool, chatting about what they might do differently at their own wedding.

She knew she should be sitting here thinking about her family and what a happy occasion this was. It wasn't that she wasn't happy for them, she would just be happier if Kyle were here with her.

Once the event was over, she could concentrate on putting all her numbers together for the spa. She had some basic numbers thrown together from her years of research of what it would cost to build out the space—the equipment they would need and the additional staff. But if the idea was about to become a reality, then she needed to put together some firm numbers to show her uncles.

It occurred to her again that Kyle had been right, and that this was her chance to make that dream come true. As much as she wanted to hate him for what he'd done, she knew that if she was going to forgive her uncles, she would have to do the same for him too.

"That's what you do when you love someone, right? You forgive them?" Drea said, breaking the silence with her seemingly out-of-nowhere comment.

"Are we still talking about your uncle or have we moved on to someone else?" Leona asked.

"Both?" She paused. "I mean, he was right, this place is my life—I don't want to be anywhere else. I just wish he was still here too."

"Here, have more rum," Dalton answered, pouring more into her cup.

"Just how much longer are you going to keep plying me with booze?" Drea asked.

"Until you no longer wish he was here," Dalton said proudly. "That's my job as comedic relief."

CHAPTER THIRTY-ONE

Kyle sat at the kitchen table in his childhood home, spinning his phone around in circles in his hands. Everything in him wanted to text Drea, tell her all about what he discovered when he arrived home in Florida. Out of sheer habit he'd started at least a dozen times, before catching himself and deleting it. The logical part of his brain knew he needed to apologize, needed to tell her he knew he was an ass and that he regretted it more than he'd ever regretted anything. But he also knew that wasn't enough. You can't just say "I'm sorry" after telling someone "to have a good life."

He'd meant what he said. He did hope that she had the best, most wonderful life possible. One where she was happy and got everything she ever wanted. A life where the spa was a massive success and turned everything about the Indigo Royal on its head. More than anything else, though, he wished he could be a part of that fantastic life. But it was too late now. Maybe if he had stopped thinking about himself for a moment longer when she was in his room that day, they could have figured out a way to make it all work.

She had been right on some level—Miller and Grayson had been perfectly accepting of their relationship. But as long as at least one of the uncles wasn't, it didn't matter how the other two felt.

Taking a quick peek at the time on his phone, he realized they would be right in the middle of the wedding. He wondered what dress Drea had decided to wear. She had pulled out a bunch from her closet a few nights ago and had them lying on the back of the couch. The one that had caught his eye had been a charcoal, almost black, silky material, with thin little straps and what he thought was referred to as a sweetheart neckline, not that he was all that good with women's fashion. The skirt of the dress had angled outward so that Kyle imagined spinning her around on the dance floor and it poofing out just a bit. The thoughts had made him excited to take her to the wedding, even if it was under the guise of being her best friend.

He wondered now if she had picked that dress or if she had gone with the black and white one that kind of draped itself, clinging nicely to her boobs. It occurred to him that he could text Dalton to check in, see how things were going, get a picture of him and the girls all dressed up. He'd sent a text to his buddy as he was getting on the plane coming back here asking him to watch out for Drea, make sure she was taken care of, so he knew that Dalton was right there with her tonight.

The refrigerator came to life with a hum, and that inspired him to grab a beer. A pity party for one called for beer. Actually, what it really called for was bourbon, but there wasn't any of that in the house. There hadn't been any beer, either, until Kyle ran to the corner store this afternoon for the six-pack that was currently chilling in there. Seems his mom had taken to only drinking club soda these days.

He was happy to see her taking her health so seriously, but in this moment, he wished she still kept a little something hidden in the house.

Just as he was closing the fridge door, the overhead kitchen light came on, lighting up the entire room. His eyes burned for a moment as they adjusted to the light, but he recovered quickly, reaching for the bottle opener magnet on the side of the fridge.

"Why are you sitting in the dark?" his mom asked, walking in and standing behind one of the chairs at the kitchen table.

"Just didn't seem worth the effort to turn on the light," he retorted. He realized he sounded like an ass, but didn't have the energy to even apologize.

"What the hell is the matter with you, Kyle?"

"Nothing." He took a long pull on his beer, and leaned against the counter.

"You don't lie very well. You never have. Now sit," she said, snapping her fingers and pointing to the chair he'd been in moments ago.

He did as he was told and sat. She joined him at the table, pulling her chair in so close she almost looked squished in between it and the table.

"You have been sulking around this house for three days, young man. This is after you show up out of nowhere, unannounced, with no real reason for being here. So, out with it," she demanded.

"I told you, I was worried. I got a text from Mrs. Maury that you weren't answering your phone, so I came to make sure everything was okay."

"Without calling first? I raised you better than that."

"She said she hadn't seen or heard from you in days. I was worried you were unconscious or something."

"Kyle, that woman is a nosy old bat. I've been avoiding her for months."

"Ever since you took up with him?" he asked accusingly.

"I will admit that Brian might have been part of the motivation to finally do it. But I'd been meaning to do it for years."

"You could have mentioned that. You know, on those once-a-week phone calls we have. You could have mentioned you were trying to avoid her. Oh, and that you have a gentleman friend," Kyle said, not trying to hide the snark in his voice.

If his nerves hadn't already been shot from being fired, fighting with Drea, and leaving St. Thomas so abruptly, walking in on his mother *in flagrante* with her new boyfriend on the couch would have certainly done it. The house had been quiet and dark when his Lyft had pulled up, causing Kyle to dig out his keys to let himself in. He had called out her name, but apparently not loud enough to pierce whatever bubble the two of them had been in. Flipping on the switch to turn on the living room light, he promptly turned it off again as soon as he registered what he was seeing—his mom, straddling a man on the couch, much like Drea had straddled him just a week ago. Her shirt was crumpled on the floor and from what Kyle could tell, her bra was damn close to joining it.

"I had every intention of telling you about Brian. I promise. But it was also nice to have a little secret as well," she said, with a mischievous little smile.

"Who was I going to tell, Mom? I was over a thousand miles away!"

"I know, baby. But I know you, and you would have found something to worry about. When you told me you and Andrea were starting something, I wanted you to be able to focus on that, not on me."

Kyle sighed. Focus on Drea, that was what got him into this trouble in the first place. Had he been better about his priorities, maybe he'd be twirling her around the dance floor, listening to her giggle right now, rather than sitting at the kitchen table with his mom.

"What's going on, Kyle? You said that you came to check on me. Okay, you checked. You can see I'm just fine. Why haven't you gone back to the island?"

He sucked in a deep breath. Now was as good a time as any to come clean with her. "I got fired from the Indigo Royal."

"What? What happened?"

"Wednesday morning at breakfast, Drea found out she was an equal partner with her uncles in the resort."

"How exciting for her!"

"Yes, very exciting for Drea. Well, in that moment of excitement, I kissed her."

"So? Isn't that what a good boyfriend does?"

"In front of her uncles."

"Oh."

"Yeah...and it was not well received. Well, Miller and Grayson didn't care. Vaughn, however, lost his mind and fired me. Said that I was taking advantage of her, was only interested in her because of her money, and that I'd been leading her on for years."

"Oh my goodness. Does Drea believe any of that?"

"No, thankfully. But, we had a fight after. She told her uncles to buy her out and we would go into business together, and I told her no, that I couldn't ask her to do that, because I know the Indigo Royal is her life. It's where she belongs."

"But you didn't ask her, she offered."

"Now you sound like she does," Kyle said, laughing at the irony.

"Lady logic is a little bit different than man logic," his mother told him. "So, where does all this leave you two?"

"We're over. I came back here. I can't get another job on the island after being fired from there and I don't have enough money to do my own thing yet. So, I kinda told her to have a good life, and I left."

"Kyle Joseph Egan! You did not tell that sweet young lady to have a good life!"

"I did," he admitted, hanging his head.

"Oh Kyle. Every man has jackass moments, but that...that is a serious asshole move, kiddo."

"I am aware, Mom, thanks."

"It needed to be said," she replied, shrugging. "So, now what?"

"Not sure. I plan on staying here for a bit if that's okay and then—"

"No, that's not okay," she said quickly, cutting him off. "Let me rephrase the question. How are you going to fix this with Drea?"

Kyle looked up, surprised. "Fix? Pretty sure there is no fixing this, Mom."

"See, this is your man logic coming through again. Do you love her?"

"Mom..."

"Do you love her?"

"Yes. I love her. She's..." he trailed off.

"It? She's it? She's your lobster?" she asked him, linking her hands together via circles made from her forefinger and thumb like Phoebe did on *Friends*.

"Yes, she's my lobster," he admitted.

"Oh, baby." She reached out and grabbed his hand. "Then why the hell are you still here?"

"I told her to have a good life, remember?"

"Baby, true love is a gift, and it doesn't come along very often. If you really love her, if she's your lobster, then you need to go fight for her. Grand gesture, groveling, whatever it takes."

"I'm not sure she'll ever forgive me. I'm not sure *I'll* ever forgive me."

"I bet she'll surprise you. Love is a very powerful thing, Kyle," she said. She took in a deep breath before starting again. "Kyle, I loved your father with every fiber of my being. I know you were cheated out of the chance of knowing just what an amazing man he was, but he was. He was my everything. I would have stopped the world and spun it backward for him. The only thing that kept me going after his death was you. And I see so, so much of him in you. You look just like him, but beyond that. Your fierce loyalty, your independent spirit, your overprotective nature —that's all your father. He was my lobster and there isn't anything I wouldn't do to get him back."

"You mean Brian isn't your lobster?" Kyle said sarcastically.

"No. Brian is a great guy, you'll see. But he's not your dad. Just like I'm pretty sure I'm not his late wife. But, that is one of the things that binds us—we both understand the loss of a spouse." Kyle nodded, taking a sip of his now warm beer.

"Wait here," she said, pushing away from the table and scurrying down the hallway. When she came back, she slid a small blue box toward him on the table. It looked like it had once been covered in velvet, but it was well-worn and showing its age.

"I'm not saying to give this to her now—that's a cop-out move. You need to figure out your own thing. I highly suggest lots of groveling," she said, looking down her nose at him. "But, this is my engagement ring. If she's really your lobster, she should have it." She flipped the little box open and Kyle saw the ring that he'd seen his mother wear until he was in high school.

"Mom, I can't take this," Kyle said, pushing the box back toward her.

"Kyle, you seem to have a very bad habit of telling us girls what we can and can't do. I know you mean well, but stop. I am giving this to you. Take it. Hold on to it for when you win back your girl and finally decide on forever."

"She likes that word, forever," he said, recalling the words she said to him in his room. His heart had skipped a beat as she told him that, and it hurt now thinking about how he shoved it back in her face.

"Most girls do, baby," she replied, looking at him lovingly.

He leaned back in his chair and closed his eyes. His mom was right, as always. He needed to go win her back. He needed to grovel and beg and prove that he loved her, no matter what. He just wasn't one hundred percent sure where to start.

"I think I have a few phone calls to make," he said, sitting back up and looking his mom in the eye.

"Yeah?" she asked.

"I think I know exactly what to do."

"That's my boy."

CHAPTER THIRTY-TWO

TIME SEEMED to drag the next couple of days, no matter what Drea did. One would have thought that since they were shorthanded that the opposite would be true, that the days would fly by from being so busy. The problem was that it seemed like at every turn there was a reminder of Kyle's absence. He was the reason they were shorthanded, after all.

Grayson had filled in as captain for the first couple of days, and she enjoyed running the tours with him like they'd done when she was in high school. It'd been a long time since they'd worked together, but thankfully they slipped back into their old routines. Of course, having Dalton there to provide entertainment for the guests certainly helped.

Today, however, Dalton was playing captain as Grayson had some "administrative matters" to handle. Part of her wanted to know what exactly that meant, but another part of her knew it was that he was searching for Kyle's replacement and that made her heart ache all over again. She knew that eventually it wouldn't hurt as much to think about him, but for now, she was learning to live with the pain. Maybe once things got underway with the spa, she really would be too distracted to notice the hole he left in her life.

The spa was going to be stunning. She and Vaughn had sat down the day before to go over Drea's ideas and all the numbers she had figured out regarding build-out, construction time, equipment, staff, etcetera. The look in her uncle's eyes when she pulled out her folders of research and inspiration photos told her just how impressed he was with everything she put together, and she had to admit she was incredibly proud of it all. The idea had been festering inside her for so long that it took almost no time to pull all the papers together with her ideas. Vaughn had run the idea by Grayson and Miller at dinner that night and they were both in agreement that a spa would do great things for the Indigo Royal as a whole. The only thing left to do was meet with the accountant to figure out just what the budget would be, and she'd be on her way to breaking ground.

Drea was relieved when she saw the resort's docks come into view. They had run a tour to Turtle Cove today and it was the first time she'd been back since the whole mess with Kyle. It took all her resolve not to burst into tears as they pulled into the cove to anchor. Lucky for her, none of the guests seemed too put out that she wasn't joining them in the water today, leaving her to have a brief pity party behind the bar with the bottle of rum.

Now that they were back at the resort, she figured once she got everything cleaned up and prepped for tomorrow, she would just find Leona and the two could sit on Big House Beach and complain about how much men suck. Cullen Cruz had pushed out the date of his visit by about a month, but in doing so, he also sent a list of additional requests since the resort would have time to accommodate them. Drea thought Leona might explode on the spot when Randy, the night manager, handed her the document. Nothing got under her skin quite like the superstar athlete, although Drea was pretty sure it was for reasons other than the ones that Leona insisted on. Nonetheless, Drea was more than happy to let Leona have a night of word vomiting on the subject. *It'll be nice to hear about someone else's man problems and not think about my own*, she thought.

Dalton helped Drea off the boat, watching as she made a face as she heard her phone chime with a text. Looking down, she found a text from Grayson.

Grayson: Found a new marina manager, just need your approval, others already on board. Meet me at your place?

He found a new marina manager already? That was fast, she thought. She typed back to him that she needed to change, so to let himself in whenever he got there. She hadn't realized that he'd even put the word out yet that there was an opening, but it seemed that news traveled fast around the island. Not that she would be working the sailing tours much longer once everything with the spa got moving, but she hoped for Dalton's sake that it wasn't some douche who thought he could just come in and change the whole feel of the tours.

Making quick work of changing out of her swimsuit and shorts and into one of her sundresses, Drea made her way into her living room, wondering where her uncle was. It shouldn't have taken him this long to get over here from the main building—part of her had even been expecting him to beat her here. When she felt the breeze hit her, she looked over to find her patio door open and what looked to be tea lights lit and placed along the railing. The setting sun made it hard to tell they were lit, but the breeze caused the little flames to flicker just enough that Drea could see them.

What the hell? she thought as she walked closer to the door. It wouldn't have been strange to find Grayson on the porch, but the candles made no sense. As she drew closer, she heard the sounds of a guitar playing softly, although she didn't recognize the tune. She paused right before walking out the door, a little freaked out about what was going on. Could Dalton have done something trying to cheer her up? He'd been full of all sorts of bad jokes and such ever since the wedding, trying to keep her spirits up. But she couldn't imagine him lighting candles on her porch, not to mention he'd just been on the boat with her.

Turning the corner slowly and apprehensively, she was met with the last person she expected to be sitting on her porch, playing an acoustic guitar.

Kyle.

He must have heard her step outside, because he looked up at her, registering the shock on her face just as she came to a halt. Taking this as his sign, he started to play in earnest now. She was frozen in place, unable to move or think. After a moment she realized he wasn't just playing, he was singing too.

Kyle continued to play Daughtry's "Life After You," a song Drea had enjoyed when it was on the radio but hadn't heard in years. A slow smile crept across Kyle's face as he sang, slowly and slightly off-key.

After the first couple lyrics, Drea couldn't hold in her laughter. Kyle was a horrible singer. This wasn't really news —she'd listened to him butcher so many songs over the years. But it was certainly highlighted now that it was just him and a guitar.

Tears started to prickle in the corner of her eyes as she

listened. She couldn't believe he was here. A quick glance around let her know they were alone, and this was a private show just for her. Kyle was such a classic rock guy, she had no idea he even knew this song, much less would have had the time to learn to play it. The tears that had simply been prickles started to slither down her cheeks now. Was this really happening? She wanted to run over to him, pull the guitar from his hands, and throw her arms around him. Almost as much as she wanted to bash him over the head with that same guitar.

"Kyle," she gasped.

He stopped playing and leaned the guitar up against the railing. Standing up slowly, he walked a couple of steps, closing the gap in between them. "Drea, I'm sorry."

"What the hell is all this?"

"This is me trying to grovel and beg and apologize for being a first-rate jackass. Just like the guy in the song."

"I don't follow," she said.

"It's literally a song about a guy who's a jackass and gets into a fight with his girl, leaves, realizes he was wrong, and comes crawling back. Because he realizes he doesn't have a life without her."

"Oh."

He recited the lyrics, this time more like poetry rather than attempting to sing. They told the story of a guy who was obviously regretting his choices, reliving the argument and kicking himself for all the things he'd said. That he knew that the woman he loves was more important, and that without her, he had nothing.

"Kyle, I don't know what to say."

"Then don't say anything, just listen. I know that I made a mistake. The biggest mistake of my life. I need you to know that I'm serious, that I don't have a life without you.

And I know you must think I'm crazy, out here trying to sing, but I needed to make sure I had your attention. I actually considered standing at the edge of the dock, holding a boombox over my head, as your tour came in today, playing that song on repeat," he started.

"I hate that movie."

"I know you do," he said, stepping closer to her. "Which is why I reconsidered. Because I know you hate that movie, and that you can't stand John Cusack, but you adore his sister and how quirky she is. Because I know you, Drea. Sometimes I think I know you better than I know myself. Which is how I know just how badly I hurt you."

"But you were right," she whispered, looking away from him and out over the porch railing at the beach. She quickly wiped away some of the tears from her cheeks, trying to pull herself together.

He stepped closer, cupping her face in his hands and looking her straight in the eye. "No, sweetness, I wasn't. I was so, so wrong. I thought I was doing the right thing by letting you go, telling myself that I would just hold you back. But it doesn't work like that. We're in this together."

"You said this place is my life, and you were right about that," she said, smiling a little. "I can't leave here—I belong at the Indigo Royal. The resort is my life."

"And you're mine, Drea," he said, leaning in so their foreheads touched. "No part of me handled things properly that morning. I should have stood up to your uncles and told them just how much I love you and that you are my entire world."

"You love me?" she asked, pulling away to look at him. Her heart sped up and her stomach tensed, her whole body seeming to hang on every beat of the moment, waiting for him to confirm.

"Oh, did I not mention that?" he smirked. "Yes, Andrea Lorraine Miller, I love you. It's been on the tip of my tongue for what feels like forever and I should have said it a long time ago. I love you more than anything, and you are my forever."

THE MOMENT he said those words, Kyle felt himself relax and tense all at the same time. It felt so freeing to finally say them out loud—he just hoped he wasn't too late. The tears that were now streaming down Drea's cheeks gave him hope, as long as he was reading her right.

"I love you too, Kyle," she finally managed to say through her tears.

He grabbed her around the waist and lifted her up, spinning her around as she giggled, holding on to him for dear life. When he put her down he wasted no time in leaning in and capturing her lips in a deep kiss. When they finally parted, Drea looked at him with a quizzical look on her face.

"But what about my uncles?" she asked.

"I have spoken to all of them. You were right, Miller was on our side the whole time. Turns out Grayson was too. And Vaughn, well, he and I have made our peace."

"So, are you coming back to the Indigo Royal? At least long enough to save up the rest of the money for your own charter business?"

"That's the one piece of the puzzle that isn't in place yet."

"Oh no. Grayson sent me a text telling me that he found a new marina manager. Do you have to wait for his approval? Because I have to vote on whether we hire him and I'll say he has to hire you if he wants the job," she offered up.

"I've met the guy your uncle mentioned and I think you'll like him, actually. Maybe even love him," he commented, smirking at her.

"Love? Why would you think that I'd...wait...you? It's you?"

"If you'll have me," he answered.

"What about being your own boss?"

"Turns out Grayson and I were very much on the same page about a lot of the things I wanted to do with my own boat. He agreed to let me bring in my own vessel to run however I want, as long as I also manage all the other boats in the same manner we've been running them. So we can do tours that are Indigo Royal only, plus some that are open to the public and/or contracted with cruise ships. It'll be a lot of work, but I think it'll be worth it. It'll be the best of both worlds; I can run things the way I want, while having the financial backing of the Indigo Royal. Of course, I do have to get the vote of the fourth partner before I can officially take over." He looked at her knowingly.

"Hmmm, I'll have to think about it. Talk it over with my uncles. We wouldn't want to just take the first candidate that comes along," she teased.

"Oh, really?" he asked, teasing her right back. Grabbing her by the waist again, he tickled her sides until she squirmed and giggled in his arms.

"Okay, okay! You're hired!" she said, gasping for air in between laughing fits.

"Good, I was starting to get worried we might not live happily ever after," he joked, stopping the tickling and pulling her in so their bodies were flush.

"Loved ever after," Drea said, correcting him.

"Huh?"

"Loved ever after," she repeated. "Kinda like in that song. But it was what my mom wrote in her journal under the photo of her and my dad at their wedding—'and they loved happily ever after.'"

"I love that. Almost as much as I love you," he said. "Now, how about we go curl up in that hammock over there and plan our forever?"

EPILOGUE

Four months later...

Drea ducked under the caution tape that indicated the start of the construction zone. Making sure that her hard hat was set firmly on her head, she walked down the hallway to what was to be the spa reception area. The builders were making excellent time on the project and they were slated to be finished on time. Drea's grand opening was planned for just over two months from now, and she couldn't believe that something that had been a dream for so long was so close to being reality.

The drywall was all hung, and they had started painting the walls the deep amethyst purple that she and Simone had picked out. The lighting fixtures should be arriving any day and she just couldn't wait to see how they looked hung up.

"You—I should probably be really upset with you that your dream is basically another ten thousand square feet for me to clean," Leona said, coming up behind her.

"I'd apologize, but I'm too giddy over this coming true," Drea responded, laughing a little.

"I know, and you should be. You worked hard for this! And speaking of working hard, it's almost two o'clock," Leona said, pointing to her watch.

"Oh crap! I better get to the dock! I'm a dead woman if I'm not there!"

Both women hightailed it down to the dock, where they found Drea's family, as well as the marina staff, Dalton, and Kyle. They all stood in front of the brand new 56' catamaran that Kyle was unveiling as the newest part of the Indigo Royal fleet this afternoon. He'd been so excited about buying this boat and held steady in not revealing what he was going to name her to Drea or anyone else at the resort.

"Ready for this?" Grayson asked her as she joined the group.

"So ready. I've been dying to find out her name, but Kyle has refused to tell me!"

"Are we taking bets on what he names her?" Vaughn asked.

"How's that gonna work?" Drea asked.

"Winner gets a free pass at not wearing the shirt next time they lose?"

"I like that!" Simone said, mostly since she had lost last week.

"Ok, I'm gonna go with...*Take On Me*," said Vaughn.

"*Wake Me Up Before You Go Go*," Simone said.

"He is not naming one of our fleet after a Wham song!" Grayson groaned. "He knows better than that. He went with something good, like *Sweet Child O' Mine*."

"*Can't Fight This Feeling*, duh!" Drea threw out there.

"*Hungry Like a Wolf*," Miller answered.

"It's the *Love Shack*!" Dalton announced jokingly.

"It better not be!" Vaughn remarked.

"Well, now that everyone is here, and apparently all your bets are placed, who is ready for the unveiling?"

"Just get on with it!" Simone said, impatient to know if she won.

Kyle laughed, but as he did so, he tugged on the little strings holding the sheet in place that was obscuring the name. As it fell away, there were oohs and aahs from the entire group. All but one person.

Drea looked at the bright blue font written on the back of the catamaran. The simple print text read *Brown Eyed Girl*, and she felt tears start to form in her own brown eyes.

"You know that song isn't from the eighties, right?" Vaughn asked. Simone elbowed him sharply, eliciting a small reaction from him. "What? It's not!"

"Rule was it had to be after a song. Grayson didn't dictate what decade," Kyle responded.

"Kid's right," Grayson said. "I like it."

Drea walked up to Kyle, trying to hold back her happy tears. She wasn't doing a very good job and the closer she got to him, the closer they got to spilling over. When she was right up next to him, she whispered, "I have brown eyes."

"I know, sweetness, I named it for you." He leaned down and kissed her lightly. "Now, how about we sail off into the sunset?"

"I'd love that," she answered.

"And I love you."

BONUS EPILOGUE

Drea laced her fingers through Kyle's, swinging their arms back and forth as they sauntered through the lobby to meet up with her family. The last little bit of sun was still peeking over the horizon, and the glow of the bonfire had started to overpower it, giving the air an electric feel that could only mean one thing. It was Tuesday night and there were bets to be made.

They found Miller in the same place as always, leaning against a pillar overlooking it all, a happy smile on his face. One of these days she was going to have a sign made and posted in the spot that read, "Miller's Pillar," so that the legacy of him standing in this spot would last forever. A giggle escaped as she thought about it and just how hard he would roll his eyes at her as she had it installed.

"What's so funny?" Kyle asked.

"Nothing," she answered. "I just think I'm funnier than I probably really am."

"That's genetic," Miller cut in. "Your mother and aunt were the same way, always laughing about something."

"It's a pretty good giggle," Kyle told her with a wink. He

pulled her into him, the heat radiating off his body enveloping her, instantly making her heart skip a beat. It didn't matter what they were doing or where they were, being with him made her the happiest girl in the world. She couldn't imagine her life without him or him ever not making her feel this way.

Kyle leaned down and captured her mouth in his, kissing her sweetly, like it was the most obvious thing in the world. His touch was soft, yet left no room for her—or anyone else—to wonder whom she belonged to.

"Get a room!" Grayson teased, giving Kyle a little shove, pulling him away from the kiss.

Drea let out another giggle, and Kyle smiled in return as he turned to shove her uncle in response. She loved seeing how well Kyle fit in with her family. All of the awkwardness that had been there after Vaughn's initial freak-out was gone, and in its place was the love and acceptance she'd always dreamed of.

"Simone's on her way. She got stuck in a meeting," Vaughn said, his eyes glued to his phone as he walked in from the pool area.

"Are we starting without her? Or waiting? Because the rules state that no bet is an automatic loss," Grayson said.

"Since when is that a rule?" Kyle asked.

"I have never heard that in my life!" Drea added. "You just made that up!"

"He's just mad because he's lost the last two weeks in a row, and he knows what happens if he loses a third," Miller chirped.

"There's a rule about losing three weeks in a row?" Kyle asked, looking confused.

"If the same person is awarded the shirt for three weeks in a row, then the rest of the family can decide on a different 'prize,'" Simone said, sauntering up to the group. "It's only happened once in all the years we've been doing this, but it was a doozy. Sorry I'm late."

"It was shortly after my eighteenth birthday, and Uncle Vaughn lost three weeks in a row, so Uncle Gray made him spend a day dressed like Simone. Heels, lipstick, the works."

"And payback's a bitch," Miller commented.

"But I'm not losing this week, so it doesn't matter," Grayson said with a confidence Drea wasn't really sure he was feeling. "Tried and true answer this week—we're gonna see a staff hookup."

The group let out a collective groan, but Grayson just shrugged his shoulders. Drea couldn't remember a time when he'd lost using that bet, so it was probably a pretty safe one for him to go with.

"I'm thinking we're gonna see some tears tonight," Miller followed up with.

"You can keep your tears," Vaughn said. "I think there'll be someone celebrating."

"They could be happy tears!"

"I like the theme we have going...I think I'll stick with it. If there's celebrating, there will be champagne," Simone added.

"I think the young couple from Germany on their honeymoon ends up in the pool," Drea offered. "With or without clothes."

"I think we're gonna see a proposal," Kyle finally added.

Drea whipped around to look at him. That had been guessed before, but every time someone had used that, they'd lost. It was almost a running joke that you were asking for the shirt by using that as your bet.

"Is Uncle Gray paying you to take a dive?"

"No, sweetness, I just have a feeling I could be the first person to be right about this."

"Dude, if you are, then you shall be held in high esteem," Grayson told Kyle, clapping his hand on his shoulder as he walked away.

Kyle let out a booming laugh, and it sent a round of butterflies off in her stomach. Damn, she loved this man. She turned into him, looking him up and down, trying to figure out his logic. Bets were always kind of out there—that was part of the fun—but this was off the wall for him. He wrapped his arms around her, pulling her flush against him again, placing a kiss on her forehead. The warm breeze that ruffled her skirt did nothing to stop the shiver that went up her spine as Kyle continued to hold her, making her feel safe and loved.

"He's paying you, isn't he?" she asked again when the rest of her family had walked away.

"He isn't," he assured her. "But let's go grab our spot. We have a lot to watch out for tonight."

―――――――

NERVES RUSHED through Kyle for what must have been the hundredth time today. This plan had been in motion for weeks, and he'd never felt more right about anything. But now that the day was here, his emotions were all over the place. One thing remained true though—that this was what he wanted. That *she* was what he wanted.

As they reached what had become their usual spot, just past where the concrete disappeared into the beach, Drea stopped suddenly, spinning in a circle as she looked around. The look of confusion on her face was absolutely adorable, and Kyle couldn't wait to kiss it off of her.

"What?" he asked, playing into the moment.

"Where's Leona? She *always* beats us here."

"I'm sure she just got caught up in something...or someone..."

Drea shrugged, accepting his answer at face value. He loved how trusting she was—it made pulling off surprises like this so much easier. Her happy, easygoing spirit, though, took a back seat to her great big heart, and he still had no idea what he'd done to deserve her.

Pulling over the lounger that they usually sat in, Kyle sat down and quickly tugged Drea into his lap. She let out a giggle as he wrapped his arms around her. He loved the sound of it and wished there was a way to bottle up the feeling that it gave him.

"I love the bonfire," she mused, twisting in his lap so that she was facing the blaze. She snuggled back into his chest and continued, "There is just something magical about it."

"There is."

"You know, I never thought a day would come where we'd be able to be like this at the bonfire. Dreamed of it, yes, but I didn't expect the dream to come true."

"Oh, I did. It played out a little differently, but I always saw moments like this," he said, happy for the perfect segue. "Did you know that my original idea for a name of my boat was 'Brave Beauty'?"

"Brave Beauty?"

"Yup. Since I thought I was going to be independent from the resort, I hadn't been thinking song titles, but it still needed to be something that was important to me. Andrea means brave in French, or so that French guy told us that day, and you'll always be the most beautiful thing I've ever seen. So Brave Beauty it was."

"You were going to name the boat after me?" she asked, twisting again to look at him. Her eyes were wide and glassy, like she was fighting back tears. Damn, he hoped those were happy ones.

"If you recall, my brown-eyed girl, I did name the boat after you."

"Yes, but I didn't realize that was always the plan."

"It was always the plan," he said, kissing her softly. "I had this whole big idea to surprise you with the name once I had the boat and everything was good to go. I imagined walking down to the pier, holding your hand, doing this whole reveal where you laughed and cried and leapt into my arms. There were kisses too, of course."

"Of course."

"In every version of this story in my mind, I told you how much I love you and how it wasn't just a boat, but the start to the rest of our lives together. But in some of the versions, I also asked you a question..."

He slid Drea out of his lap, scooting himself off the chair as nonchalantly as possible. He really hadn't thought about how awkward this part would be when he'd pulled her into his lap earlier, but he was making it work. Once he was standing on the beach, he turned back toward her and knelt down on one knee.

Drea gasped, her eyes going wide all over, her hands flying to cover her mouth. She was on to him now, which made his heart race, feeling like it could beat right out of his chest. He loved this woman more than he knew how to express, so he'd been practicing the words in his head for weeks. It was now or never.

"Drea, you are my everything. Whether we are out on the boat, dealing with some sort of resort drama, hanging with our friends on the beach, or placing bets with your family before the bonfire, you are what makes that moment special. You are what makes my world turn. You are my lobster, my forever. And I can't wait to see what adventures life has in store for us. I love you, Andrea Lorraine Miller. Will you marry me?"

"Yes!" Drea choked out, nodding furiously, tears streaming down her cheeks. Kyle reached into his pocket and pulled out the old, worn, blue box his mother had given him months ago. Flipping it open, he heard Drea gasp again, a whole new round of tears making an appearance.

"It's not much," he said, slipping the simple solitaire onto her finger. "But my mother gave me this a couple of months ago, thinking it might come in handy."

"I love it. I love *you*, Kyle. I can't wait to be your wife."

"I love you, Drea. And I can't wait to be your husband."

For more by Claire Hastings, including a FREE Indigo Royal Resort short story, please:
www.clairehastingsauthor.com

ABOUT THE AUTHOR

Claire Hastings is a walking, talking awkward moment. She loves Diet Coke, gummi bears, the beach, and books (obvs). When not reading she can usually be found hanging with friends at a soccer match or grabbing food (although she probably still has a book in her purse). She and her husband live in Atlanta with their fur-child Denali.